D0987907

 Greenwich C
Library & Information Service

IN HOUSE
QUALITY
SYSTEMS

**Mobile and Home Service at Plumstead Library
Plumstead High Street, SE18 1JL** *B*
020 8317 4466

Please return by the last date shown

- - MAY 2011	/ / JAN 2014	T Grange
	- - APR 2014	- - AUG 2018
_ _ JUN 2011	_ _ MAY 2014	- - NOV 2018
	- - NOV 2014	ARass
- - AUG 2011	_ _ DEC 2014	- - JAN 2019
- - OCT 2011	- - MAR 2015	
- - APR 2012	- - SEP 2016	
- - AUG 2012	- - DEC 2016	
2 6 MAR 2013	Willy	
- - SEP 2013	- - MAY 2018	
- - OCT 2013	Thank You!	

To renew, please contact any Greenwich library

Issue: 02	Issue Date: 06.06.00	Ref: RM.RBL.LIS

DISTANT HOMELAND

*Kay Stephens titles available from
Severn House Large Print*

A Rare Beauty
Lost and Found
Late Harvest
Silver Harvest
Sea Changes
Set in Stone

DISTANT HOMELAND

Kay Stephens

Severn House Large Print
London & New York

This first large print edition published in Great Britain 2006 by
SEVERN HOUSE LARGE PRINT BOOKS LTD of
9-15 High Street, Sutton, Surrey, SM1 1DF.
First world regular print edition published 2004 by
Severn House Publishers, London and New York.
This first large print edition published in the USA 2006 by
SEVERN HOUSE PUBLISHERS INC., of
595 Madison Avenue, New York, NY 10022.

British Library Cataloguing in Publication Data

Stephens, Kay
    Distant homeland. - Large print ed.
    1.   World War, 1939-1945 - Aerial operations, British - Fiction
    2.   Women air pilots - Fiction
    3.   Fighter pilots - Fiction
    4.   Love stories
    5.   Large type books
    I.   Title
    823.9'14 [F]

    ISBN-10: 0-7278-7504-3

Printed and bound in Great Britain by
MPG Books Ltd, Bodmin, Cornwall.

One

The sun was low in the September sky, blinding Sally as she turned to fly west to the airfield. The Messerschmitt soared towards her, head-on, machine guns spitting fire. She flinched, feeling the impact as the Spitfire was hit somewhere beneath her.

'God, no!' she cried, and tensed, every sense alert for signs that her plane was gravely damaged. 'Just let me get there,' she prayed. Getting there was more vital even than avoiding injury. One of the few women entrusted with delivering aircraft to RAF bases, dying en route seemed preferable to having her plane wrecked.

Her Spitfire wasn't losing height dramatically, but its performance told her the fuselage had suffered, and that Messerschmitt had circled for a second encounter. This time another plane was on its tail. Sally thought it looked like a Hurricane, and hoped that it was. She loathed being discouraged from undertaking active warfare herself, but needed to rely on others.

It was a Hurricane, and the pilot knew his

stuff, blasting the German plane until it lurched and began to spiral down out of their bit of sky.

The RAF pilot drew level with her, close enough for Sally to acknowledge his grin with a swift 'thumbs-up'.

Quelling any resentment that she hadn't been the one to engage the enemy, she flew on, thankful that her aircraft remained fairly stable. That Hurricane still was hanging around. Providing escort? An escort that Sally neither needed nor wished to have. In common with all female pilots, she cherished the ability to fly alone. In this instance, beginning to doubt that her landing gear was fully functional, she had no desire for additional spectators on arrival.

When the Hurricane again came close enough to see her signal, she indicated that she was all right: he should fly on.

He was off into the distance far swifter than she had anticipated. Sally noticed then that her plane was losing power, but this area was familiar, she reckoned she would make it to the airfield.

Landing was another matter. As she had feared, the undercarriage was damaged, one wheel refused to engage: shuddering and scraping, her Spitfire slewed right off the runway despite all her massive efforts to hold the thing straight.

Grimly, Sally completed landing procedures, closed her eyes, willed her emotions under control, and steeled herself to go and report in. This autumn of 1940 was not the time for arriving with a crippled plane. Unable to face the full extent of the damage, she turned her back when she'd clambered out of the aircraft. Snatching off her helmet, she steadied legs reluctant to support her, and strode towards the watch office.

'I am so sorry,' she began before the officer seated there could say one word. 'A Messerschmitt came out of nowhere.'

'They always do,' he said dourly. 'How bad is it? I heard how it sounded.'

Sally guessed that he would have dashed to watch that landing as well. But he seemed more philosophical than she'd expected. Sally risked reminding him that she had managed to bring the Spitfire down.

'And I gather that you were lucky that you weren't shot out of the skies.'

She gave him a feeble smile. Evidently that Hurricane was from this base, and its pilot had filled in a few details after putting down. She ought to be glad, but couldn't help feeling that her capability had received an additional knock.

'Better get on with the paperwork,' she was told. 'I'll have someone check her over, find out how serious the damage...'

His voice trailed off when Sally leaned over the desk to begin completing documents.

7

Blood was dripping on to the paper from the wound recently released from the rim of her flying helmet. She raised her left hand to her head. Blood smothered her fingers. Determined to ignore the gash, she stretched out her other hand for a pen. Pain shot from her shoulder, through aching neck up into her head, and down the arm towards the elbow.

'Oh, hell!' Sally realized now that she'd been too distressed about the damage to her aircraft to notice how badly she had wrenched that shoulder.

'Wrestling to keep her on the runway?' the officer suggested. He'd never willingly have sanctioned having women fly, but he wasn't unsympathetic when they succumbed to injury.

'That must have been it. But I'll be all right, really.'

'Not like that, not on my territory. Just clean that hand up a bit, use my washbasin over there. You'll have to sign with your left. And then, young lady, you're off to see the medics.'

Sally would have argued, but the pain from her shoulder was intensifying. She couldn't believe concern for her Spitfire had kept her unaware of being hurt until she'd reached the office. Her head wasn't much better, the handkerchief she was using to stem the blood was saturated before she'd wiped clean her mid-brown hair and the waxen face staring out from the mirror. And if her injuries weren't sufficient to cause this sudden unsteadiness, the shock of that air attack was taking effect.

A chair awaited her when she'd cleaned off most of the blood. She was being watched with a concern that confirmed her own dread that she might make an utter fool of herself by passing out.

The hospital was in the nearest town, accustomed to casualties arriving by RAF ambulance. Compared to many of the personnel they treated, Sally was suffering only minor injuries. She was thankful for their cheerful assessment and swift repair to the cut on her head. The damage to her shoulder prompted a certain amount of manipulation which, although excruciating, seemed to lessen the pain afterwards.

Her brown eyes clouded with disappointment though, after she was stopped as she began preparing to set out on the journey home.

'You're not going back to base tonight, I'm afraid,' the young nurse told her.

Sally smiled. 'I wasn't, actually. Due on leave, said I'd be home tonight.'

'And home is...?'

'Halifax, the West Riding.'

'Yorkshire! Sorry, but Doctor would never countenance that. If you'd said elsewhere in Kent, he might have been persuaded.

Travelling any distance would be most unwise with that head injury, plus the shock you had.'

Sally sighed. Evidently the RAF had filled in the hospital staff on earlier events.

'We'll soon have you settled into a ward, rustle up a meal of sorts. I bet you haven't eaten a thing for hours.'

'I'm not hungry.'

'We'll see.'

'What I could use, though, is a phone call. My father's a terrible worrier.'

'There's one over there. Help yourself, I'll see about allocating you a bed.'

Henry Downing was not best pleased to learn that he wouldn't be seeing his daughter that night. He'd had another fruitless day at the mill and, worse, was struggling to cope now his right-hand man had left to run a munitions factory.

'Can't you get a later train, or something?' he asked Sally, who was carefully avoiding mention of being hospitalized.

'Afraid not. But I should make it tomorrow,' she assured him. 'And then there'll be a good few days with you.'

'If you're not recalled, all of a sudden, like.' That had happened more than once, and Sally didn't seem able to understand how intensely Henry loathed that hazardous job she was doing.

'Got to go now,' she told him, exhausted

10

further by the strain of speaking with him while concealing her true situation. 'Take care of yourself, Dad.'

'Have to, shan't I? Nobody else does. And everything here is getting worse – David's left us, gone to manage a munitions place, of all things.'

'Really? David Saunders?'

'Who else?'

'Good for him.'

'You would say that. Well out of it, aren't you?'

The call to her father had not improved her mood. The only thing that made her smile even slightly was donning the massive nightgown that the nurse issued to her.

Sally obediently ate the supper provided, then closed her eyes, determined to catch up on a bit of much neglected sleep while the opportunity was presented.

'You have a visitor...'

Sally hadn't slept at all, had scarcely settled her aching head more comfortably, when the very junior nurse startled her.

Opening her eyes, she stared up at a blue uniform that looked somehow strange. Raising her gaze further, she took in sun-tanned features, unsmiling, plus a deep forehead topped by golden hair.

'Hello,' the man said, tentatively, and continued to stand there.

'Should I know you?' Sally enquired. She

was in no condition for guessing games, and if the chap was some kind of hospital visitor, a do-gooder, she'd no need of him.

Again, she looked at his face. *Did* he seem familiar? But if he was someone she'd met through her Air Transport Auxiliary job, why wasn't he reminding her of the circumstances? And how did he know that she was in this hospital?

'Hello,' he said again. This time he smiled.

Sally had seen that smile before. The pilot who had grinned from the rescuing Hurricane.

'I owe you a big thank you, don't I? For my life, I dare say, certainly for getting me out of a tricky situation. You'd better sit down, can you find yourself a chair?'

Blankly, he stared at her, remained standing, looked even more uneasy. Sally glanced again at his uniform, realized that it wasn't standard RAF issue.

She smiled warmly. 'You're not English, are you?'

'No English, no.'

'Polish?'

He shook his head.

'*Êtes-vous Français*?' She knew several free-French pilots had made their way across to serve in Britain.

He shook his head. '*Non, mais je parle français...*' He hesitated, indicated a small quantity with his long fingers.

12

'*Asseyez-vous*,' Sally suggested.

He smiled, located a chair and came to sit beside her bed.

'*Je m'appelle* Sally Downing,' she told him.

He pointed at his own chest, seemed lost, sighed. 'Vaclav Capkova,' he announced, then added something in his own language.

Sally recognized only one word. 'Did you say Czech?' she asked him.

Vaclav nodded. 'I am pilot in Bohemia – you know as Czechoslovakia.'

'How did you come to England?'

Again, he looked bleakly at her, eloquent hands indicated that he did not understand.

Sally smiled ruefully. 'Sorry,' she apologized, and tried to gather the right words in French. '*Comment venez-vous en Angleterre?*' she managed slowly, and sighed. Would he grasp her meaning? She was sure she'd got the tense all wrong.

Vaclav smiled again. '*Je – échappe à France... après –* er, *beaucoup mois... beaucoup pays...*' he told her haltingly, and waited for proof that she comprehended.

Sally understood, could picture the prolonged, dangerous journeys Vaclav must have endured in order to get away to fight over here. Czechoslovakia had been overrun by German forces almost as soon as the war had begun.

Vaclav enquired how badly she was hurt, and Sally demonstrated the shoulder injury,

13

and tried to explain how quickly it should heal.

'*Et vous* – er, *votre tête?*' he continued, his blue eyes dark with concern.

'*C'est rien.*' She shrugged.

Still hesitantly, for her French was half-forgotten since her schooldays and his a smattering of the language acquired en route to England, they talked for a half-hour or so. Sally told him that she had been fortunate to qualify as a pilot while at university, and added that flying was what she had enjoyed most during her years there. She couldn't be certain Vaclav fully understood, but he went on to explain that he had flown with the Czech air force.

From her sketchy knowledge of how bad the situation out there had been since the Munich Agreement, Sally could appreciate that Vaclav would have been determined to make his way through Europe to England.

Trying to win a smile from him again, she suggested that being here must feel good, that flying again must feel blessedly familiar.

The desired smile didn't appear. When Vaclav sighed, she felt perturbed. He began explaining then, as best he could, how troubled he was by too many differences.

In his own country, Vaclav was proud of all that he'd achieved. Sally gathered that he was well respected for the alacrity with which he had learned to fly. Over here, most

14

of the aircraft were new to him, and many of the RAF phrases he encountered seemed even more foreign to him than the English in general use. Such words were not to be found in any dictionary.

She could believe that, she'd had to familiarize herself with a whole fresh set of colloquial terms as soon as she began delivering to airbases. During a flight a certain amount of basic English might be used, but that didn't help with service expressions like 'scramble', and 'prang', to say nothing of some of the more colourful RAF vernacular.

Vaclav eventually looked at his watch and rose. 'I report back,' he managed in English.

'Thank you so much for visiting me, you are very kind,' said Sally, and translated her thanks into French, as they shook hands.

'*Mais non – je vous remercie.*' Vaclav added that he'd never before admitted to anyone how uneasy he was made by coping with so much that felt strange to him.

The grasp of his hand on hers was firm, while his blue eyes seemed to will her to understand him. Sally asked him how long he had been in England. She thought he was trying to say two weeks, but his reply was so halting that she couldn't be certain.

The only certainty on which she could rely was her own response to him. Those eyes of his appeared so magnetic, while the warmth conveyed by his fingers was urging her to learn more about him. A charge of sheer attraction began pulsing through her, and more than that – the compulsion to permit some expression of the affection that she already was feeling towards Vaclav Capkova.

Sally expected that by the following morning she would be rationalizing their meeting, convincing herself that only the circumstances bringing her and the Czech pilot together were responsible for her reaction. He had rescued her, hadn't he? Then followed that up by his thoughtful visit to her bedside. No woman could have remained impervious to all that, especially while suffering from the shock of an encounter with a Messerschmitt.

When her first thoughts on awakening were of Vaclav and how he might be coping at the RAF base, Sally appreciated the effort he must have put into visiting her. But she ought now to forget him, she was late starting this trip home to Yorkshire.

She had been given the all clear to leave hospital. Although still painful, her shoulder was gradually improving, and a slight headache was all that remained of her head injury. Sally's chief problem was finding the best means of travelling north.

Quite often after delivering an aircraft she would be offered a ride back to the ferry pool where she was based or, more rarely, to

16

her home when due a spell of leave.

On this occasion, she'd be obliged to travel by rail, not something she relished, with trains inevitably crowded and subject to delays. The only good thing, this trip, was having no luggage to contend with, but that same absence of possessions also meant that she couldn't change the uniform shirt which she'd worn throughout the previous day.

The journey up to London through the Kent countryside was much as she'd expected, with evidence of damage inflicted by recent Luftwaffe raids, although also enough wrecks of enemy aircraft to witness that they too had suffered. Crossing the capital itself became so harrowing that Sally willed herself to look away from the innumerable ruined buildings, many of them still smoking. Somehow, though, she couldn't quite avoid staring towards the destruction. By the time she had reached the train that would take her to the West Riding, she was feeling thoroughly dejected.

Sally hadn't needed anything to witness to the fact that the planes which she helped to take into service were vital. The damage to that Spitfire might not have been her fault, but nothing alleviated her feeling of being responsible. Before leaving the base yesterday one of the officers had assured her that any investigation was likely to exonerate her. That did not prevent Sally from blaming herself for delivering a plane that wasn't ready for service.

She really had needed to explain how she was feeling. There had been no opportunity for that. And would she have known what to say? The inability to express her reactions to the incident made her think of Vaclav again. How must it feel to be unable to talk to anyone about any of the highs and lows experienced daily with the RAF?

Sally had been touched when Vaclav had revealed that only to her had he admitted the difficulties he was encountering as a foreign pilot serving in a strange land. And here she was miles away from him already, and soon to be much farther from him in the north of England.

There were several delays en route when local air raids enforced a stop, sometimes out in the countryside, sometimes in stations. But they at last were running through her beloved Yorkshire valleys, where even the soot-blackened buildings appeared reassuring, especially so for remaining intact.

Sally never ceased to be thankful that her father lived in this still relatively safe area. Today, being glad to be relieved of alarm on his behalf extended to include her own appreciation of the quiet. Coming back to her home county felt to be regenerating her, endowing a tranquillity all the more effective because of being undisturbed by

18

enemy attack.

She wished, inexplicably, that she could have brought Vaclav to Halifax, that he might use their peace to help him to adapt more readily to a country where he must feel very much the new immigrant.

Henry Downing was not at home, and nor was Mrs Holbrook, the elderly woman who had kept house for him since his wife had died in 1934. Sally didn't pause to change her shirt before setting out for the mill. If her father left before she arrived there, they might waste an hour or more passing each other en route. Henry would most likely still be using his pre-war Humber, whereas she herself would have to rely on the bus.

Sitting gazing from the bus window, Sally wondered why ever she hadn't opted instead for waiting at Downing House until he returned. The substantial Victorian villa at Highroad Well was very comfortable, and she was exhausted. The truth lay, she supposed, in her own feeling of discomfort in that house, an emotion which she was only beginning to admit, even to herself.

Since the awful days following her mother's death, Sally had grown steadily more aware of Henry Downing's possessiveness. During every vacation from university, and afterwards whenever she was on leave, she had felt stifled by his dependence upon her.

19

Justifiable though such reliance upon an only daughter was, she had yearned to break free of that yoke, no matter how tenderly it might have been imposed. And, latterly, any tenderness had been scarcely tangible. In anyone else, she would have recognized Henry Downing's manner as overbearing. But he was nevertheless her father, and very, very dear.

At his desk in the office of their mill, Henry was letting every line of his weary face reveal how disgruntled he was feeling. Slumped there, his six-foot frame looked diminished. Until he glanced through the doorway and saw Sally approaching.

Grey eyes brightening, he stood up and strode to greet her with a fierce hug. Sally just wished that the welcome could feel warm without being so stifling.

'I was that afraid you weren't going to make it at all!' Henry exclaimed.

Sally kissed his cheek, gave his shoulders a squeeze. 'I told you I would, Dad.'

'Aye – well ... There's many a slip, isn't there? These days. What held you up yesterday, then?'

'Had a bit of a difficult landing, wrenched my shoulder and did this cut on my head. They wouldn't let me say no to being checked out by a doctor.'

'But you are all right now, love?'

'Shoulder's a bit stiff, that's all.'

'Good, good.' Henry smiled. He could accept his daughter's assurances so long as she was here. He couldn't allow himself to do otherwise. Her lengthy absences from home were the times when he gave in to worrying: if he didn't rely on the evidence of his own eyes now, he'd never know any let-up from anxiety.

'Do you always work this late nowadays?' Sally asked him, concerned about his apparent weariness, which seemed to have increased the lines beneath his greying hair.

'Quite a lot. There's not much to go home for, is there?'

'Anything I can do?' she enquired. She had helped out in the office pre-war.

Henry shook his head. 'Not really, out of touch by now, aren't you? And it's all changing, any road. The last carpet orders came off t'looms earlier this week.'

'And have you started manufacturing stuff for the forces yet? You said that was on the cards.'

'Oh, aye. And a boring business it's going to be, if you ask me.'

On their way out to the car Sally asked what would happen to all their workforce.

Her father sighed. 'I suspect that, in the main, them that haven't joined up will eventually have to go and work on munitions and the like.'

'Even highly skilled people – designers and

so on?'

'Some of them are doing different stuff already, in our own factory – camouflaging tents, and what not.'

'Hardly a satisfying use of their skills.'

'Not much choice about it, though.'

He continued to bemoan the limitations that the war was placing upon their business, only letting up when they arrived at the house.

'I've just got one phone call to make,' Henry announced as he unlocked the door and waited for Sally to precede him through into the hall.

'Fine, Dad. I've got to change, anyway. With having to see a doctor, I wasn't able to pick up any of my gear. Good job I've plenty of things here.'

When she had freshened up and put on a jumper and skirt, Sally went downstairs to find her father in the sitting room. He was looking very pleased with himself.

'That was David I had a word with. He's coming to have a bite to eat with us.'

'Tonight?' Sally was disappointed. She was too tired to want to see anyone, even an old friend like David Saunders.

'Can never be sure how long you'll be stopping, can I? And he did say he wanted to see you, particular like.'

She didn't respond. Sally knew her father, and she knew David Saunders: if they were permitted their own way, they would have her married to David. She had been struggling for ages to keep their friendship to just that – friendship.

Inwardly, she smiled. She couldn't believe that her exhausted appearance would do much on this occasion to encourage David to deepen the relationship!

David himself wasn't looking too brilliant either when he arrived just as Sally was heating up the pans of vegetables prepared by Mrs Holbrook before she'd left for her own place. Always entirely at home in Downing House, he came striding through to the kitchen after only a brief word with Henry.

Kissing Sally on her cheek, he slid both arms around her waist from behind. 'My word, you smell good!' he exclaimed.

'Hello, David. You wouldn't have thought that when I got here,' she said ruefully, aware of his touch, which seemed to jar on her nerves. 'No chance to change before setting out this morning. How are you, anyway?'

'Better for seeing you.'

David sometimes tended to speak in clichés, and always seemed a shade too polite for expressing deep emotions. *Verbally*, at least, Sally reflected. He still was standing very close to her, and didn't move his arms away until he was obliged to let her open the oven door. Even tired as he sounded, his broad shoulders could make her feel dwarfed by him – or *smothered*.

She often was thankful for his reticence with words, coping with his impulsive hugs was strain enough. Always appearing something of a loner, David Saunders seemed more at ease with her than with any other female, but Sally could be pleased that he relaxed without wishing him to become more intimate.

'Did Henry tell you I've been landed with fresh work?'

'Aye. I gather you'll be running a munitions place. Have you started there yet?'

'Last week. I'm afraid at present the factory seems to be running me! Luckily, there's a sound foreman there, and the managing director knows engineering inside out. So far, they've prevented me creating too much of a crisis.'

'And you do have some knowledge of maintaining machinery, don't you, from keeping the looms running?' David had worked his way up through the carpet mill until becoming Henry Downing's second in command four years ago when he was twenty-eight.

'There is that. Trouble is, it's all so different. And you wouldn't believe the regulations, on account of everything being for the war.'

'And where is this place, is it local?'

24

'Sowerby Bridge.'

'No bother getting there then.'

'You'll have to come and have a look round. How long are you home for?'

'Only a few days. In any case, are you permitted to show visitors around – with it being war work?'

'Maybe not. I wasn't thinking. We'll have to go somewhere else then, make the most of your leave. How about the pictures?'

'I'd rather go for a walk. Happen on Sunday afternoon, what do you say?' She recalled too many cinema visits with David Saunders when he'd expected the darkness to encourage a lot of kissing.

The meal that evening was congenial enough, with her father in high spirits because of David's presence. Sally's too, of course. Henry frequently mentioned how grand it was to have her home, and how greatly he missed her when she was absent.

'Do you two chaps get together of an evening, then?' Sally enquired. 'When you're both on your own...'

The exchanged glance and their shrugs confirmed that they did nothing of the kind. Sally's spirits sank. Her assumption that her presence alone had prompted the invitation issued to David did nothing to increase her comfort.

Later, leaving for his own home a short distance away, David reminded her that he would see her on Sunday. Sally willed herself not to reveal her reluctance. David Saunders had always been a reliable family friend who had been especially helpful during the dreadful period surrounding her mother's death. There had been times, years ago, when she had been glad that he was those ten years her senior. That had made him more like the older brother she would have loved to have.

Unfortunately, with time, the difference in their ages felt to have levelled out, leaving the problem that Sally seemed to be alone in wishing to ensure that nothing deeper should develop between them.

Despite all her reservations, their walk on the following Sunday became very pleasant. The weather had obliged with a touch of warm sunlight to take the edge off the autumn breeze wafting across the hilltops.

Walking briskly, they reached one of Sally's favourite places, the Albert Promenade, where its height on top of the rocky causeway provided a view across neighbouring valleys towards wooded hills. Almost out of sight lay the factories and rows of houses, along with the river and canal, but it was the slopes ahead which drew her gaze, as they had ever since childhood.

'I'll never grow tired of this, nor even sated by it,' Sally admitted. 'It's all but inspirational to me – makes me believe that – well, happen that because I can walk these hills, I might tackle most things.'

'As you will – as you do – look at the way you've learned how to fly aeroplanes. I'm that proud of you, Sally love.'

'I suppose it was something of an achievement. Didn't think much about it at the time, with quite a few of us at Oxford taking it up together.'

Flying had been a challenge, and fun as well. There had been no thought then of the skill being used for war work. The hostilities had seemed to appear suddenly, just when she and her fellow graduates looked forward to enjoying their freedom. Sally had wondered since how education could have left them less than fully aware of where Europe had been heading.

'They wouldn't take me, you know,' David confessed gravely, brown eyes clouding. 'I was determined to join the air force. My eyesight let me down first of all, then there was the fact that I'd had rheumatic fever when I was a youngster. Heart not a hundred per cent, they said.'

Sally had heard all this already, from her father. 'Never mind, you'll be doing your bit making the weapons all the lads out there are getting desperate for. And while you're around Halifax like this, you can keep an eye on Dad for me.'

'You can count on that. You can count on me for anything, Sally love.'

It wasn't entirely what she wished to hear. She only needed somebody to see that Henry Downing was all right. And now she felt under an obligation to David. When he reached for her hand as they turned to walk down through the woods, she steeled herself not to flinch.

She couldn't help not fancying this man whose pleasant features and wavy dark hair would delight most girls. Sally refused to feel guilty about not wanting him. This place always did her good, she mustn't spoil today. In fact, while they had been looking out across that glorious view, she'd been thinking.

Her part of Yorkshire really did always make her feel better, its effect couldn't be tarnished, even by this war. While the hills challenged her to do her utmost, the beauty found whenever she walked through these woods or over the nearby moors restored her by evoking its own especial peace.

And she no longer felt happy about keeping its benefits for herself. This *would* be just the sort of place to bring Vaclav Capkova, she had been right to think so – a place to share, to make him feel more at home in England.

Two

Sally was feeling fit again, glad to be returning to work. Her visit to Yorkshire hadn't entirely had its usual effect of empowering her to tackle everything and, even trying to be fair, she couldn't avoid blaming her father for that. His invitation to David on the day she'd arrived home had been followed up by further suggestions that he join them in the evenings. Sally had considered that Sunday afternoon walk with David sufficient, his frequent appearances in her home felt to be preventing her from relaxing.

She'd made herself unpopular with both Henry Downing and David on her last evening when she went out instead of sitting with the two men, but calling to see Emma Francis proved to be just what Sally needed.

An old school friend who'd also been at Oxford, although in a different college, Emma had married young, even before graduating. Now the mother of girls aged three and thirteen months, she had adopted the easy-going attitude which helped her to cope with young children. It also made her the ideal person for welcoming surprise visitors. Sally smiled as she relived the ease of that pleasant evening.

With a bottle of wine between them, the two women chatted for hours, interrupted only occasionally by demands from the girls, whose adoption of Emma's attitude was revealed in the number of times that they got up again after being put to bed.

'Paul would go berserk,' Emma confided, laughing. 'He claims it's high time a three-year-old learned a bit of discipline, if only regarding a sleeping pattern. But he's not the one who most often packs them off to bed!'

A regular in the navy, Paul was serving somewhere in the Mediterranean, his long absences from home only compensated by Emma's reliance upon her many friends.

Smiling again now as she boarded the train that would take her back to base, Sally recalled Emma's reminder to get in touch as soon as she was home again.

'I've known your dad for years, haven't I – and the way he'll always try to claim every hour of your time in Halifax! There'll always be a place for you here, even if I've got hordes of people around.'

Sally wished that she had some of her friend's facility for gathering a crowd of like-minded folk together. She herself seemed never to have acquired that ease, and tended as a result to have a few close friends, but

30

hardly any acquaintances. Although she supposed she could count the people she met through her ferry pool base: the men and women of the Air Transport Auxiliary who delivered aircraft to RAF squadrons.

In some respects, the job tended to generate a certain isolation. Deliveries quite often were made alone, and there rarely was enough time at any one airfield for getting to know aircrew or ground staff.

'Are you sure about that?' Emma had asked last evening while Sally was trying to explain this. 'I know how hopeless you are. If it was me, I'd make certain I happened to be around whenever a dance was on in the mess.'

'No, you wouldn't, not when you're a much married lady!' Sally had laughed.

'I would have, though, in my single days. There'd have been no stopping me.'

Dismissing her friend's words, Sally virtually forgot their conversation long before she was reporting back for duty. Even with a husband in the forces, Emma didn't really understand how seriously everyone was obliged to take their role in this war.

This seriousness certainly came back forcefully to Sally when she was greeted on arrival at base with the information that 'her' Spitfire had been restored, and was waiting to be delivered.

'I'm sure you will wish to make up for what happened by returning it to them as good as new,' her commanding officer suggested.

'Of course,' said Sally quickly, while she pushed any reservations to the back of her mind. There would be time enough during the flight for overcoming potential embarrassment induced by landing at that particular airfield again.

Common sense had told her all along that there was no possibility that she could avoid visiting that base throughout the duration of the war. Maybe getting the ordeal over and done with would be the best way of putting that unfortunate incident behind her.

Once in the air again, and pleased to sense that the Spitfire still felt familiar, Sally gave all her attention to the actual flight, and forgot about looking ahead to her possible reception on arrival. She was determined to ensure that, this time, no enemy plane would take her unawares. Sally still felt ashamed of the way that she hadn't noticed that Messerschmitt before it came at her head-on. Checking and re-checking to all sides of her, she flew on until the airfield was in sight below her.

Holding her breath, and willing every part of the machine and her own body to co-operate, Sally landed immaculately. After verifying twice that everything in the cockpit was in order, she clambered out on to the runway then headed towards the watch office. Infinitely relieved, she could feel how light her step was.

The same officer happened to be on duty – he smiled wryly when Sally announced that the Spitfire was delivered intact, this time.

'And you yourself?' he enquired, pushing paperwork across the desk towards her.

'Reconditioned, and all in order, sir.'

'Good, good. Glad we don't have to pack you off to hospital tonight. Don't know quite when you will get away, though. It's been pretty quiet, so far, but everything airworthy is on stand-by until dawn.'

'That'll be all right, sir. I could make my own way back tomorrow.' A bed of sorts was always available on camp for stray personnel like herself.

'You could make enquiries in the mess, see if anyone due off on leave might oblige with a lift,' he suggested.

The sounds flowing out from the mess as she approached told Sally that dancing was in progress. She was tempted to forget about seeing anyone else, and head off for a few hours' sleep. The strain of piloting that Spitfire again while deeply concerned that there should be no further attack seemed to have exhausted her.

A couple of WAAFs were standing just outside the doors, smoking Woodbines and chatting earnestly. They had been watching

Sally and called to her.

'You're coming in, aren't you? It was you brought in the Spitfire, wasn't it? Can't be much fun on your own on a strange station.'

Ignoring their welcome would be churlish. Sally smiled and followed them indoors. The place was crowded, mainly with uniformed men and women, but with a scattering of girls in civvies. Airmen away from home always tried to ensure that they enjoyed the company of any local girls.

He was the first person she recognized, from the far end of the room. He was standing near the bar, but a pace or two away from the other airmen. Vaclav knew her instantly, came striding through the throng of dancers, making his way between couples as elegantly as if he himself were dancing.

'Sally!' he exclaimed, blue eyes gleaming. 'I pray that I see you again.'

Something in his tone told her that Vaclav didn't use the word 'pray' lightly. Sally smiled and said 'Hello' as she held out her hand to shake his.

Warm fingers grasped hers and he raised her hand to his lips. His gaze was seeking her own, his smile confirming a delight to match the pleasure surging right through her.

'I learn some English,' Vaclav confided swiftly. 'Is because I hope to talk with you.'

'But you couldn't know you would see me again,' said Sally, feeling bemused.

'I hope. I know that I have to see you.'

'Are you with somebody tonight?'

'With?' Vaclav might have acquired more English, but he did not understand her question. 'With all of these persons that are here.'

Sally recalled how solitary he had appeared near the bar. 'You are alone in the mess?'

'No longer alone. Now with you, I am never alone.'

She told herself she was silly to feel touched by his words, that his limited knowledge of her language was responsible for the phrases. But Vaclav was leaving her no time for thinking. Still grasping her hand, he drew it to his chest, placed his other arm around her.

'We dance, yes?' He allowed no opportunity for discussion.

Within moments Sally was realizing how foolish she would have been to resist dancing with him. She had been so right to class his walk towards her as graceful. The quickstep into which he swept her was as elegant as any she'd ever experienced, so stylish that she wondered if Vaclav could have been taught professionally in his own country.

He understood enough of her question to laugh at such a notion. 'No, nothing like it. When small boy at school they learned me how.'

'They taught you very well.'

He sighed, rolled expressive blue eyes

heavenwards. 'I say the wrong word, yes? It has to be "taught", not the other word.'

'It doesn't matter, Vaclav, I knew what you meant.'

'But I wish always to do everything right for you.'

'You are doing,' she murmured under her breath, aware of the intensity of the attraction already coursing through her.

Vaclav had heard what she said. He drew her even closer against him, whirled them around in an exhilarating spin turn. But that track of the record was ending. Sally's sudden regret that they must draw apart surged in to replace her excitement.

Still holding her hand, Vaclav led her off the floor. While they stood together at the side of the room, his fingers moved ceaselessly, caressing her own.

The next number was a slow foxtrot, but the mess was too crowded for anyone to indulge in elaborate routines. She wasn't surprised when Vaclav drew her closely against him once more, shortening his steps to accommodate the lack of space.

He held her easily in his arms, but firmly enough for her to feel almost – *cherished*. Recognizing her feeling, Sally was amazed: she had known him for so short a time, and she was the last person to let such emotions run away with her. Where was her common sense disappearing to? This did all feel so natural, though, so very right.

They danced and danced, speaking little now, except each in turn to say that they hoped there would be no call for aircrews to halt dancing and prepare for take-off. Granted this opportunity to savour being in Vaclav's arms, Sally knew she would feel torn apart if he was removed abruptly to take to the skies.

They were fortunate. No crisis brought the dance to an end, but by the time that the music eventually finished even they were compelled to admit to feeling tired.

'I do not let you to go away,' Vaclav said when they were obliged to venture out into the cool night air.

'I'm afraid I have no choice,' Sally reminded him gently. 'I have to report back tomorrow.' And during an interval in the dancing, a pilot she knew slightly had offered her a lift to her base, which meant departing early next morning.

'You must not look so sad,' she continued when Vaclav sighed heavily. Smiling affectionately, she reached up and stroked his cheek.

He caught her to him, hesitated for only one second, then kissed her full on the mouth. His lips were firm and smooth, and she felt the slight scratchiness of his chin, revealing that he was due for another shave. Somehow, awareness of this intensified his masculinity for her, reawakening Sally to the full significance of the sensations their dancing created.

Sally kissed him back, fervently. Driven by an impulse beyond her conscious will, she could not resist testing his lips with the point of her tongue.

Vaclav sighed, blissfully, his teeth parting, welcoming her to explore. He drew her nearer still, his hands pressing into her back, asserting his need of her.

'We go together, alone, yes?' he suggested.

'How can we? I hardly know you. And besides, there's nowhere that we could go.'

'There will be somewhere, for *us*, one day. I will go with you to where the world is finished.'

It sounded romantic, but that was all it could be. A bit of a romantic dream. For the present, the reality, the best they could locate was the doorway of a hut that seemed to be neglected.

Vaclav leaned with Sally into its rough wall, held her close against him once more, showered her cheeks with feather-light kisses, and then his mouth again sought her own, his tongue began delving between her teeth, thrilling her. Against her, he felt firm and warm, the stirring of his hips conveying more than a hint of the attraction generated between them.

'Somehow, we are going to have to stop,'

38

Sally whispered regretfully, at last.

'I know. I do know that. When I make the loving to you, it shall not be in an awful place like it is.'

Strangely, she could believe that they would make love some day, that they might have a future. But she could not even venture to examine the question of where that might be or when. This, she feared, was the magic of their night, not even remotely connected with the reality to which she ought to hold on.

'We'd better say goodnight then, Vaclav.'

'With the goodnight kisses, yes?' His voice held a hint of mischief, yet the mouth that closed over her own seemed seriously intent on making her a promise.

She had to steel herself to insist on leaving to find her accommodation for the night.

When Sally finally undressed she was reflecting on what had become a lovely interlude that they had shared. And that was the way in which she must think of it. An interlude, one of many which for others like themselves – the diverse people engaged in this war – must remain no more than a tantalizing memory.

Trying to adapt her restless body to the camp bed, Sally found her brain remained active, producing reminders of how dramatically Vaclav's command of her language had improved. And, much as English would be necessary for his work, this amazing improvement did indeed seem eloquently to express his feelings for her.

After leaving the airfield the following morning, Sally began to find the ride back to the ATA ferry pool far too undemanding. The pilot beside her in his Morris Eight was little more than an acquaintance, and their conversation soon dried to nothing after an initial exchange of pleasantries. Left to her own thoughts, she had no alternative to reconsidering the previous evening, and to admitting at last that her fondness for Vaclav Capkova did seem based on sparse knowledge of the man. They had met only the twice, and with that first occasion so brief that there had been no real introduction to each other. Even despite last night's passionate embraces, she knew hardly any more about who Vaclav really was than she had after his visit to her hospital ward.

Allowing herself to indulge in such intimate kisses wasn't usual for Sally, and certainly not with someone who indisputably was still a stranger. A stranger in her country, she reflected, remembering how he had stood a little away from the other airmen at the bar. A stranger who had admitted to her that his new life with the RAF presented difficulties. She could only conclude that his air of not quite belonging among his fellow pilots had aroused her sympathy, and had softened her heart.

But it must not soften her head, she decided. Being excited by all the passion that Vaclav generated was a distraction Sally could ill afford. She had been one of the fortunate ones to be selected for the Air Transport Auxiliary, the only means by which she was likely to operate as a wartime pilot. Holding on to her job while there doubtless were others ready to compete for the work did mean that she had to keep ahead of all that might be required of her.

Before this Czech pilot had come into her life, she'd already been fully occupied. Never quite free to follow every whim: alongside the commitment to her job, there always existed certain responsibilities towards her father.

Henry Downing might have a good housekeeper, but that didn't relieve his daughter of constant concern for his well-being. Neglecting him would be unforgivable. She could never dismiss the opposition he'd put forward from the moment that she'd expressed her intention of acting as an ATA pilot. Sally had always known that she wasn't only lucky to have been accepted for that work, she was luckier still to have won the freedom to take it up!

Arriving back at base, Sally was despatched immediately to fly a Hurricane to Biggin

41

Hill, the fighter station in Kent which over several weeks had received fierce bombardment from the Luftwaffe. Now struggling to continue operations, they needed to be re-equipped with the same speed as the airfield itself was being repaired.

Although she had heard about the massive damage incurred there, and the terrible loss of life, Sally was shaken as soon as Biggin Hill came into sight. She had been told of the WAAF girls having their shelter destroyed about them and the wrecking of workshops, the NAAFI and the sergeants' mess; none of the news had prepared her for the general destruction awaiting her.

Coming in to land, the evidence of craters hastily repaired along the runway was very obvious, and it looked to her initially as though every building on site had been ruined.

'Thank God for that,' she was greeted when she reported in to the makeshift office. 'We're as desperate for machines as we are for men to crew them.'

'I believe I'm scheduled to deliver you a few more of these.'

Sally refrained from suggesting that a shortage of fighter pilots might be alleviated, if only temporarily, by engaging women like herself. She'd had months of learning to accept that these male fliers would, in the main, need years to recognize how capable their opposite numbers might be. For the present, she could only express her genuine sympathy regarding their losses.

'I was dreadfully sorry to learn how severe the damage here is, everyone connected with the RAF would be shaken by what happened. We can understand that a great many people will be feeling upset.'

The officer nodded. 'But we are fighting back, becoming used to getting everything operational again after an attack.'

Delivering to the hurriedly reconstructed Biggin Hill airfield and others like it became a routine, and one which kept Sally too busy to give in to her distress whenever she witnessed appalling devastation. Sometimes, though, there was no avoiding evidence of the men and women for whom life had ended when their RAF base became an enemy target.

Sally had to will herself to carry on, and to confine her tears to the nights. At least, giving in to emotion then was not preventing her from helping the Allied cause.

Those nights began to occur all too frequently and, going to bed exhausted if dry-eyed, she would awaken abruptly, and in tears, from dreams that were ferociously vivid. She would lie awake, wondering and worrying, and all the while deeply concerned for one airman, Vaclav Capkova. She was finding it hard to believe that he might be

43

spared when so many were being lost. Anxious for him though she was, Sally knew that she couldn't just go off to see Vaclav, she had another duty. She ought to seize the first opportunity to visit her father again.

Through his phone calls she recognized that Henry Downing was becoming really depressed about the use of his mill for war work. Originally a carpet designer himself, he hadn't realized, until it was taken from him, how greatly he relished seeing good designs coming off his looms. For him, there wasn't an ounce of interest in any of the stuff they were obliged to produce now, and no amount of assurances that they were aiding the war effort could help him.

Sally's next leave was short, a mere forty-eight hours. Initially, she still caught herself wishing that she might somehow use it to be with Vaclav, just to learn that he was all right. All the early resolve to be sensible about her attitude towards the Czech pilot was evaporating with the nightly dread that he might suffer a similar fate to the others who had perished. She would miss him so terribly.

She could try to ignore the feelings of attraction which Vaclav generated in her even while they were separated by this distance of many miles. What she could not control was even stronger feelings of affec-

44

tion and concern. And the depth of such emotions disturbed her more greatly than any degree of passion.

Not knowing the man well no longer really counted, except that it created enough bewilderment in her own head to force her repeatedly to re-examine his impact upon her life. Perhaps it was as well that she had this other demand on her free time!

Disciplining herself to take the train up to Yorkshire seemed hard, but once she was on her way, Sally resolved that this would mark a turning point. Hadn't she already concluded that devoting too much attention to Vaclav was anything but sensible?

Giving her few free hours to her father would certainly force her feet firmly back on to the ground.

Henry seemed better than during her last telephone conversation with him. He might eventually accept the changes to the production his factory was turning out – if not gracefully, at least with rueful common sense. As he said, by going along with such inevitable changes, he was avoiding being directed into even less congenial work. His mill was close to home, an advantage which, even on the bad days, he could not deny. And since Sally's last leave, he had insisted that David Saunders spend more free time with him. He had missed the man's company more than he'd admit, and was pleased

45

to think David benefited from being able to talk through problems of adjusting to his new position at the munitions factory.

David was at the house when Sally arrived in the evening. Since she recalled mentioning that the two men might spend more time together, she could not complain. She was too tired, anyway, to do other than fall in with whatever arrangements had been made following her earlier phone call.

Mrs Holbrook had laid on a wholesome meal, which, if a little plain, was far superior to much of the food that Sally managed to snatch at one airfield or another.

David appeared tired also, less chatty even for him; she sensed that she wasn't the only one to feel oppressed by the war enmeshing them all. When it was time to depart for his own home, he did suggest that she might wish to go somewhere on the following day, but he seemed unperturbed when Sally declined.

'I'm glad you didn't arrange anything with him, love,' her father confessed as soon as they were alone. 'You get so little time with me. I like it well enough when David joins us here, but I'm afraid, when it's only a forty-eight, I don't want to let you out of my sight.'

Sally could go along with that for what remained of the two days, and limited her contact with Emma to a chat on the phone, just to keep them in touch. As it happened, one of the children had gone down with the mumps and was keeping Emma fully occupied.

'I will see you next time I'm up at home,' Sally promised.

The only occasion she went out was for a walk with her father after chapel on the Sunday morning. Mrs Holbrook had come over from her own house to cook for them, freeing Sally to enjoy her leave.

Henry asked where she wished to go, but Sally was content to let him choose, and was pleased when he set off in the direction of West View Park. Another of her favourite spots, and filled with childhood memories, she would never tire of revisiting the place.

Reaching the terrace that overlooked the valley and backdrop of hills, they stood shoulder to shoulder, relishing the sunlight if not the cold wind that tugged at their clothing.

'You've always liked it here, haven't you, Sally love? And that's important. We've all got to have somewhere that matters. A bit of territory that's a part of what "home" means.'

'That's right, Dad,' Sally agreed.

Suddenly, though, she could not look at him. Henry would have seen the tears welling in her eyes, and he wasn't a man who'd neglect to enquire as to their cause.

She was fast becoming far more vulnerable

47

than she liked. Speaking of places that represented home was enough to remind her of how disturbed Vaclav must feel so very far from *his* home. From his people. It seemed as if, no matter how strong her resolve, she could not switch off her concern for him. And, again, her emotions did not make sense – why in the world should she experience this longing that he might find his home where she was?

Surrendering to her father's ideas for the rest of their time together was, in a way, an escape from her troubled feelings. Always someone who enjoyed carrying out his own wishes, Henry Downing was happy in the present. During this visit of hers, he refrained from complaining about the time he was obliged to spend without her, and emphasized instead his satisfaction with the hours they spent together.

'I'd thought David might have called round this afternoon, to see you afore you had to go back, but happen you don't mind that he hasn't?'

'Not in the least, Dad. This has been fine.'

'That goes for me an' all.'

Driving her to Halifax station for her train, Henry surprised her with a generous offer. 'I've been thinking as how it isn't so good for you to have to keep trekking back and forth on railways that have uncertain schedules, and in trains like as not packed. I've a mind to set you up with a car of your own. How would that suit, Sally love?'

'That sounds a lovely idea, but why would you? I'm not without funds of my own, you know.'

Her father smiled. 'Let's just say I want to do something to make life a little easier for you. I might not like the work you're doing, you know, but it does my heart good to see how well you tackle it.'

'I don't know what to say – I do appreciate the thought, Dad, but should we be buying cars in wartime?'

'I wasn't contemplating setting you up with anything the size of mine. There's an Austin Seven I have my eye on. One of the chaps from the mill belongs it – he's in the navy now, it's stood there doing nothing. And his young wife has indicated she'd be glad to have it taken off their hands.'

Sally thanked him, naturally, before he dropped her off for her train. By the time she had reached her platform she had pushed all thought of a car to the back of her mind. She wasn't at all certain that she wouldn't have preferred to buy a vehicle herself, if she really needed one. It seemed years since she had felt indebted to her father, she didn't fancy finding herself in that situation now.

The car, when it arrived, took her by surprise, but no more so than having her father and David Saunders deliver it. Fortunately, Sally was somewhere around the house on that particular Sunday. Rarely for her, she'd opted for spending a few hours in the billet where she had a room. A couple of weeks previously she had moved there, pleased to take up the chance of getting away from life on the base. She was quite enjoying the opportunity to experience a bit of more normal, civilian life.

When her landlady Mrs Congreve tapped on her door and announced that she had visitors, Sally frowned, puzzled.

'Are you sure they're here to see me, Mrs Congreve? Nobody knows where I'm staying, do they?'

'Your father does, dear. At least, that's who he says he is. And there's another gentleman with him.'

'Oh, of course – I had to let Dad know where he could contact me when I'm not on duty.'

They were waiting in the old-fashioned hall, occupying chairs that were set against the wall to either side of the umbrella stand, looking for all the world like bookends.

'What's brought you here then, Dad?' Sally enquired after kissing him.

'That car I promised you! Leastways, David here insisted on driving that. I came in my own, to make certain of getting us back home, like.'

50

'Well, I don't know!' Mrs Congreve exclaimed. 'This is the right sort of a father to have, and no mistake.'

'He is indeed,' said Sally. 'I'm ever so grateful, Dad.'

Mrs Congreve tagged along when they went outside to inspect the Austin Seven, and she enthused repeatedly about the car. Still retaining a few reservations about not purchasing the car herself, Sally tried to sound equally enthusiastic. She was Henry's only daughter, after all, she might expect he would wish to indulge her.

'David will explain all the workings of it,' Henry told her. 'You should find it easy enough after handling an aeroplane!'

'If you're going to have a bit of a drive round, I'll be making a pot of tea ready for when you get back,' said Mrs Congreve, as happy as anyone to have a hand in making arrangements. 'You must come indoors to wait, Mr Downing.'

'It's good of you to come all the way down south to bring this,' Sally told David.

'No trouble at all, love. Soon as I heard your dad asking one of the chaps retired from the mill to accompany him, I insisted it had to be me instead. You know how glad I always am to see you. And we didn't manage that during your last visit.'

David opened the driver's door and indicated that she sit behind the wheel. Sally slid on to the leather seat, and grasped the steering wheel, glancing about her for the controls. She hadn't driven her father's car for years, and this looked very different.

As he got in beside her, she noticed how large David seemed in his outdoor coat, quite overpowering with his shoulder right against her own. He was leaning across now, pointing out the speedometer, and where the car started up.

'You've driven that monster of Henry's, haven't you? The principle's the same, of course, regarding the clutch, brake and accelerator. Not that you'll find much else that's similar, there's so little power here, by comparison.'

'But it'll get me around.'

'Happen it'll encourage you to make it up to Halifax more often. Here's hoping, anyway ... I miss you, you know, Sally.'

She hadn't wished to hear that. Having David miss her was as bad as her father bemoaning her absence, and far more complex.

Starting up the Austin and negotiating carefully to pass her father's car took her mind away from David's statement, if it failed to distract her from his overwhelming presence. Growing accustomed to the controls, she was thankful to drive out of the narrow street into a wider road where she could increase her speed slightly.

'I like the feel of this. Were you happy with her on the way down, David?'

'Yes, yes. But then I'd insisted on vetting this little beauty before Henry put in an offer. Wanted to be certain you got the best.'

'Thank you,' said Sally, wondered if she ought to say more, but decided she wasn't about to lead David to read anything deeper into whatever she might add.

Today, he had plenty to say; initially, about the car, but then regarding his own concern for her. 'I could only make sure this car was safe for you, but I wish with all my heart that I could ensure that every flight you make ended safely.'

A short distance ahead Sally saw a place where she might draw in to the kerb without causing problems for other motorists. Slowing to a halt, she contemplated saying something to leave David with no illusions regarding her wishes. She always recognized the signs that he was pushing to strengthen their relationship. Suddenly though, Sally felt unable to summon words which might clarify without hurting. She resorted instead to switching off the engine, and smiling as she opened her door.

'You'd better show me how to use the starting handle, hadn't you? If I don't learn how, the odds are I'll soon find I can't get her going without it!'

The relief of being out into the air, away

53

from such close contact with him, was immediate, and lasted only until David's hands closed over her own on the starting handle. Sally wondered what she had let herself in for. The good thing was that this drive wouldn't last more than another few minutes. And she was sure already that having this useful little car would amply compensate for today's awkwardness.

Back at her billet, Henry and Mrs Congreve were enjoying tea and toast, both eager to be assured by David's assessment that Sally handled the Austin splendidly.

By the time that the two men departed for the long journey home, their spirits were lightened by Sally's genuine appreciation of all that they had done for her.

David seemed absolutely delighted, and evidently was taking her thanks as referring especially to his decision to come to see her. *I do wish I could like David more, that I could find him attractive*, thought Sally as she checked that the Austin was locked securely when she turned away from waving off her father's car.

Life might be so simple if she could eventually settle down as Mrs David Saunders. She would be close at hand for her father, and with a man who already thought highly of him.

The trouble was, she never had longed for a simple life. All her experiences since leaving home were encouraging her to look for something greater: work that would always satisfy, and a relationship that would bring complete fulfilment. Sally had a strong feeling that she would not find any of that very close to Downing House.

Three

Sally had not been particularly keen to have her father purchase the car for her but before the end of 1940 she was thankful to have the ability to get around more easily.

Vaclav had persuaded her to give him a telephone number where she might be reached whenever she was at her base.

Although it often seemed to Sally that she was more frequently in the air or en route back from delivering an aircraft, there were several occasions when Vaclav succeeded in contacting her. Ever since she had witnessed the terrible damage to the airfield at Biggin Hill, her worries about the safety of the Czech pilot had continued. Being aware of the dangers he faced while flying was bad enough, adding in the hazards of possible bombing by the Luftwaffe increased the anxiety.

Her relief each time Vaclav's voice came down the line combined with the excitement that was generated by listening to him. Even her own name gave her a thrill when he was the one who was speaking. His English was still improving and they often talked at length. Sally found comfort in relieving the tension of her job, and she was delighted when Vaclav said he was glad to have one person to depend on, in this land that still felt rather strange to him.

Vaclav currently was based at one of the Kent airfields. When they both had weekend leave that coincided, he asked her to spend some time with him.

'You can stay in a room in the local inn, can you not?' he suggested.

Reassured that Vaclav had no illusions that they might be staying somewhere together, Sally was content with the arrangement.

They were into winter now, and she certainly was pleased to have her own transport for the trip and, since she hardly ever used the Austin, enough petrol to drive off to meet Vaclav.

Excitement was an understatement of her emotions. She hadn't felt so elated for weeks, and seemed to hear his voice in her ears as she pressed on through Sussex towards the border with Kent.

After first agreeing to their meeting, Sally had cautioned herself to remain wary of attaching too much significance to the potential for their relationship. Their telephone calls had revealed very little more about Vaclav, and in any case this war brought its own reminders that complete certainty must be imperative before making any commitment to someone.

All such reservations evaporated as soon as her own identity documents had secured her admission to Vaclav's base at Manston. He was waiting eagerly for her arrival and in no time at all she had turned the car and was driving them off into the late afternoon sun.

They were chatting rapidly, exchanging details of recent flights that each had tackled, while assuring one another that nothing could be more fun than getting together again. Sally suspected that Vaclav was editing out some of the more alarming encounters in which he'd engaged while airborne, but she could sympathize with that. Experience had taught her how much to withhold when recounting her own exploits to anyone who was close.

And she and Vaclav were close in affection, they had hugged and kissed immediately on seeing each other.

They ate that evening in the pub where she was to stay, and were glad to sit up to the open fire afterwards. Her little car was un-heated, not the most comfortable of vehicles in which to spend much time after the sun had gone down.

They were just congratulating themselves on having an air-raid-free day when a siren sounded. The landlady announced immediately that drinks would continue to be served in the cellar, which also functioned as a shelter.

'But do you have to report back on duty?' Sally asked Vaclav. She knew there was a possibility that all pilots might be needed back at base.

Smiling, he shook his head. 'They would not call on me, my plane is out of action since two days. And we do not have the surplus aircraft until more are delivered.'

'Don't tell me we Air Transport Auxiliary folk have let you down,' Sally exclaimed with a grin.

'I do not believe any shortage is for that reason. The manufacturers are not supplying swiftly enough to cover losses, yes?'

'That's true.'

When they followed everyone who was heading down to the cellars, Vaclav noticed that one door at the far end was labelled 'garage'.

'I think perhaps we might ask if your car could be placed in there for safety, if the garage space also is underground.'

Enquiring, they learned that there was indeed room for the Austin there. One of the barmaids took them outside to show where the entrance to the garage was.

As Sally drove inside they discovered that the only other vehicle was a Morris of similar size to the Austin, which left them more than sufficient parking space. They had been shown how to close the outer doors, and told to knock on the inner one to be let through into the main cellar.

Sally was about to head in that direction after Vaclav had secured the other doors when he detained her with a gentle hand on her shoulder.

'Do you really wish to spend all our time with more persons, when you have your comfortable car, and in here it will be quite warm, I think...'

Settling into their seats once more, Sally felt Vaclav's arm going around her as he drew her closely to him. His lips still felt cool from the wintry night, but their pressure against her mouth quickly generated their now familiar ecstasy.

'I have longed for you so much, for so many long days,' he told her. 'Even when I make for me new friends among my comrades, I think constantly of you, and ache to be with you.'

'That goes for me too,' Sally admitted, no longer so wary of conveying how much Vaclav meant to her. Why had she supposed that this war made people aware of how unstable the future seemed, no time for commitment? It surely created the need to make the most of each day, of every hour.

'If we were in a different world,' Vaclav continued, 'a world that was ideal, we would have our own place in it, somewhere to be together. But I would not need you more than I do this day. Do you understand what I am telling you?'

Sally understood, just as she recognized in her own racing pulse and surging emotions that this pilot here attracted her more fiercely than anyone she'd ever encountered anywhere.

They kissed and kissed again, she felt his fingers at her breast and silently willed him on to increase the excitement. Beside her Vaclav was stirring, despite the confines of the little car, pressing a thigh against her own, his warmth urging her to cling to him. Beneath her sweater one of his hands was tracing the column of her spine, the other still was caressing her breast.

Vaclav drew her yet nearer across his lap, holding her to him, willing her to comprehend his need. His tongue darted between her teeth, savouring her taste as he ached to savour the whole of her. The cruel months since he had held a girl this close felt like an eternity. Inwardly, he groaned, suspecting that even longer months could elapse before he might find contentment.

He loved Sally so much tonight, but would he love her tomorrow, and for a succession of tomorrows? If he were able to choose, would she be the one with whom he would wish total commitment? In this strange land, she anchored his life, her strength was the tenderness which created his compulsion to join them irrevocably.

Her hand rested on his thigh: if he knew Sally better he could perhaps beg her caresses ... if he knew her less well, he might have expected she would comply.

Even as things stood, her nearness was wonderful, heightening all senses, promising fulfilment, inducing dreams of what might be. Aware like this, *attracted*, he felt fully alive, exhilarated by sensations.

'We'd better go in, join the others,' Sally murmured.

'One more kiss,' Vaclav protested.

The deepest kiss of all, it continued on and on, her sweetness and her warmth urging that he must not falter, this was opportunity. Mouth and arms alone must somehow convey how he would love her for ever, love her completely.

'Remember this,' he told her, before, finally, they went through to the rest of the pub.

Memories of that night were to be all they had as evidence of their closeness. Back at his base, Vaclav tried to sleep, while in her upstairs room at the inn Sally wrestled with her emotions. Had she been so intensely cruel as she feared? Acutely conscious of Vaclav's need, how had she refrained from giving the love which she already believed she felt for him?

There was to be no ready solution. The

following day allowed them even fewer opportunities for private moments. Despite having spent the night under cover, her car seemed to have succumbed to either the cold or the underground damp. When she'd had breakfast and greeted Vaclav as he strolled into the pub, Sally was compelled to ask his assistance.

'As soon as I came down this morning I went to start her up, and I couldn't get a spark out of the ignition.'

'Did you try the—' He paused, seeking the English words. 'The handle to make to start? You do possess such a thing?'

'Of course. And I'd made sure of being shown how to use it. Today, nothing did the trick.'

Vaclav went with her to the garage, smiling to himself as he thought how he would demonstrate his superior prowess. It wasn't that he'd ever resented Sally's ability to pilot an aeroplane exactly – but he would not regret this opportunity to master this tiny car's starting handle for her.

The situation refused to yield to him. Neither his greater strength nor his advanced experience proved of use. Vaclav soon was obliged to admit that they would need to seek help elsewhere.

The pub landlady pointed them towards a tiny petrol station where the aged mechanic agreed reluctantly to come out to her car.

'If you weren't in the forces, dear,' he told her quite sharply, 'I'd be showing how much work I've got waiting already. Far too many people are being compelled to keep their cars running long after they're really past repair.'

As the day dragged on it became apparent that Sally and Vaclav would be the ones waiting for attention. The fault proved to be a discharged battery, and the mechanic didn't have a suitable one in stock.

'I'll not see you stuck, I will get a battery for you, but it can't be before I close for lunch so's I can drive over to Ramsgate. And I'll have to bill you for my petrol in addition.'

They planned to take a walk, see something of the Kent countryside while they were prevented from driving anywhere, but even with her hand in Vaclav's, Sally could not avoid feeling deflated.

The day was extremely cold, their situation too near the east coast to find much shelter. When a thin drizzle began to fall, Sally found remaining cheerful difficult. Snow might have been better, she reflected, even though the iciness of the surrounding air would have chilled them even further.

It was late afternoon before the mechanic found time to come out to the pub and fit the battery that he'd obtained. Vaclav had waited with her to make sure that Sally had the means of returning to her own base, but half an hour later he was compelled to leave her and report for duty.

'I think that very soon I shall be moving from Kent,' he said while they were saying goodbye. 'As you may know, there are many pilots from my homeland in Britain now. Our own Czech squadrons are being formed.'

'I had heard something. With your own senior men in charge as well?'

'But yes. We too possess pilots of squadron leader calibre, and others more highly qualified than that, you know.'

'I'm pleased for you then, you'll be happier with men from your own country.' But behind her words Sally was disguising a sudden unease. Vaclav would no longer need her so greatly. Living and working among his own people, he easily might forget her...

'I shall contact you again, but in another new place I will need more time perhaps before obtaining a leave pass.'

Vaclav had done a lot of thinking overnight. He had thrilled to the passion aroused between himself and this lovely English girl, but had no wish to behave unfairly. Towards *anyone*.

The delayed start of her journey from Kent meant that there was no time for going to her billet at Mrs Congreve's house. Approaching the familiar ferry pool, Sally felt relieved, and not solely because her car had performed immaculately since acquiring the new battery. She had needed time in which to allow her emotions to cool, and that was precisely what the long drive on a winter's evening had provided. With no part of her could she regret the attraction which had soared between herself and Vaclav, she had relished every exciting minute. But she still experienced this gnawing concern that she had done nothing to provide any release for Vaclav. She couldn't remain oblivious to the frustrations that service life often created.

Sally knew her upbringing was largely responsible for this sudden preoccupation with sex, making it enter her life with such impact. She'd never in the old days had much cause for even thinking about desire. The daughter of strict parents, who had left her in no doubt that she must remain chaste until the day that she married in their Methodist chapel, her mother's death had only increased her own resolve. Hadn't Henry Downing implied that respecting his wife Gwen's memory tied in with such principles? Until meeting Vaclav, Sally hadn't been greatly troubled by the prospect of reserving full intimacy until after getting wed.

'I hadn't understood that could be so hard,' she murmured aloud inside the car with her base now in sight, while she

66

resolved to give her full attention to work.

Perhaps it would be for the best if Vaclav's move to a different station were to prevent them from meeting frequently? Or even from meeting at all?

Contemplating the possibility of not seeing him again was beginning to seem less appalling. This second day of their weekend had been such an anticlimax. And although the rain had cleared during her drive, Sally's spirits had not lifted with the weather.

Reporting in provided an instant distraction from all personal emotions.

'I hope you've rested for your whole leave,' she was told. 'You're to grab a brief snatch of sleep, plus something to eat, then you're on your way. There's been another hit on Biggin Hill, where they're reminding us that their squadrons are not yet up to strength.'

Following the intense bombing of so many of the south-eastern airfields, this shortage of aircraft seemed insuperable. For days and days Sally flew off repeatedly to deliver planes, with barely sufficient time for sleeping and grabbing a meal between one flight and the next.

Christmas was fast approaching and with it the short leave Sally was promised after working a lot of additional hours. Henry Downing finally caught up with her in a phone call insisting she must spend her time at home.

'Of course, Dad,' she promised. 'I wouldn't go anywhere else.' She'd never been in doubt that this was one time of year when he relied very greatly upon her. There was a further reason too for her need to go home. A bomb had landed recently in Halifax, devastating the area around Hanson Lane; eleven people had died and several had been injured. The incident, rare though it was, had reminded Sally that no one anywhere was invulnerable.

'At least you've your own transport now,' Henry continued. 'Though I suppose you'll remind me you can't promise what time you'll get here.'

Although looking forward to Christmas with nothing more in mind than being able to relax for a short while, Sally used a precious couple of free hours to shop for gifts to take with her to Halifax. She would be ensuring some time with her friend Emma and the children, and chose presents for them as well as something for Paul. Emma hadn't said if he would manage to get home leave, but his gift would be there when he next came back from sea.

Finding something to give David Saunders was less easy. Still living in the house inherited when his parents died quite young in an accident, David possessed a home that was already fully equipped. He also seemed disinclined to update anything within it. As for David himself, he had no taste for what he called 'frivolous luxuries'. Sally decided to wait until she arrived in Yorkshire, and ask her father's advice regarding David's present.

Reporting to base following her brief shopping trip, Sally was greeted by one of her fellow ATA pilots, who announced that there had been a phone call for her.

'Who was it?' she asked, worried, wondering if her father was ringing through with a problem.

'The man didn't say. He just left this number. It was only ten minutes since, why don't you call him now?'

'I have been standing by the telephone, praying that you would call me!' The voice was unmistakably Vaclav Capkova's, and Sally found she was smiling.

'How are you, Vaclav? I take it you're with one of your own squadrons now? You must be very happy.'

'I am with a Czech outfit, yes,' Vaclav replied slowly, but not sounding exactly thrilled to be with his own people. 'Is simpler, of course, to speak with one another, but...'

'But?' Sally prompted, his voice had trailed off so drearily.

'You must take no attention of what I say,' he went on hurriedly. 'Is not important.'

69

'What isn't? Important, I mean...?'

'We talk *too much* now perhaps, all of us together here. About our homeland, about how it is at Christmas there, in the old days.'

'Oh, I see.' Sally could understand their being homesick, especially for a country where the German occupation was likely to be imposing difficulties on the local inhabitants. All Czech airmen must be deeply concerned for their families.

'There is an idea, I have, a hope – Sally, could you spend some time with me? We are in nice countryside, here in East Anglia, and I am promised leave at Christmas.'

'Sorry, Vaclav, I couldn't. I've already made arrangements—'

His sigh interrupted her. 'You are angry with me, yes? Because I do not speak to you in long time.'

'I'm not angry at all, nothing like that. It's just that I've promised Dad that I'll go up to Halifax. There's only me, you see...'

'You are fortunate to be sure that he is safe. No one of us here can know if our people are alive.'

Sally couldn't let Vaclav remain so unhappy, especially over Christmas. 'You could come with me, up to Yorkshire.' Hadn't she visualized taking him there?

His evident delight was enough to suppress her qualms about such an arrangement. She would phone through and explain to her father. Henry knew what it was to dread being alone, he would understand.

Vaclav agreed to phone her again nearer to Christmas, when they would finalize details of their journey north.

Vaclav began his leave one day earlier than Sally, which provided him with time to make the journey to her base. She was living in there again, no longer billeted with Mrs Congreve, who had been taken ill. Someone had found Vaclav a bed for the night, enabling the two of them to set out early in the morning of Christmas Eve.

Sally had been pleased to see how cheerful Vaclav appeared when he arrived, and felt well rewarded for the difficulties she'd encountered when ringing to tell Henry that she would be bringing a friend with her.

The hope that her father might be understanding when she explained this friend was another pilot who had no chance of getting home for Christmas, had proved over-optimistic.

'So, I'll have to share you, I suppose,' Henry had remarked heavily. 'And your time here short enough, as it is.'

'But at least you will have company,' she'd reminded him.

'Aye, aye,' he'd said hastily. He had hung up before Sally had told him that their guest was male.

71

Despite strong winds and intermittent rain, the drive up to Halifax was pleasant enough. She and Vaclav were too busy catching up with each other's lives to be greatly perturbed by the weather. Stopping once for a meal and a second time to buy hot drinks, they managed to ward off the effects of travelling in the unheated Austin.

Vaclav was in uniform, proudly displaying the badge of his recently formed Czech squadron. Sally was pleased for him now that he could work among fellow citizens of his own country. Today, he seemed quite happy, less preoccupied with the situation in Prague. She couldn't have been more thankful that she had invited him to come away with her.

Mrs Holbrook opened the door to them. Wearing her coat and hat, she evidently was just leaving for her own home.

'Miss Sally, I'm right glad I haven't missed you! Come on in, both of you, and let me get this door shut afore we have the wardens after us for showing a chink of light. Your father's getting changed, he'll be down any minute.'

Smiling widely, Mrs Holbrook shook hands with Vaclav when they were introduced. 'I've got the front spare room warming nicely, with a fire in the grate.'

'That's good, thanks,' said Sally. 'And are we going to see much of you over Christmas,

Mrs Holbrook?'

'Bless you, no, love. I'm off to my daughter's now. But you'll find I've left everything as near ready as I could.'

'I'm sure you have, you always do. But before you rush off, I've got a bit of something for you.'

Suspecting they might see her only fleetingly, Sally had kept the housekeeper's gift near to hand. 'Not to be opened till Christmas Day, think on,' she insisted. She hoped Vaclav hadn't noticed another present, labelled with his name. She had shopped hurriedly the previous day in order to give him something.

Henry Downing came slowly down the staircase as the front door was closing behind Mrs Holbrook. His gaze shot straight to Vaclav, and looked so astonished that Sally was afraid her father might miss his footing on the next step.

'So – you'd better introduce us, hadn't you?' said Henry as he strode towards them across the tiled hall.

Smiling in the hope that she might counteract Henry's potential indifference, Sally took Vaclav's arm and encouraged him the pace or so to meet her father. 'Dad, this is a friend of mine, Vaclav Capkova. Vaclav, I want you to meet my father, Henry Downing.'

'How do you do?' said Henry while Vaclav

gave a courteous bow over Henry's hand.

'I hope that you are well, Mr Downing.'

'Well enough, thanks.'

Sally hugged her father and gave him a kiss, then showed Vaclav where to hang his greatcoat. She noticed Henry was scrutinizing Vaclav's uniform.

'Not British, then. Polish, are you?'

'Czech,' Vaclav announced, in a tone challenging him to fault his nationality.

'Didn't know they had an air force.'

'Not many people do. They will learn.'

'And "Vaclav" – what sort of a name's that?'

'A saint's, sir. St Wenceslas, you sing of him at Christmas, I believe.'

Henry's eyes narrowed. Sally recalled that he'd never liked people who had a swift answer for him, and Vaclav's had seemed very swift. She suspected that her Czech friend had needed to arm himself with the translation of his name, one which should have made for smoother relations with his English host.

'I gather from Mrs Holbrook that one of the spare rooms is ready. I'll take Vaclav up, shall I? What time do you want to have our meal, Dad?'

'As soon as David gets here. He won't be long, said he can't wait to see you.'

'David's a family friend, used to work with my father,' Sally explained, leading the way

74

upstairs. She was determined nothing Henry Downing said or did should convey a wrong impression.

'Not *your* especial friend then?' said Vaclav lightly.

'Not mine, no.'

Sally was pleased that their housekeeper had created a warm welcome in the room which she herself always thought was enhanced by its peach-toned fabrics and mahogany furniture. Vaclav's smile revealed instant appreciation.

'You have a lovely home, I think.'

She showed Vaclav where the bathroom was and left him to unpack the few things he had brought to Halifax. After hastily freshening up, Sally threw on a green woollen dress and hurried down to her father. She needed to have a word with him before they were joined by either Vaclav or David.

The voices from the living room told her that David had arrived anyway, and she sighed over the missed opportunity for a straight talk,

Both men were standing near the living-room hearth. David turned and strode quickly across to take both of her hands in his own.

'Sally, lovely to see you again! How are you? And did the car behave all right on the way here?'

She manoeuvred his kiss on to her cheek,

but hadn't succeeded in extracting her hands from David's when she heard Vaclav entering the room behind her.

'I'm fine, thanks, and we had a good journey. Didn't we, Vaclav?' she added, freeing herself to include him.

Introducing the two men, Sally noted thankfully that neither of them appeared overtly disturbed by the other's presence. She hoped this indicated that Vaclav accepted her explanation of David's friendship with the family. And that even if David resented the pilot who had arrived with her, he would not attempt to assert any imagined rights over her.

The meal already waiting in the oven was hot, but the atmosphere in which it was eaten remained no more than cool.

Vaclav was trying hard to justify his place there by interesting them in the customary family gatherings on Christmas Eve in his home. 'We always had carp soup, and then ate carp some more, fried perhaps with potato salad. And for something sweet we would have fruitcake.'

'Never tried carp myself, never wanted to,' Henry observed. 'Can't beat a nice bit of haddock.'

'We give presents to each other also on this special evening,' Vaclav continued. 'Before we attend the Christmas Mass.'

'Catholic then,' Henry murmured. A

further difference, said cold grey eyes.

'Henry's family are all Methodists,' David explained gently. 'But I'm C of E.'

Vaclav understood from the church parades witnessed since being involved with the RAF. 'Is not always so very different perhaps from my cathedral.'

''Course it's different,' Henry insisted. 'Got to kowtow to the Pope, haven't you?'

'But we all believe in the one Christ,' said Sally. She could see where her father was leading this, and she didn't mean to have him advance his tactics one step further.

David rescued the moment, turning to Vaclav and beginning to explain how he now was managing a factory where they made arms for use in aircraft. Listening, the Czech pilot nodded and smiled, inserting the occasional 'that is good' to emphasize that he comprehended.

'Vaclav knew hardly any English when he came to England, Dad,' Sally revealed. 'He has learned a tremendous amount very quickly.'

'I dare say he had in mind to better himself when he decided to come over here,' said Henry.

'No, it was more a matter of managing to reach somewhere where he could do his bit to fight the Germans,' she contradicted. 'In life and death situations, bettering yourself doesn't enter into it.'

Henry didn't like that, but was prepared to let it go. He could wish to antagonize this stranger in his home without wanting to annoy his daughter.

Silence soon began to express the unease between the four of them again, and Vaclav tried to introduce another topic.

'Do you have any customs here for early December? In my country, parents or uncles dress like the devil, or like St Nicholas, to ask if the children have been good. They then leave gifts...'

'We give our presents on Christmas Day, naturally, like everybody,' said Henry, interrupting. 'But, this time, we're doing that tonight.' He wanted this chap to see what fine gifts he'd provided for Sally and David, and expected he'd feel chastened by not being included. Not his fault the arrangements Sally made were last-minute.

David seemed to have been unaware that Sally was bringing someone home with her. He had brought presents for Sally and his old friend, but was quick to point out that he hadn't known Vaclav was to join them.

The young pilot smiled reassuringly. 'Is of no consequence. I do not expect to receive from anyone, I am thankful for the kindness of being welcomed here.'

But Sally did have a gift for him, a scarf which she had purchased in a shop close to the ferry pool. What she had overlooked was the fact that she had forgotten to put right her earlier failure to find something suitable for David.

Making matters worse, David was handing an exquisite pearl necklace to her – one which she suspected was inherited from his mother. It was far too valuable a gift, and would have embarrassed her normally. She could only thank him, then apologize and hope to convince with explanations of how hastily she had prepared for coming home.

David looked hurt by her omission, and Sally could not blame him, but Henry Downing was furious. So furious that he hardly glanced at the antique silver photograph frame that she'd located for him. Refusing to study the picture of herself that Sally had chosen especially, he set the frame aside with perfunctory thanks.

Nothing improved, but a few hours later, when David was about to leave, he turned to Vaclav. 'I shall be going to my church tonight for midnight. If you want to come with me, I'd like that. You might be able to follow some of the service.'

'That's a lovely idea, David, we'll all go,' said Sally, thankful that one person at least was showing Vaclav some consideration.

'That we won't,' Henry contradicted, glaring at his daughter. 'I gave my word that we'll be at the chapel, same as always.'

Vaclav smiled, gave a tiny shrug. 'I am sure

that we should not need to argue in this way. I am happy to go wherever you suggest, Mr Downing.'

'That's settled then,' Henry stated.

'It's not, actually, Dad,' Sally protested. 'You can't speak for me every time. And I wish to try the church, as David suggested.'

'Please yourself.'

Henry would not waver. He wasn't pleased by loss of face, he never had been. No one need learn how distressed he would be to be forced to attend chapel without his daughter.

Vaclav and David began getting ready to go out, and still the atmosphere remained unhappy. Henry and Sally met in the hall when she came down the stairs.

'I shan't forget this, not in a long time,' he told her gravely. 'First, you neglect your old friend David—'

'I haven't neglected David, I wouldn't.'

'You have – by not buying him a decent present, nor a present of any sort. Then you choose to neglect me, an' all, refusing to go to chapel with me. On Christmas Eve, of all times.'

'Haven't you reflected that I might believe the spirit of Christmas was more faithfully expressed in considering folk that are denied the comfort of their own home, and of their own family? I'm sorry, Dad, but I don't think your behaviour tonight is particularly

80

Christian.'

The other two joined them as Henry was thrusting on his heavy coat and opening the door.

'Make sure you lock up properly as you go,' he snapped over his shoulder.

'I am so sorry,' said Vaclav. 'I would not wish to create any contention while you are so thoughtful of me.'

'You're not creating anything bad, it's that old so-and-so,' Sally told him. 'He's always liked his own way, he's not going to adapt readily to anybody else's.'

'I'm afraid that may be true,' David agreed. He could like his former boss and old friend without being blind to his behaviour.

'Come on, you two,' Sally urged them, switching off the lights then opening the door. 'If we have to rush to the church, we shan't have breath left for singing.'

Out in the icy night air, she slid a hand through an arm of each of the men. 'It is such a pity about the blackout,' she told Vaclav. 'In the old days you'd see masses of lights twinkling from all these glorious Yorkshire hills. Viewed from a distance, even gas lamps can add a picturesque aura to the scene.'

At her own words, she quelled a sigh. There seemed nothing picturesque about her home county tonight, and would she have recognized any such quality anyway, while Henry Downing was set to ruin everything?

Sally didn't want to hate her father, but he did seem to be challenging her to do just that. She could only pray that, from somewhere, some of them might succeed in locating a little of the spirit that was meant to grace this season.

Four

The midnight service that Christmas began to compensate for the unfortunate atmosphere in the Downing household. Wedged between Vaclav and David in one of the crowded pews, Sally found she finally was unwinding. Although she couldn't avoid thinking about her father, who would now be seated in their familiar chapel, she resolved that he must not be permitted to spoil their worship.

The hymns were familiar to her, if the order of service was not, and the ease with which Vaclav seemed to kneel or bow or stand in accord with David and the rest of the congregation suggested he was following everything readily. In fact, he appeared able to understand more of what was happening than Sally herself. This was High Church, she knew, and, although it was Anglican, appeared to have enough affinity with the Roman Catholic Church world-wide to bridge the few inadequacies in Vaclav's English.

Travelling to Yorkshire the previous day she

had marvelled at how rarely he had needed her to translate even an occasional word. She was impressed by the effort he had put into learning her language, of which he had known so little only those few months ago.

When David accompanied others towards the altar, leaving the two of them alone in the pew, Vaclav grasped Sally's hand.

'This is right for me,' he whispered. 'Not too very different from my own church, and being here with you is an occasion to remember.'

It was becoming a memory to cherish for Sally also, because of the man beside her. No matter what obstacles future events might insert between them, she could not have felt any closer to Vaclav. Close, and – despite the sanctity of this place – overwhelmingly attracted to him. If this was love, perhaps it was not too wrong of her to be experiencing such depth of emotions here?

The service ended in a crescendo of singing, the choir forming a procession as their notes soared to the rafters. Vaclav joined in, and if his voice faltered at times over more obscure words, it remained true to every note of the music.

He sounded so good, thought Sally, and longed to have him beside her always.

Flakes of snow fluttered in the wind when the three emerged; the ground at their feet was turning icy, both men insisted on steadying her as they hurried between the rows of trees and out of the churchyard. David's home was only a street's length away, and he left them with thanks for accompanying him to the service.

Alone together, Vaclav's arm went around Sally, he kissed her cheek. 'Do you regret that because I come to your home, your father is angry?'

'I'm sorry he's angry, but not that you have come here. You mustn't think that, Vaclav. I've suspected since Mother died that he is over-possessive. Having that proved leaves a nasty taste, but we'll get over it. I'm a bit sad that he's like this at Christmas, but that's his choice.'

She felt even more sad when they went into the house. Henry's coat, hat and scarf hung in the hall, which, despite its pale apricot wallpaper, felt stark, rather cold. He evidently had taken himself off to bed. Remembering coming in from chapel in previous years, to eat mince pies and sip warming brandy, she yearned for her father.

'Please do not be sad, I am here,' said Vaclav tenderly.

He had removed his greatcoat, but still wore the scarf she had given him. He slid it from his own neck to place around hers, used it to draw her close to him. He kissed her fervently on the lips, a kiss that continued on and on while delight surged right through her.

'We usually eat mince pies when we come in after the service, and drink a drop of brandy to warm us up. Would you like that?'

Smiling, Vaclav insisted he must join her in whatever tradition she might have. Sally placed the pies in the oven to heat, but discovered then that brandy was one Christmas pleasure that had succumbed to wartime shortages.

'I hope a cup of tea will do instead, or I could make coffee...'

'I shall be happy to drink tea.'

They ate their snack sitting to either side of the living-room hearth, which made Sally reflect that they looked like an old married couple. Tonight, she wished that they *were* married, she needed Vaclav so much, longed to be with him always.

He took her cup, saucer and plate when they finished eating, and placed them with his own on the low table. He reached for her hand as he came to kneel on the rug beside her feet, and then he was drawing her down with him to lie in the comfort emerging from the fire's dying embers.

Kissing her again, Vaclav held her to him while he stirred with the passion he could ignore no longer. His tongue parted her teeth while his hands pressed into her back, anchoring her more closely against him.

'You are making me to love you,' he murmured into her hair. 'One day, one day when it is right for us, I wish that you could belong with me.'

Aware solely of each other and the attraction insisting it should not be denied, neither of them heard the slippered feet descending the staircase and coming through the tiled hall towards them.

'This must stop! At once, do you hear? Get up, this instant, Sally!'

They sprang apart, immediately, stumbled to their feet, and faced Henry Downing.

'We weren't doing anything wrong, Dad,' Sally began. 'You can't expect us to have no feelings.'

'I expect you to know how to behave!' Henry turned from his daughter to Vaclav. 'Get out of my house, Vac— Vac— oh, whatever-you're-called.'

Sally went to Vaclav's side, grasped his hand, and stood firm. 'If he goes, you'll not find me here in the morning, Christmas or not. I'm an adult of twenty-three, old enough to behave as I think right. We were only having a hug and a kiss, but that's not really any business of yours, you know.'

'It is while you're under my roof.'

Sally turned to Vaclav, took his other hand as well while she gazed up at him. 'How long will it take us to drive to your base?'

Vaclav had become very pale and was frowning. 'Sally? We must not do this, you should not let me spoil this family Christmas.'

Her father noisily cleared his throat. 'Happen I have been a wee bit hasty. I – I suppose we could leave this till morning...'

Together, they faced him. It was Sally who spoke, her voice heavy with unshed tears.

'To do what, Dad? Endure a lecture from you? I don't think so, thank you. There is a lot needs sorting, but it all stems from you never accepting I'm grown up.' She sighed, turned to smile at Vaclav. 'Will you go up to your room, love, please? I only want a word or two with my father. I'll come and see you later.'

'That you'll not,' Henry contradicted. 'I'm not having such goings-on in my house.'

Sally faced him again. 'Grown up,' she repeated, very softly.

When Vaclav left them, Henry sank on to the arm of one of the chairs. Running a hand over his head, he sighed.

'It is only that...' he started, and faltered, shook his head.

'That you're having to compensate, because of being my only remaining parent? Do you think I don't know, Daddy? That I haven't sensed this ever since the two of us were left to make the best of it? It had to come to a head sooner or later, and Christmas seems to be a time when emotions are running high. But that doesn't mean that either Vaclav or I were letting our feelings run away with us. We wouldn't want that, either of us,' Sally added, and hoped that was true of Vaclav.

'You seem so young, so...'

'Immature?'

'No, no – innocent, more like.'

'Is that what you really think? After months flying back and forth for the RAF, handling planes that a man can fly. And living among men and women who have experienced more life than I ever expect to see. Men like Vaclav, that are driven from their homeland, left with only their prayers to sustain what they feel for families they haven't seen for ages. I've witnessed enough to make me grow up pretty fast, and I'm afraid the time has come to prove that it's given me sufficient judgement to decide how I behave.'

It was a long speech, Sally couldn't be sure how or where she had found the words, or assess what effect they might have on her father. At least she hadn't wept.

'I dare say you're right, Sally love. Happen you'll need to be patient with me. I'm always that worried the job you're doing will take you from me, having to contend with there being a chap who could do the same is a shock, you know.'

Sally could believe that, but the fact didn't make her any more comfortable with accepting that Henry seemed as though he would always have such a claim on her. She needed to be free, to be herself.

Vaclav was still dressed, seated on the edge of the bed, when she went to the spare room.

'I am so sorry,' he said yet again.

'There's no need to tell me. I can see that in your eyes, but we're not going to let Dad ruin this Christmas. He has to get used to me being a grown woman, living my own life. It isn't only you, Vaclav love, it's the way he'd be with any man I brought home.' She could see why Henry had encouraged David, who lived down the road.

'Have you brought no one to his house before?'

'Friends from university, once or twice.' Only that had been in a group, of girls as well as young men. Henry Downing wouldn't have read any threat in that.

Vaclav nodded to himself. He was looking serious, making Sally wonder if he was perturbed about her previous relationships. Somehow, though, that wasn't quite the concern that she seemed to read from his eyes.

'Time I went to bed, and left you to sleep,' she said. 'We'll never get up in the morning.'

The kiss they exchanged was brief. Sally hoped that the night's events hadn't eroded all the original elation generated between them.

★ ★ ★

Christmas Day was fractionally better than she had feared. Henry evidently had decided that he must accommodate his daughter's feelings, and maintain some kind of hospitality towards Vaclav.

The overt courtesy, which could have become uncomfortable, eased somewhat when David arrived in time for the meal that they were to eat mid-afternoon. Sally had been right to assume that she wouldn't rise very early and, despite Mrs Holbrook's advance preparations, cooking everything took considerable time.

David was asking Vaclav about the services he normally attended at Christmas in Prague, and was interested to learn these were in the main cathedral. The two talked for some time, comparing and contrasting aspects of the liturgy.

'I'm glad we got Sally to go to my church,' David was saying when she came into the room. 'I shall hope she'll want to be with me there whenever she's at home.'

Henry was giving David a look. Sally expected that would be followed up with a reproof for hauling her away from the chapel, but her father merely shook his head and sighed. She remembered then how highly David scored with him by being local.

When evening came and David set out for his own home, Sally suggested that she and Vaclav should visit her friends Emma and

Paul. Vaclav surprised her by proposing that they could delay calling on them until the following morning.

'We might do so perhaps on our way south. I am sure your father wishes to make the most of your company today.'

Sally hadn't anticipated that they would be returning from leave on Boxing Day. Had she overlooked something Vaclav had said when making arrangements for coming here? Or had he endured quite enough of the atmosphere in her home?

Even with Henry Downing reining in his disapproval of Vaclav while the three of them listened to the wireless, the remainder of the day wasn't exactly easy. Sally had been pleased to have Vaclav's help when she tackled clearing away and washing the dishes after their meal, but that spell in the kitchen was their only time alone together. She was tired, and a headache had plagued her all day long: not surprisingly, following the interchange with her father.

Leaving the house on Boxing Day gave her a miserable feeling. Henry had shaken hands with Vaclav and wished him well, but coolly. There had been no hint of a suggestion that he hoped he might meet him again.

Sally had been hugged and hugged again, while Henry had told her repeatedly to take care of herself. His final, 'You're all I have,' left her close to weeping.

'Let's get over to Emma's as quick as we can,' she said, as she and Vaclav got into the Austin. 'I'm desperate for somebody to cheer me up.'

Emma and Paul and the children certainly seemed to act as the tonic needed to brace them for accepting how difficult Christmas had been. In no time at all the girls were thrusting their new toys at them for inspection, while their parents enthused about the presents that Sally had given them.

'Come on and open up the parcels you've just been brought,' Paul urged the girls. 'You've had all the other stuff since yesterday.'

The youngsters had been schooled to show appreciation and thanked Sally effusively when they discovered they'd each been given a jigsaw puzzle.

'Mummy's pleased as well,' the elder girl added. 'She likes us to do jigsaws 'cos we're quiet. And I can do better ones now, not those with big pieces for babies.'

Only when the time came for them to set out on the long journey south did Sally begin to experience again all the deflation that had descended over Christmas.

'I don't know what you must think of us,' she said to Vaclav as they were driving along. 'Father certainly proved to be anything but hospitable.'

'But you were kind, as you always are to me. Kind, and very loving.'

Before they reached his RAF station, Vaclav admitted that he had encouraged Sally to leave Yorkshire a day earlier than necessary.

'I hope that you will wish to stay nearby to me for one night. I could arrange somewhere for you to sleep.'

Sally surprised herself when she declined his suggestion that she stay. She was realizing that she was wearied by too many traumas, unable to come to terms with the fact that inviting Vaclav to spend Christmas at Downing House had proved to be such a disaster.

'You are annoyed with me because I did not belong in your home,' Vaclav suggested dejectedly.

'Not in the least, none of the problems were your fault, love. It's just – well, I suppose I'd never really understood before how afraid of changes my father is.'

'But I would not change anything, you make me happy as we are.'

'All right, let's try and forget it, eh?'

'I will telephone this evening, I need to know that you have arrived in safety.'

Leaving Vaclav at his base, Sally noticed how bleak RAF stations appeared in winter, and how solitary he looked as he waved her off. She could only hope that some of his fellow Czech pilots were seeking company that evening.

Vaclav's call and those that followed during the next few weeks were all that kept them in touch. With the Christmas season over, it seemed as though the RAF were determined to make up for the few days of easing-up by calling forward all the new aircraft available.

Sally was too busy to give much thought to anything beyond her work, and was thankful for being too occupied to worry for very long about Henry Downing or anyone else.

The weather was foul and she developed chilblains on her fingers as well as feet, adding this irritation to the discomfort of taking to the skies in winter. She remained just as keen on flying, nevertheless, and relished the challenge of mastering the different controls of each kind of aeroplane that she delivered.

Sally was flying a Hurricane on the day that she returned to the station where she'd first met Vaclav. Handling a plane similar to the one in which he'd protected her from that Messerschmitt, perhaps thinking back to that encounter was inevitable. Several times, conscious as ever that a stray enemy aircraft could take her by surprise, all her senses were alerted to the drone of any engine other than her own. On each occasion, though, she was relieved to spot Allied

95

markings on any plane becoming visible in her air space.

Her descent and landing were close to perfect, and she permitted herself a private smile. Ever since that awful day when she'd brought in a damaged Spitfire, Sally had dreaded having another misfortune, especially en route for this particular airstrip. When the officer on duty in the watch office happened to be the same person as on that memorable occasion, she felt reassured by his ready smile.

'Still doing it by the text book, I see,' he greeted her. His friendliness during other recent encounters had confirmed already that she was long since forgiven for the mishap. If, indeed, forgiveness was required. No one could have blamed her for the original incident, and no one had.

'You got to know one of our Czech pilots, didn't you?' he continued while they were signing documents. 'They've gone to their own squadrons now, but perhaps you've heard? All except one chap who'd come down just this side of the Channel and ended up hospitalized. He's fine now, just waiting for a posting.'

'He'll be missing the rest of them,' said Sally. She had no intention of giving away anything about her own friendship with Vaclav. Gossip often seemed relentless on most bases, but normally among their own ranks: she didn't confide in senior officers.

It was her last delivery of the day, she would have something to eat, then try to find out if there was any hope of a lift back to her own base that night or early the following morning.

Half a dozen WAAFs were seated at one of the long tables, Sally carried her tray towards them once she'd made her selection of dishes. One or two of them looked familiar from her previous visits, and they welcomed her with a mixture of banter and cautious respect. So many of their members were restricted to tasks which they considered unexciting, fellow women who actually got to fly were that bit different.

'What did you bring in today?' asked one girl who had met Sally during her last trip.

'A Hurricane – seem to be getting used to them now. Initially, it was always Spitfires, but I guess it's only like changing from one make of car to another.' She always tried to play down any competence she might possess, especially when aware of the envy her work could generate.

Five of the women returned to discussing the dance being arranged for the Friday evening. 'You won't still be here, will you?' one enquired.

'Not unless I've another drop here Friday, shan't know till I report back.'

'We're just feeling rather half-hearted

about the dance. Freda, here, is always the life of the party and the lucky so-and-so's off on leave as of now.'

Sally turned to the auburn-haired girl called Freda. 'Going somewhere nice?'

'I wish. Home to Mother, and she's a bit of a liability, poor dear. Tends to rely on me more than I like. Not her fault, my dad died in the early stages of the war. She's never been used to coping on her own.'

'I've got a father like that, except that it's years since he was widowed. Doesn't seem to get any easier, though.' Sally recollected, sighed. 'Sorry, that must be the last thing you wanted to hear!'

Freda grinned. 'Everyone's different, aren't they? I'm trying to get my mother to do some WVS work, find herself a few friends while she keeps busy.'

'Good idea.'

'Or get her working on munitions,' one of her friends added. 'Then she really would become too tired to miss you.'

'Want to bet?' Freda said, then looked at her watch. 'Lord, I'll have to go, like it or not. She'll be chewing her fingernails down to the elbows if I'm later than she expects. Nobody'd think I drive for my living, anyway.'

Freda was gathering her belongings together when she turned to Sally. 'Is it your ferry pool I pass on the drive home to

Hampshire? I could give you a lift.'

They compared details and Sally was delighted to go with her. Freda continued chatting as she led the way to her car, convincing Sally that she was pleased to have a companion.

When the car proved to be an Austin, a year newer than her own, Sally laughed and explained how her father had bought hers as a gift.

'Sounds like your old man's loaded then.'

Sally grinned. 'He's got a bob or two, owns a carpet mill. But there's no saying what his situation will be when this lot's over. Carpet production's been halted, and he's got to turn out boring wartime stuff. Essential though that may be, with me away so much, this isn't the time for him to be bored.'

'And where do you live?' Freda asked when they had left the RAF station behind and were on their way.

'Halifax, in the West Riding.'

'Quite some distance then. Do you make it home very often?'

'Had leave over Christmas.'

'Lucky you!' Freda paused. 'Or was it?'

'Could have been worse, I suppose. He can't help needing me around more.'

'Especially while coping with changes in his factory.'

'That's exactly what I keep reminding myself. Doesn't always work.'

'Have you only ever lived at home until you began with the Air Transport Auxiliary?'

Sally shook her head. 'No. I was at university – Oxford. Where I learned to fly. Thing is, I was a bit young then to appreciate what my absence was doing to Dad. He might have been better at disguising it then, or I wasn't very perceptive.'

'And you weren't engaged in work that took you into all today's hazards. Still, you say you flew then, didn't that worry him?'

Sally grinned. 'It would have – if he'd known. Didn't let on until I'd got my pilot's licence. At least that provided evidence of some degree of competence.'

They laughed together.

'And what about you, Freda? What did you do pre-war?'

'Not a great deal. The only thing I was interested in was boats, sailing. Used to muck around the boatyard where my brother laboured for Dad.'

'You have a brother. I do envy you.'

'No need. Colin was the thorn in my side. A year older than me, and the one who was getting to learn the craft. I'd have given my eye teeth to follow Dad into the business.'

'Perhaps you will, one day.'

'You reckon? No – since Dad was lost the first day he went mine-sweeping, Colin opted out. He and Mother are selling Turners', the family boatyard. Colin has joined the navy. End of story.'

They fell silent for a time, both occupied with reflecting on the changes enforced in so many lives by war.

'So – what else do you do?' Freda enquired eventually. 'Or is flying your only interest?'

'I hadn't really started on a career, not properly. Sounds stupid, I know, and I can see it was a big mistake. I went into the office at the mill. Doing accounts, wages, stuff like that. I always was good at figures, and my father needed someone to take over when my predecessor suddenly died.'

'And your spare time – you *were* allowed time off...?'

'Of course. We were very involved at the local chapel, and I did a bit of acting with the dramatic society – amateur, naturally.'

'You enjoy theatre then?'

'I'll say! Used to get to lots of West End shows while I was at Oxford. I'd miss all that, if I wasn't fully occupied now.'

'And is there a man in your life, Sally?'

She didn't know how to reply. She never had known quite how serious the relationship with Vaclav was, how serious it might become if this war ended.

'Nothing promising to become permanent, if you see what I mean.'

Freda gave her a sideways glance. 'You mean he doesn't want to be committed to anything?'

'No, I didn't mean that.' Sally wanted to be fair to Vaclav.

'You don't have to tell *me*! I've got one like that back home. All lovey-dovey when we're together, but leaves me to guess what he's up to while I'm away.'

'Sounds like he's not in the forces. What does he do?'

'Manages a munitions factory, aircraft parts.'

'That's funny. A friend in Halifax has left Dad's mill to take charge of a place like that.'

'Is he the one – the chap who won't propose?'

'No, nothing of that sort. David's more a friend of my father's.' Except for that suspicion she'd always had that David would propose to her, given the least encouragement.

They talked on and on. Sally sensed that Freda was as glad as she herself was to have another woman's company for a one-to-one conversation. It wasn't always easy to speak about your true feelings when you were in a crowd, a situation which so often applied in the forces. When Sally learned that Freda envied her ability to fly, she did her best to encourage her to apply to have instruction.

'Mention the Air Transport Auxiliary, and they'll realize you're being realistic. Otherwise they might adopt the general idea that girls with ambition to be pilots are getting above themselves!'

They found a wayside café that was still open, and stopped for a break where they drank tea and sampled cake so uninteresting that they giggled over failing to identify its intended flavour.

Before taking to the road again, Freda asked if Sally would care to drive.

'No, thanks – unless you're desperate for a change. Your car looks newer than mine.'

Freda laughed. 'Don't say you're daunted by this when you handle the monsters you do overhead!'

Sally smiled, but still felt thankful that Freda took the wheel of her own car. They would soon be nearing her base anyway, but she had enjoyed this trip. She made a mental note to check out the WAAF personnel on any station when she needed a lift.

'Have you always been based on the same camp?' she asked when the outer perimeter of her ferry pool came into view in the light from the three-quarter moon above them.

Freda nodded. 'One of the few who have. Although I suppose it's the chaps who get moved around more than us, when their squadrons are sent elsewhere. You miss them if they go just as you're getting to know them as individuals.'

'That must be true.'

'You can have a laugh with some of the pilots, then there are a few who take themselves too seriously. On account of having got their wings.'

'I hope that doesn't apply to those of us women who fly?'

'You're the first one I've really talked to much. No – I meant the men, even some that have come from a foreign air force. That Czech who missed moving on when they set up their own squadrons. I thought he'd be glad to have a chat, but he didn't respond.'

'Maybe he didn't speak enough English for a conversation.'

'Oh, he did. When he first arrived he was showing off how much he understood. Not like his friend Vaclav. *He* turned up not knowing a word of English.'

'Would that be Vaclav Capkova?'

'Sounds right to me. And he was the only Vaclav we had on station.'

'I know Vaclav, he—' Sally paused, hesitating over how much she should confide. 'He fought off a Messerschmitt on my behalf when it tried to shoot down my Spitfire.'

'You were the one who only just made it in to land that time? I didn't realize that. Funny the way Vaclav reacted afterwards, didn't want to talk about it. Not the usual attitude when a pilot's hit his target.'

Sally was interested, but not surprised. Vaclav, during that period, had seemed rather reticent and unassuming. Except with regard to pride in his licence to fly, which he'd been eager to confirm as gained in his own country.

When Sally didn't speak, Freda continued. 'That friend of his who's still with us always claims that Vaclav had more than one motive in coming here. He spent ages teaching himself English, you know. And all so he could make the most of his time in this country: part of the major plan that Vaclav Capkova would go back to Czechoslovakia better educated after the war.'

'Nobody could blame him for that.' Sally felt perturbed, but could hardly correct Freda's assumption by stating that he had only learned English to communicate more readily with *her*.

'Quite right, no one would. I'm just saying he had it all planned out. Vaclav's fiancée is quite an intellectual, by all accounts, extremely ambitious. Sounds to me that when he marries her they'll do very well for themselves.'

Freda had stopped the car at the entrance to the ferry pool. Sally had no opportunity to question what she had been told. And she would not have queried one word. The thudding in her head, and the sudden ache seizing her heart, confirmed that she had no choice but to believe that Vaclav was engaged to marry.

Afraid that she suddenly was feeling too distracted to remember her manners, Sally thanked Freda effusively for the lift, opened the passenger door and stumbled out.

The bitter night air stung her face and neck, hands also, for her gloves had dropped to the ground, unheeded.

'Your gloves, Sally...' Freda had opened the door again to call her.

Picking them up, Sally nodded, tried to smile. With a hasty wave in Freda's direction, she fumbled in her bag for the pass she always carried.

Trudging towards her quarters, she willed herself to show no emotion. People here knew her, the last thing she needed was anxious questioning about her anguish, which must be plain for anyone to see.

If she'd been kicked in the stomach, Sally couldn't have felt more sickened. How had she been such a fool, how in the world had she failed to even think of asking if Vaclav had a girlfriend back home?

But he had said that he loved *her*, Sally Downing – or had he? Had her own eager spirit conjured those words out of nowhere, because they were all she needed to hear?

It all seemed a sham, false. How gullible she had been, how ready to believe whatever Vaclav Capkova cared to say. Nothing had been true, not even his assertion that his determination to learn English had been for her.

106

And now nothing remained, no more than a handful of memories – memories of an excess of passion. Attraction that held nothing deeper to give it substance.

Five

Sally ran towards her accommodation hut, and hurtled across to thrust her belongings into the drab locker. For once, none of the other women were there, and she couldn't have been more thankful. Even so, she couldn't risk going to pieces in a place like this where someone might walk in at any minute. She wished fervently that she hadn't been obliged to live on site again, her old billet with Mrs Congreve might have offered more privacy.

Two or three girls were lingering in the toilet block when she sped inside, but none of them were particular friends. She tossed a brief hello in their direction and dashed into the nearest cubicle.

'Must be in a bad way,' she heard one of them say. 'Something she's eaten perhaps ... Or too much booze.'

Sally wished that it was. She would give anything to have the cause of this revulsion an item of food or drink. She was obliged instead to face the fact that her own stupidity had placed her in this situation which literally made her feel sick.

Sinking on to the seat, she lowered her head into her hands. How could she have been so near to making love with Vaclav, and have given no thought to the possibility that he might be committed to some other female, somewhere? Was she really as naïve as her father believed her? How had she let her relationship with Vaclav intensify like this while knowing so little about him?

She had supposed him to be slightly older than she was; meeting any other man, wouldn't she have been at least curious to learn whether he was single? Rather than that, she had plunged on, relishing their developing attraction until...

Oh, God! She couldn't honestly confirm, even to herself, that she wouldn't have made love with him completely if they hadn't been interrupted.

She could hear her father's voice again now, overriding her present attempts at thinking, and the dreadful truth was she deserved his condemnation.

The tears didn't come, somehow they just *wouldn't*, but they might have brought some ease. Dry-eyed and raw-throated, she was too overwrought to do more than restrain a long moan of despair.

Why hadn't Vaclav revealed his true situation? They could have continued as friends, but she certainly wouldn't have encouraged his kisses, caresses. People might consider that *he* had made a fool of her. Sally couldn't think beyond the fact that she was the person who was foolish.

But she loved him.

Or wanted him? In the early days of their acquaintance, she had been intrigued by this handsome, *different* being who had appeared in her world. Flattered by his assertion that he was learning English because of *her*, she had tossed caution out of the window. When the power of attraction reinforced her interest in Vaclav, her longing for him had grown so strong that resisting the impulse to make love with him had become extremely difficult.

We *did* stop short of that, though, didn't we? Sally wondered, confused briefly by the conflict of so many emotions. For several dreadful minutes she could not feel absolutely certain that she had not given in entirely to the surge of passion.

They had been so close; close to each other and close to making love. She was correct to recall the night of her father's sudden intervention as the occasion when she could have been carried away, but she and Vaclav had been prevented.

It would be all right. She had not done anything very terrible: with time, the weeks of knowing Vaclav Capkova would be consigned to past experience. There would be nothing, *nothing* to witness to all that intense yearning.

That yearning itself, though, was active even now, despite the shock, the embarrassment, the fury. The now familiar pressure within her was testing and teasing, waves of sheer longing; a need so strong, she would believe it everlasting.

Later that night, going at last to her bed, Sally called a scarcely audible 'Goodnight' to the hut's other inhabitants. They, along with the rest of the world, seemed barely real to her. All existed only distantly, beyond this need now asserting itself in a current of desire.

Sally feared she would lie awake, but shock combined with exhaustion to provide sleep's escape from utter disappointment. The passion remained though, to torment in her dreams with a longing more intense than ever.

Towards morning, awakening unfulfilled after her dream world had depicted the loving that she needed, life felt unbearable.

Cruel chance that day brought a phone call from Vaclav. Unready with any ideas let alone *decisions* on how to react, Sally had to still the instinctive surge of delight that his voice generated. She heard her own tone sounding frigid, suspected she ought to explain, once and for all time, and failed to do so.

Sally did, nevertheless, refuse to arrange to meet him in the next few weeks. It was a start, she supposed, and could be followed by the explanation that she knew he wasn't really free to date her.

Work again offered a kind of solution, providing so many deliveries that Sally was given no time in which to dwell on the truth about Vaclav's situation. When, inevitably, she was obliged to fly to the station where his squadron was based, her emotions felt to be under control.

The weather that day was poor, troubled by patches of fog, which meant Sally had to keep ultra-alert to the surrounding sky in case enemy aircraft were lurking unseen. Fortunately, she didn't encounter any Luft-waffe.

After landing and reporting in, she headed towards the mess, where she hoped to find a snack and, if she was very lucky, the offer of transport back to her own base. No such ready escape seemed available that day, Sally resigned herself to taking the train from the local railway station and hurriedly ate her sandwich and drank the strong tea.

She was setting out to walk the short distance to catch a train, when someone called her name. Glancing over her shoulder, she saw Vaclav emerging from the doorway of a nearby mess.

Now for it, thought Sally, resolving to put an end to all of her own speculation regarding any potential future between them. The intervening weeks had failed to erode her longing for him. As Vaclav ran to catch her up, she faced him squarely.

'You are not on your way back to the ferry pool?' he asked, sighing. 'Why did you not telephone to let me know you were coming here?'

'I had no intention of trying to meet you. Frankly, Vaclav, I didn't want to – not after learning that you're engaged to someone in Prague.'

Hot colour rushed to his face then drained away to leave his cheeks ashen. Along with his pale hair, his features looked as though life was ebbing out of him.

Sally restrained an instinctive hand that would have grasped his arm, just to reassure him.

Vaclav swallowed hard, appeared to think for a minute or so. 'We could still remain friends. I believed that you were my friend, no matter what. You cannot really wish to end all that without permitting me to explain.'

'Actually, I'm sorry, but that is what I intend. You misled me, Vaclav, and I would no longer be sure that I could believe whatever you were to tell me. Such mistrust is no basis for any kind of a relationship. Even friendship.'

'You cannot be so unkind to me. If I were never to meet you again, I should miss you quite terribly. You were the very first person to befriend me in your country.'

'And now you are based with your fellow Czech airmen, in your own squadron. There is no earthly reason for you to depend on me any longer. Not for anything.'

'No reason? Do you not think of what there has been between us?'

'I prefer not to. You belong with someone else. I cannot reconcile that with anything that we have done.'

Telling him what she had decided was hard, harder than Sally had expected. No matter what Vaclav's circumstances were, she could not simply switch off all that she felt for him. She could only refuse to consider what she was feeling.

Turning away abruptly, she began running towards the main road that led to the railway station.

Having ages to wait for the next train made Sally feel even worse, but she fought down the impulse to think back over that miserable encounter with Vaclav. Dwelling on how forlorn he had looked and sounded was pointless. She was compelled to make this break now, or risk becoming more deeply involved with someone who was committed to another woman. Being fond of him

114

already was bad enough, she did not mean to allow that fondness to increase.

Knowing that Vaclav was based with one of the Czech squadrons, and likely to remain alongside his fellow countrymen, simplified Sally's task of avoiding him. She was becoming well respected within her own team of fliers, and was quite often able to arrange to take on only deliveries where there was less risk of meeting someone from his country.

Vaclav repeatedly telephoned her, as she had half expected that he might, but Sally refused to have long conversations with him. And she continued to assert that meeting him would be fruitless. Her resolve to keep away from Vaclav seemed to strengthen as she gradually grew accustomed to no longer looking forward to their spending time together.

Keeping the RAF supplied with aircraft became yet more imperative as the Luftwaffe struck repeatedly at British towns and cities. These attacks frequently generated Allied retaliation bombings, alongside the constant efforts to intercept German planes before they could reach their targets.

Sally snatched one brief forty-eight hour leave in Halifax, and was relieved to find that the town was still virtually as undamaged as reports had led her to believe. Her father was well, if still less than enthusiastic about the supplies his factory was obliged to turn out for the war effort.

'I've lost all my best men, designers, skilled carpet weavers, even good dyers. If they haven't joined up, they've gone after more interesting jobs, making munitions. It'll never be the same when this lot's ended, you know,' Henry reminded her.

'But David will still come back to Downing's after the war. He'll be there to rely on.'

'Happen so. Certainly, he doesn't seem to have taken to that engineering place. Although I'll give him his due, he's putting his back into making a go of it there.'

This was confirmed when David joined them for their meal that evening. Sally noticed that he now was well versed in production of armaments, and proud to relate that they were increasing output month on month. If Henry hadn't protested, he would have spent the whole evening describing the work engaging him.

David laughed when checked by his former boss. 'I do go on, I know, it's just that it's so different from what I was used to at your place. And I'm not shy of admitting that it is satisfying to learn a new trade. But enough about me, Sally – how are you coping? Busier than ever, from what your Dad tells me...'

'That's right, but I don't mind. Better to keep busy than spend too much time fretting about what this war's doing to folk.'

'And your little car, is it behaving well? I saw it parked outside.'

'Ran perfectly all the way here. I was glad to have an alternative to trains and buses.'

'You'll have to resort to those, I suppose, to get you back to your ferry pool after flying off somewhere,' said David.

'That's right, except when I'm lucky to get a lift. Doesn't happen often enough though.'

'But you're still enjoying the work?' Henry asked her.

'It's the best I'll get, Dad. The RAF are not likely to send women pilots into action – or if they would, that's news to me.'

Henry's frown told her that having his daughter flying against the Luftwaffe was the last thing he wished to contemplate.

The weather during that weekend in the late spring of 1941 was good, mainly dry and reasonably warm. When David suggested that they should take a walk on the following day, both Henry and Sally agreed.

As it happened, Henry was prevented from joining them when a phone call telling of a problem at the mill sent him rushing there, complaining as he went that even Sundays couldn't be relied on as a break.

Setting out with David to walk, Sally was surprised to see that people were heading towards the church they had attended on Christmas Eve.

117

'Thought you'd have been joining them,' she remarked.

'They'll still be here when you're not. Of course, you could go there with me.'

'Why not?'

Sally wondered what the ordinary Sunday services would be like in a High Anglican church. She was afraid she might seem rather out of her depth there, but she did feel in need of some sort of anchor while still troubled by so many emotions.

The liturgy soon proved to be only a shade less elaborate than the one used at Christmas. There were some hymns she knew, but also a lot of music from the choir, and incense filled the cool interior.

Her going there with David pleased him, she could see that in his frequent smiles, but it was thoughts of Vaclav Capkova which surged through Sally as soon as memories returned of how at home he had seemed with the Anglo-Catholic services. He might have belonged here, in a more true sense than she herself ever would.

Sally felt torn – a part of her relished the sensation that in this place she could be closer in spirit to Vaclav, yet all the while she must remain aware of his Catholic heritage. They believed in marrying for life, didn't they, surely this suggested that they would regard an engagement as an equally firm commitment? And she had no right to even begin to question that.

By the time that she and David emerged into the sunlight, Sally was experiencing a strange conflict of feelings. This church had quieted some of her dismay, but it also deepened her conviction that she had been wise to keep well away from Vaclav. Unfortunately, doing the right thing had not, in this instance, eliminated her feelings for him.

There was little time left for walking, but she and David strolled side by side as far as West View Park where they admired the freshly opened leaves turning most of the trees into brightest green.

'I've been seeing quite a lot of Henry these past few weeks,' David told her. 'It'd be daft not to, I couldn't help missing him ever since we've stopped working together, and he seems happy that we can have a good chat.'

'Dad will be pleased that's continuing. He could do with more company, stop him fretting about stuff.'

'About *you*, you mean? I'm afraid he'll never do that, not so long as this war continues and you're doing such a risky job. Neither of us will be happy until it's all over, and you're back here with us for keeps.'

For keeps? Sally reflected, the words startling her because of being ones she had heard only infrequently during all the months that she'd lived away from Halifax. She couldn't dismiss the expression for the casual phrase it was. *For keeps*, when she was a child, had been used often enough to express ownership of some object, perhaps a toy or other treasure swapped during a deal with a friend. The words today seemed to denote ownership still, but of herself. Whilst almost certain that David hadn't intended to imply any such meaning, Sally couldn't ignore the dread evoked. When this war finished, she had no wish for anyone to keep her. In any sense of that word.

'Time we were getting back for that salad, Dad will be famished. I take it that you are coming to lunch, even if the meat's only leftovers?'

In retrospect that leave generated a peculiar mixture of feelings. There had been a certain tranquillity imbued by the church service, but that was tarnished by memories of Vaclav Capkova. And somehow the rest of her stay in Yorkshire had failed to provide any of its old balm. There had been too little time, of course, the quantity and quality of time which she'd taken for granted pre-war. Strolling for half a day or longer through woodland slopes or over purple-heathered moors was what Sally really needed.

She could be grateful, and she was, that her father was relatively fit and living in a part of England which seemed to be escaping the worst of the bombing. Since David had revealed that he and Henry still were spending more time together, she ought also to be relieved that someone was there for her father.

No matter how hard she tried to think only of Henry's well-being, Sally could not avoid feeling deprived of all the qualities she once had relished around her home. She hadn't been really homesick ever, certainly not since the first few days at university, but that was not preventing her from having this yearning for her beloved West Riding hills. This latest visit seemed to her to have lacked so much that she most associated with her part of Yorkshire.

Being in the air again, and tackling each day's challenge of flying aeroplanes to wherever they were most needed, soon restored her normal sense of purpose. Nothing outshone the satisfaction of being capable of handling these machines, and if her work resurrected thoughts of Vaclav, she was schooling herself to live without seeing him.

Vaclav himself evidently had no reservations about the place their friendship should continue to have in his life. He telephoned consistently to chat with Sally, eager to catch up on her news, and to relate his enthusiasm for each fresh posting, quite recently his move to Bomber Command. On most occasions he would end by inserting the suggestion that they could still meet.

Sally held out against his persuasiveness. When he seemed particularly adamant that he needed to see her, she would resort to reminding him that he was not quite so free as he had led her to believe.

'I can only apologize again for that small deception,' he said down the line one evening. 'I was wrong to assume that this war, with its abnormal existences, might excuse my longing to be with the one person who understands me.'

'The one person over here perhaps,' Sally corrected him. Face to face instead of over the phone, she would have spoken more strongly. 'And I'm afraid I can't ignore the insistence somewhere inside me that *I* would be distraught if I had a fiancé who was seeing too much of some other woman!'

Sally could well have never seen Vaclav again, but for the news of an RAF Wellington bomber that crash-landed shortly after taking off from an East Anglian station. For days the only word filtering through, even to those engaged in flying, was that the plane belonged to a Czech squadron, and several of the crew had perished.

Sick with anxiety for his safety, she could not get Vaclav out of her mind. Names of the crew members involved appeared to have been withheld, Sally certainly had difficulty discovering further details. She did learn that one of the men had escaped death by actually being blown clear of the aircraft, but he was reported as a radio operator rather than a pilot. She couldn't think that was Vaclav.

Rationalizing that she had no real reason to believe that he might have been a member of that particular crew was useless. Sally could not rid herself of the gnawing dread that he had been killed.

On the night that Vaclav next telephoned her base, she could do nothing to conceal her relief. Tears ran down her face as soon as she heard his voice, and her own words were choked with emotion when she responded to him.

'Thank God you're alive. I've been so afraid that you were one of the men in that dreadful crash-landing.'

'Oh, Sally – what can I say? But you must not be sad now. As you hear, I am well, quite safe. And I long to make up to you for your anxiety. We must meet quite soon, and I will show you a happy time.'

She could no longer hold out against her own longing to see him. Without meeting him she would not be certain that he was alive. On Vaclav's insistence, Sally finally let him know the date when she would next be delivering to the base where he was stationed.

Vaclav had flown on operations during much

123

of the night, but nevertheless contrived to be around at the airstrip when she landed. Hugging her to him, he kissed her forehead and both cheeks, then gazed affectionately into her glistening brown eyes.

'I worry also, you understand,' he told her, and she saw his own eyes were moist. 'I would not bear it if anything were to occur while you are in the air.'

They separated only while Sally went off to go through the routine of handing over of the plane that she'd brought in.

'We walk now, I think,' Vaclav suggested when she rejoined him.

He had been planning for her visit. Their stroll took them into a tiny rural village where its pond and a scattering of cottages seemed eloquent of a quiet that once had been undisturbed by the aircraft now frequently heard overhead.

'I have a billet just along the road here,' he told her. 'I show you how nice, not at all like being in a hut at the base.'

'And how did you wangle this?' asked Sally, as they approached a thatched house.

'Wangle? I do not know that word, what do you mean?'

'Succeed in arranging something good.'

'Ah – so. The lady who owns this house serves in the NAAFI, and was telling how she hates to stay each night alone. Three persons of our squadron asked permission to

billet with her. Was not difficult, accommodation on site is very overcrowded.'

'No doubt she spoils you. What is she like?'

'Fat, very jolly, and quite old. Forty-five at
least.'

'I'm looking forward to meeting her.'

'But no, Hilda is on duty today. Although
perhaps you meet when we go back to base.'

'I can't stay long here,' Sally told him. 'I
must catch a train this evening – got to
report in first thing tomorrow.'

The interior of the house was as pleasant
as its outward appearance. A little entrance
hall gave on to a cosy living room where a
large sofa predominated together with two
armchairs.

'We all eat in the kitchen,' said Vaclav.
'There is another room for dining, but now
has a bed for one of my fellow pilots.'

Vaclav seemed to have thought of everything. Enquiring if she was hungry, he
hurried towards the larder and reappeared
with bread and cheese. 'I bought these
especially for us, I know how hard it is for
Hilda to provide the meals for her pilots. Of
course, most of the time we eat in the mess.'

Sitting together at the kitchen table, Sally
had difficulty reminding herself that she
must not be quite so at ease with Vaclav as
during previous meetings. He seemed no
different to her – unless, that was, in being
all the more dear, because of recent fears for

his safety.

When they had finished their meal, he rose. 'Please – I wish that I show you the room that I have here.'

Sally shook her head. 'I don't think that's a good idea.'

'Please. Then, in your mind, you may see this place where I am sleeping.'

'No, Vaclav.'

He shrugged, smiled, and led the way instead back into the living room. Drawing her down on to the sofa beside him, he placed an arm around her.

Sally could not move. His arm was only loosely about her, but her own need to be close to him was holding her firmly to his side. And that was one impulse which she must not heed. Stifling her sigh, she eased away slightly.

'This is all wrong,' she told him. 'You have a fiancée, remember. I'm not going to be the one who encourages you to forget that.'

A flush of colour soared from his uniform collar, his blue eyes hardened. 'Why do you suppose that I would wish anything of the kind? I think only to be your friend, to find some comfort for each of us amid this cruel existence.'

'Sorry, Vaclav, you've chosen the wrong person here. I may be too old-fashioned: whatever the reason, I'm not letting this go any further than it has already.'

126

'And how does that agree with all that you said to me when we were with your father? How that you expected him to treat you like an adult person. What is so adult now, when you are frightened to even sit at my side?'

'I didn't know at Christmas that you belonged to someone else. I *can't* pretend that nothing's changed, and I won't. You may be no different, but I know your true situation now. I cannot let anything happen between us.'

'You do want me then?'

She had revealed her real emotions. Sally cursed her own careless words which clearly displayed the effort she was exerting to resist the urge to be near him, to...

Vaclav smiled to himself. 'I shall content me with that. My dear, innocent, English girl.'

Their being together was spoilt. Unable to relax, haunted by the unseen presence of his fiancée, Sally decided to leave.

'I'm glad I've seen you, Vaclav, very thankful that you're alive and well. But now that's confirmed, it's time I was on my way.'

'You cannot mean this. I arranged especially to take time with you. I do not fly again until the morning. I cannot let you leave me.'

'I'm afraid you will have to. My decision's made.'

'But we will meet again, you must give your word...'

Sally began to shake her head.

'Do not say "never",' he protested. 'I show to you that I am a good person. We shall see each other next time where other people are present. We go to drink in an inn somewhere, to the cinema, to one of your very respectable tea shops...'

She shook her head again, this time ruefully at her own inability to refuse him completely.

'We'll see, Vaclav. It will depend on the circumstances.'

Their walk to the railway station was subdued, and Sally felt sorry. She had no wish to make Vaclav miserable, but she equally had no intention of letting herself in for the distress she would deserve if she continued to permit their friendship to progress. She knew herself too well, was aware that only by seeing him very rarely, and in company, would she contain the urge to love him.

He kissed her goodbye as she boarded her train, a kiss on her lips, fervent and sincere. He might have been promising the world. A future.

Passion surged within her, desire and a love all the more intense for the need for its restraining.

'Take care, my Sally,' he murmured.

'And you, Vaclav.'

There wasn't one vacant seat. She struggled through the packed corridor, leaned against a carriage window, refused to gaze and gaze towards Vaclav waving from the platform.

Someone once, somewhere, had said that watching a person until they were out of sight brought bad luck. Wrong or not, her friendship with Vaclav meant too much to her to risk tempting Providence.

Six

The year continued with further bombings of German targets, while from the war zones at sea came news of vessels belonging to both sides being destroyed. At home, by the end of 1941, single women were being drafted to serve in the armed forces, fire service or the police. Once again, Sally was thankful that she was well established in her job. Flying remained her greatest love and, with ever more opportunities to pilot different aircraft, her skills continued to be tested.

The satisfaction this brought compensated for the shortcomings in her social life. Occasionally, she would attend a dance at a RAF station somewhere, less frequently at her own base, where it was rare for anything to be arranged, as so few of their pilots could guarantee being around on a given day.

Vaclav still phoned her from time to time, but less frequently now, and this somehow enabled Sally to accept his calls more readily. Even she could no longer condemn those occasional chats as becoming an obsession.

Sally was schooling herself to worry less about his safety. She knew herself, and her tendency to grow preoccupied with concern on Vaclav's behalf. She could steel herself now to let him go out of her life – although *not*, please God, ever because his own was ended.

Word that he was alive should be enough: she suspected that she really was preparing herself for a time when she wouldn't necessarily see him at all.

Vaclav evidently continued to regard their friendship much as he always had, turning to her whenever he had something to say. Or so Sally gathered when he telephoned to discuss news of the Japanese attack on Pearl Harbour. They talked that December evening for several minutes, about the latest word that President Roosevelt had declared America at war with Japan. Vaclav considered this could mean massive changes in the direction the Allied fight would take.

Feeling unsure how this would affect their own part in the conflict, Sally added very little to what he was saying. She never seemed to have sufficient time to keep up with all the reported implications of events, even major ones. As for thinking things through herself, her work often left her too tired for considering anything very deeply.

Vaclav was well aware that her attention also lay with the effect of this war upon

131

family and friends, and he had not forgotten his experience of the previous Christmas spent in her home.

'Will you have home leave this year for Christmas, Sally?'

'Not certain yet, but I doubt it. What about you?'

'I am afraid that I shall not get away at Christmas. In fact, I could be moved on before then.'

Sally quelled the sudden surge of anxiety. Where would he be sent? Could that be abroad somewhere? To an area providing access to one of these fresh war zones? There was a difference between neglecting to meet him, and being denied the opportunity to do so.

'I do have a forty-eight coming up next week,' he told her. 'Any chance of getting together? Somewhere very public?'

Despite all reservations, Sally laughed. Vaclav Capkova was adept at foreseeing her potential objections and countering them.

'I'm due leave too,' she admitted. 'But only a twenty-four hour—'

He interrupted swiftly. 'I shall come to your base, take you out for a whole day. To anywhere that you suggest.'

Vaclav was eager to see the place from where she set out to deliver planes. He reminded her that he had the necessary identification papers. He would be allowed on site, and arranged to meet her there early on her free day.

Despite her determination that she would not become deeply involved with him, Sally was looking forward to spending a few hours in Vaclav's company, and was thankful when the dawn brought a clear sky, where the winter sun was rising between the perimeter hangars. She was glad also that they would meet on territory that she regarded as hers, where she felt sure she would have more control of the situation between them.

Dressed in the civilian skirt and sweater that felt strange because of being rarely used, Sally ate breakfast at a more leisurely pace than on work days. She was crossing to finish getting ready to go out when a colleague called her to take a telephone call.

Vaclav can't make it, she thought, and was dismayed by the sharp sinking of her spirits. She ought not to be so greatly disappointed.

The voice on the other end of the line was not Vaclav's. Henry Downing was ringing her, and he sounded utterly distraught.

'Something terrible's happened, Sally. And I don't know whatever to do. I had to talk to you...'

'Whatever's wrong, Dad? You haven't had an accident? You're not ill, or anything, are you...?'

'Not me, no. It's David. He's had a heart

133

attack, it's bad...'

'Oh, no! *How* bad is it?'

'It's serious, Sally. I'm afraid they don't know if he'll pull through. I'm at the hospital now. He was with me, you see, when it happened.'

'When was this?'

'Last night. He'd come over to me for a bit of dinner after work. I thought he looked overtired when he came in, but he said he was all right. Then he just keeled over, soon as he got up from the table. Worst of it was, I'd gone into the kitchen. He went down with a crash, so, naturally, I went running to him. He was face down on the rug, I didn't know what to do for the best. It took me long enough to shift him slightly so's I could see his face. Poor chap was clutching at his chest, moaning with the pain.'

'Did you get his doctor to come to the house?'

'The ambulance. Thought it might be quicker. They were very good, took over and got him to hospital in double-quick time. Just as well, the doctor here said, or he'd have been a goner.'

'Have you been there all night with David?'

'Couldn't do anything else, could I? There's got to be somebody here for him besides the hospital folk. Don't mind admitting, it has been a bit of an ordeal though.'

'I'm sure it has, Dad, but it sounds as if

134

you've coped very well.'

'Happen so, just wish I didn't feel that helpless! Then there's the house – had to leave it in a state. David brought all his food back, you see – not that he could help that, of course. Trouble is, there's no Mrs Holbrook, she's gone down with the flu.'

'I'd better try and get up to Halifax. I have got leave, as it happens, but it's only a twenty-four. I'll have a word here, try and get it extended on compassionate grounds or something.'

'Eh, Sally love, I'd be that thankful if only you could. I know you're doing vital work and all that, I didn't like to ask.'

'You leave it with me, I'll see what I can do. If I can't make it, I'll let you know – you'd better give me the hospital number. If you don't hear anything further, expect me sometime today.'

When Sally turned away from the telephone, she saw Vaclav watching her. In all the upset of hearing about David's heart attack, she hadn't given a thought to how she was meant to be spending that day.

'Oh, Vaclav, I am sorry. I'm afraid I've got to cry off. That was Dad with some dreadful news. David's had a severe heart attack. I had to say I'll try to get up to Halifax and give a hand.'

Vaclav frowned. 'But – is he not in hospital?'

'Of course, Dad got the ambulance and—'

'Then there is nothing for you to do,' he interrupted sharply, his blue eyes hardening. 'It must be the task of the doctors now.'

'I can show a bit of concern, help out somehow. Poor old Dad's been at the hospital all night. I am sorry about our arrangement, and that I couldn't put you off before you'd set out, but you see how it is.'

'I see that you are more concerned to be with David Saunders than with me.'

'He's very ill, might not survive.'

Vaclav seemed about to shrug, but straightened his shoulders. 'Can you travel as far as Yorkshire and back in one day?'

'If I have to. I'm on my way to see the CO, try to get my leave extended.'

'But Saunders isn't a relative, is he?'

'He's a very dear friend, someone I care about. And now, Vaclav, I do have to get moving. I'll phone you after I come back here.'

'I would not wish you to go to any trouble on my behalf,' said Vaclav stiffly.

'Why do you have to be so unreasonable? I've explained.' Sally was furious. 'I cannot imagine why you suppose I should care nothing about an old friend like David – while you assume it is all right for you to have a fiancée at home in Prague. A fiancée who is kept secret from me, until – until...' Sally clamped her lips together, and stopped

136

just short of admitting that she had grown fond of him.

Very briefly, a smile that looked triumphant curved Vaclav's lips. Sally's fury increased. He seemed determined to make her want him!

'Oh, think what you like!' she snapped, and left him standing there.

The December daylight had waned, leaving only a glimmer from a crescent moon to augment the heavily shaded platform lighting when Sally left the train in Halifax. She had travelled by rail, believing it should be quicker than driving up to the West Riding, but the journey had proved otherwise.

She had been obliged to change trains three times, and each one had halted at least once, for air raids in its vicinity or to take on forces personnel at unscheduled stations. She was weary and she was hungry. There had been no time to seize food for the journey before setting out.

Trudging up Horton Street towards the town centre, Sally sighed as rain began falling. The last thing she'd thought of snatching up was an umbrella, and she was still wearing the smart shoes she had put on for her planned outing with Vaclav.

Her luck changed when she saw that a bus which would take her to the general hospital was waiting. At least it wouldn't be too long now before she reached David and her father.

The good fortune seemed to be holding: as soon as she entered the ward she could see David, and that his eyes appeared to be open. Henry Downing was seated on the chair beside the bed. To Sally, *he* looked far worse than the man he was keeping company.

Both men smiled on seeing her, but she saw then that for David even smiling required quite an effort. She kissed each of them on the cheek, then leaned away slightly to take a thorough look at David.

'How are you today, love?'

'Better,' David murmured huskily. 'And for seeing you.'

Henry stood up, gestured that she take his chair, and went to fetch another. 'He is improving, but not out of the wood, they say.'

'That will take time, of course.' She smiled at David. 'Main thing is you're surviving.'

He nodded. 'I just feel so weak, even talking's a struggle.'

'Then don't. I'm just thankful to know that you're coming round a bit.' Sally turned to her father. 'Have you been back home at all?'

He shook his head. 'Did you come by car?'

'No. Why? Isn't yours here, Dad?'

'I came in the ambulance with David. I'll have to try and get us a taxi, not just yet though.'

David was looking from one to the other of them, and began trying to insist that they should feel free to go back to the house.

'No need, love,' Sally contradicted. 'Dad can take a break now, I'm stopping where I am for a while.'

Henry was still hesitating over whether or not he should leave, when they heard a voice from the foot of the bed.

'David? What are you doing in here? Whatever's wrong?'

Turning, Sally recognized the vicar of the church she'd attended with David.

'Heart,' he was telling the priest. 'Happened last night.'

Henry Downing was introduced to the vicar, who smiled as he renewed acquaintance with Sally.

'Well, if you're stopping with David for a while, I might pop home, have a shave and so on,' said Henry.

The vicar sighed. 'Ah – actually, I can't stay more than a few minutes. Church Council meeting, and I've just spent longer than I should have with old Mrs Thomas. But I will be back tomorrow, David, without fail.'

The clergyman offered Henry a lift, relieving Sally concerning her father, who was looking drained.

'I'll hang on here, at least until David's ready for sleeping,' she told them. She also meant to have a word with the ward sister, if not his doctor. She had got to try and learn what the prognosis was for her friend's recovery.

David seemed on the point of going to sleep, anyway. They talked hardly at all, but the hand she'd placed on his wrist remained where it was, and Sally liked to believe that it was conveying some comfort. He must have had a terrible scare, she could only imagine how traumatic this whole business must be for him.

Sally had accepted David as a part of her life for so many years that she rarely took the time to consider how much exactly he did mean to her. He was a dear friend, of that she never had any doubt, but because she hadn't experienced any compelling attraction towards him, she had felt no need to analyse their friendship very deeply. Her long-established suspicion that David would love their relationship to become total commitment had originally seemed to her somewhat amusing. His attempts at introducing an element of passion between them had embarrassed her at times, or had simply been annoying. Today, she felt obliged to re-examine everything.

Vaclav's jealousy was largely responsible. Until that had flared, Sally hadn't considered seriously the possibility that David's friendship might evoke envy in anyone. And she reminded herself now that, in this instance, there was no reason that it should. Engaged as he was, Vaclav surely had no right to be questioning any of her relationships.

David was sleeping now. She smiled fondly towards him. He'd always been kind to her, and to her father, she wasn't sorry to be here for him tonight.

When Sally spotted the ward sister, she crossed quietly from the bed to enquire how David was progressing.

The grey-haired sister sighed. 'Doctor isn't too happy with him, as yet. His blood pressure isn't coming under control as we'd like, and that heart rate's still erratic. However, he is resting quite well, that may help restore an even keel. Naturally, we're doing everything we can. Only time will tell if it will be completely effective.'

'I see.' Sally had hoped for something more positive.

The sister smiled. 'It is early days, you know. You're Mr Downing's daughter, aren't you? Is Mr Saunders your—?'

'Very good friend,' Sally told her swiftly.

'He's going to need those. Recuperation could prove a very long process, even when he's discharged from here.'

It was Sally's turn to sigh. 'And I'm afraid I shan't be around in Halifax very much then,' she began, and explained about the work she was doing.

'If you've dashed up to Yorkshire today, you ought to be getting some rest. Mr Saunders is stable at present, you could go home, you know. We have a number for contacting your father.'

Sally remained at David's bedside for a further two hours, but only after being directed to somewhere where she could buy a meal. By the time she was leaving the hospital, she felt better for having eaten, and was trying to concentrate on the fact that David was said to be stable.

Only as she eventually walked up the path to the door of Downing House did Sally remember that she had intended to help her father clean the place up. She need not have worried – he met her in the hall, a smile brightening his weary face.

'Is David still all right?' he asked, then went on to tell her that he had had help in clearing up. 'That minister of his has been an absolute brick. He sent his own housekeeper round to give a hand, soon as he heard that Mrs Holbrook's laid up. A really *genuine* chap, that parson is.'

Sally and her father chatted for a short while after she had made a hot drink and a light supper for them. She was thankful to go up to bed, where, setting the alarm clock for six a.m., she slept almost immediately.

Henry was up and around before her, and reported that his call to the hospital had elicited the fact that David had had a good night.

'I want to be there when the doctor has done his rounds, Sally love. Somebody's got to keep track of what they really think about David's condition. How about you? I don't think you said how long you were stopping.'

'I really ought to set off back sometime today. It was only as a concession that my leave was extended beyond twenty-four hours. It's not as if David's a relation.'

'Happen that's right, but it always feels as though he's more than a friend, doesn't it?'

Sally didn't answer, she hoped her father would not pursue that aspect. This was not the time for going into details of what she was feeling.

David did appear rather better when they visited that day, and one of the nurses passed on the doctor's belief that he could, in time, make a good recovery.

Sally tried to hold on to those few optimistic words as she set out on the laborious train journey south.

Being unable to take Christmas leave that year, Sally had to be content with reports of David's progress which her father phoned through to her quite regularly. His doctors were pleasantly surprised by the speed with which he had become sufficiently fit to be discharged from hospital, and his local doctor appeared confident that he might eventually recover sufficiently to return to his normal life.

Sally was pleased to learn that, now they had been reassured, her father and David were relying on each other's company a great deal. She sensed that Henry Downing was benefiting from having a role in his friend's recuperation.

By the time that she was beginning to forget the awful shock that David's illness had brought, she was adjusting also to never hearing from Vaclav Capkova. His telephone calls had meant more to her than she'd believed, but worst of all was her disappointment in his attitude. He had made her determined to forget him.

On several occasions as 1942 wore on, Sally nevertheless thought of him again, and wondered where he might be serving, especially when the RAF were in the news a great deal. This occurred at times like the Cologne devastation, which was the biggest raid by aircraft ever recorded. Later that year, she caught herself reflecting that Vaclav could have participated in the bombing of certain Italian towns currently reported.

Sally's own work continued as busily as ever, while increasing raids on enemy territories inevitably resulted in heavier numbers of RAF planes being lost or damaged. A few additional women pilots were being taken on

144

for delivering aircraft, and Sally was delighted one day to meet up again with her old acquaintance Freda Turner, who was relishing her hard-won ability to fly.

The two women were pleased to get together for a chat, catching up on each other's news, and bemoaning all the restrictions enforced upon everyone in Britain.

'I couldn't believe it when they rationed soap,' Freda exclaimed. 'And then they even began telling us we can't have any lace or embroidery on our knickers!'

Sally laughed. 'Just as well we don't have much time for showing off our undies to chaps, anyway! Or for dressing in civvies, now we're not supposed to wear decent stockings.'

'Never mind, we might end up all slim and elegant – since they've introduced rationing of sweets and chocolate!'

Having another friend around, even though they weren't always on their base together, made Sally feel less pessimistic about the way the war was progressing.

It was from Freda, however, that in 1943 Sally eventually heard news of Vaclav Capkova.

Word was filtering through within the RAF of a massive raid carried out on Peenemunde on the Baltic coast, reputedly a German development site. Freda was trying to keep up with what was going on. She had been interested in the place ever since one of her fellow WAAF officers had spotted something extraordinary around Peenemunde in photographs she was interpreting.

Freda returned late one night from a delivery and happened to meet Sally next morning as she came away from a very early breakfast.

'Wasn't it you who'd got to know some of the Czech pilots?' Freda asked. 'One of their crews made a nasty forced landing following that raid on Peenemunde. The only good thing about it was that they managed to hang on until they were over English soil. Came down just this side of the North Sea, from what I've heard.'

'I did meet some of them, yes. But it was ages ago. Did any of them survive the crash?' Sally enquired, while her rocketing pulse witnessed to her dread that Vaclav was injured. Or worse.

'Oh, yes. I don't know that any of them bought it. But they were all badly hurt. Rushed to hospital, then some of them were transferred for specialist treatment, at East Grinstead, I suppose, places like that.'

Sally was due to take to the air and couldn't delay to ask anything further. It chanced that her trip that day was to deliver to Biggin Hill. She began enquiring at the airfield about the kind of injuries being treated in the Queen Victoria hospital in

East Grinstead, which wasn't all that far from there.

As she supposed, Archibald McIndoe's unit at that hospital often received airmen who needed facial surgery. Some inner compulsion seemed to be insisting that this was where she might find Vaclav. From that day onwards Sally continued to make enquiries.

Someone at his old base did have news, and it was not good. As her intuition had suggested, Vaclav *was* one of the men involved. He reportedly had been piloting the plane, and was dragged from it as the wreckage caught fire. His hands were badly burned, and one arm was fractured, along with several facial bones.

The fact that she so uncannily had sensed Vaclav was hurt made dismissing him from her mind impossible. Sally yearned to go rushing off to visit him, but she was too heavily committed with work to find any opportunity to even check where exactly he was hospitalized. She was obliged instead to carry out orders from her own ferry pool, and set out on her next delivery, and then the one after.

Having to delay seeing Vaclav ensured that Sally returned to thinking about him consistently. By the time that she was able to take a few hours off and make the trip, her old obsession with his well-being had returned in full strength. But she had used the few

147

spare minutes during the intervening period to discover that he was, indeed, being treated at East Grinstead. She had been unable to ascertain anything about his condition.

The ward felt very different to Vaclav from what he expected of an English hospital. From the day that he arrived, the camaraderie had been marvellous. That alone had prevented him from developing the depression which he had been afraid could prove inevitable.

They should not have allowed him to see a mirror, but he had insisted, ranting at the nurses until they were obliged to resort to any means of quietening him. The shock had been worse than any experienced at the time he'd realized controlling his damaged aircraft was beyond him. Then, there had been some warning – too long a period while he had felt the unresponsive plane rebelling against instruments, against his grip on the joystick. Even after shouting to his crew to bale out, minutes had seemed suspended while he hung on grimly, willing some miracle to intervene.

To a degree, his God had saved them, if only from sudden death. Every man had been injured. Vaclav had cursed himself for failing to prevent their being hurt, making no allowance for their individual decisions to ignore his command to quit. The whole team had suffered that abysmal landing, to stagger as best they could from the immediate inferno.

He had been so proud of his team – throughout every flight, especially so through their resolve to stick with that last one. He was proud of them still, gleaning news, when he could, of their progress, a couple in this hospital, others undergoing appropriate treatment elsewhere.

Vaclav had yearned for home, for dear, familiar Prague, where, to his own people, he might have confided this appalling responsibility for failure, which was hurting infinitely more deeply than all of his wounds. With family, with friends, with his dearly loved Magdaleny, he would have found understanding. But then he had confronted his own face...

That cruel reflection had jolted him to earth, its impact sharper than the one earlier, of his plane's battered undercarriage. Dreams of home shattered amid visions of Magdaleny's potential reaction.

The blackening of both eyes would heal, he knew, but who could confirm that any of the rest might do so? Ever. The eyebrows and eyelashes singed away gave him a vacant look, thought Vaclav, an appearance worsened by one eye seeming twice the size of its partner. And there was more: a bullet had smashed his jaw, displacing bone until even the resultant swelling did not conceal this hideous irregularity.

They had taken the mirror from his bandaged hand, and he'd resisted the impulse to finger the chin where his incipient beard was irritating skin that was scorched.

He was fortunate, he'd been told, the facial burns were minimal and should leave little scarring. Until the surgeons had used such terms, he had been preoccupied with the damage to his hands, fearing that the severe burns might cripple the tissue and prevent future flying.

Vaclav hadn't believed himself vain, but was compelled now to recognize vanity in his reaction to the damaged face, with its ludicrous complement of hair cropped to a bristle by the flames.

'All right, mate?' A fellow pilot, not of his own crew, paused beside the chair where Vaclav was required to spend the majority of each day.

He tried to smile back, winced as he did repeatedly with each facial movement.

'OK, yes. Thanks – mate.'

They laughed, as best they could, grimly.

'Care for a game of cards?' the other pilot invited.

'Not for the present, thank you. Some other time perhaps.'

Vaclav was learning to rely on the ready friendship on offer, had no wish to offend.

But he had never played card games in his youth, and worried that he might not cope with unfamiliar rules in a language that was not his own. Since that crash-landing, his brain was neglecting to run on full power.

Left to himself, Vaclav reached again for the newspaper discarded hours ago. Leaning forward, he used the bed to support its pages while he opened them out. Having one arm in a plaster cast and both hands bandaged, rendered every task difficult. Vaclav had read all he wished of the paper anyway, had had enough of this war!

He tried very hard not to envy the men from British forces hospitalized along with him. They were so obviously more at ease within this place. Most fortunate of all, they had a steady flow of visitors.

Vaclav tormented himself with thoughts of whom he would most love to see walking towards him through the ward. His parents, naturally, either of his young brothers – or *both*! His dear, sweet Magdaleny...

He had dreamed of them all, while this wretched conflict deprived him of even a smattering of news about what was happening in his homeland. He tried to phrase a prayer, but praying came less easily now, while he grew afraid that his God might no longer provide the answer that he needed.

Seven

Vaclav had seen her yards away the instant that she came into the ward. Her face looked pale at first, and was flushing now with anxiety, or confusion. He watched while she glanced to each bed in turn, frowning when she recognized no one.

He quelled a sigh, allowed himself a rueful smile: perhaps it was good that she thought him more attractive than this wretched creature that he'd become?

A nurse had turned from another bed, Sally paused beside her, spoke his name. The moments of savouring her approach were ending, Vaclav did not intend she should find him resting on the bed: upright in a chair, he might at least appear a little more presentable.

The move was ill-conceived. He reached out to steady himself, missed, slid clumsily to his feet. Scarcely believing he'd overlooked the broken arm, Vaclav gestured despairingly with the rigid limb, flopped inelegantly on to his chair.

'Attempting too much again?' the nurse

suggested, smiling.

Sally bent to kiss his damaged cheek. 'Hello, Vaclav. How are you?'

'Thank you so much for coming to be with me. You see how I am! But how are you? And what of David Saunders – did he recover?'

Prepared during those moments while Sally had searched him out, Vaclav was resolved to get this one right. This final opportunity for healing the rift between them. He would prove that he sustained some thoughts beyond his own self. How otherwise would he manage to prevent her leaving his life again? All illusions were gone, he certainly could no longer draw on charm or good looks for influencing any woman.

'I'm OK, thanks, love. And David seems very well from what I hear via Dad. I don't see David that often, no need now he's back at work. As you'll guess, I'm kept pretty busy still, especially since that raid you were involved in. Yours was far from being the only plane that was hit, you know.'

Vaclav nodded. 'I gathered that, from what I have heard – in the other hospital and since then in here.'

'Quite hush-hush, wasn't it? Can we talk about that raid, between ourselves?'

'I wouldn't know. Have not taken that risk, so far. Some of the other chaps were on the same mission, but we err on the side of caution. However, do not let us discuss the wretched war, I cannot believe how fortunate I am to see you.'

'It was Freda who told me you'd crash-landed. Do you remember Freda Turner – a WAAF from a base you were at earlier on? She got her wings, is doing the same job as me now.'

'Can't be sure I do know her. There have been so many...' New faces, men as well as women, and most of them foreign, *to him*. It was strange how he felt that more keenly, now, than ever since those initial few days over here.

'We weren't going to talk about the war, were we?' said Sally, and wondered what she could say.

Inhibited by the irregularities of his face, she was concentrating her mind on *not* speaking of how different he seemed. And how deeply she loved him.

'The bruising around the eyes will fade, I'm told, they certainly ache less today. And the surgeon tells me he has fixed the jaw successfully. It does not feel that way, but I shall be here until he is sure it is OK.'

'And your hands, the arm...?' Sally enquired gently.

He glanced down at his bandages. 'Quite badly burned, but with treatment, care – they will mend one day. The fractured arm should be fine – "simple", they tell me.'

'Meanwhile, you're incarcerated here,

154

unable to do very much. Bored?'

'Some of the time. In fairness, the other patients are the very best. So kind, because that I am far from home. The doctors and nurses also. But, here, I feel to be more strange – more, that is, than when I am with other pilots, always flying.'

'Are you the only Czech here?'

Vaclav shook his head. 'Two members from my crew also, and one other from our country, but he is very sick. The men from my team go to sit with him and talk, but I – until today, talking is not very easy.'

'You mean – is speaking like this hurting?'

Vaclav gave his new, crooked smile. 'You think that I would waste one second of your company? But no – while you are here, we must communicate.'

Sally reached out, grasped his sound arm above the wrist. 'There are other ways, if you must rest your – your injuries.'

'Is what I need, to know that you are here. But also I wish to learn how life is for you. If you are happy...'

'None of us are, are we? And won't be, I suspect, until we've beaten Hitler. The Japs, an' all. Since they've come into this war, everything seems gloomier.'

'Tell me how your father is – still hating the commandeering of his factory for wartime production?'

'He doesn't say so much about that now,

155

think he's had to accept that nothing will change there till the fighting's over. Any road, he's spending a lot of evenings and so on with David, that does him good.'

'And relieves you of some pressure perhaps?'

Sally smiled. 'Until duty resurfaces and I go up to Halifax again, check Dad out.'

'How do you spend what leisure you have while you are based so far south?'

'Much as ever, a night at the pictures, or going for a few drinks, an occasional dance on some RAF station somewhere.'

'I wish that I could dance with you.'

'You will again, one day, when this lot has healed.' She couldn't long for anything more fervently.

'You promise?'

'Of course.' Sally couldn't do otherwise, seeing Vaclav badly hurt was twisting her guts, she would promise him almost anything.

He was very evidently tiring, though, and without using the war as a topic there certainly seemed little to say. They had never been like this in the past surely? Sally herself was so tense, inhibited by the strain of *not* revealing how distressed she was by his injuries.

'I shall have to be going soon,' she told him, and silently cursed her own cowardice, but she couldn't endure much more of sitting there, seeing him so cruelly injured.

'You will come again?'

'Naturally. Got to keep an eye on you!'

'Especially while my own are not very good.'

Sally loved him for the joke, but it did alarm her. 'You *can* see all right, can't you, Vaclav?'

He tried to laugh, and winced. 'My sight is fine, Sally.'

Her hand tightened over his arm. 'You are being valiant, that will get you through.'

Rising to leave, she released his arm. Tenderly, she placed a hand on either side of his face, kissed the gravely injured cheek.

'See you again, Vaclav.'

That prospect kept Sally going for weeks. But only after permitting her emotions some release. Seated in the car outside the hospital, she wept as if her heart were being ripped out of her. Vaclav looked so appalling, and all she could think was how handsome he had always seemed. Physical appearances might be meant not to assume too great an importance, but she had loved the golden-haired young Czech as much for his beauty as for his personality. Today, she simply loved him.

She must be there for him when the going was tough. Vaclav must not be allowed to experience any of the depression which might seem inevitable, the least she could do was take his mind off his injuries. Afraid they could be slow to heal, Sally conditioned herself to enduring the recovery process with him.

During her next visit, Vaclav seemed brighter, could speak with less evident pain, and explained that his hands were healing, however slowly.

Further visits culminated in late autumn with her taking him out for a whole day in the car. Vaclav was looking forward to a promised discharge from hospital, making plans for returning to his old squadron.

They drove over the Sussex countryside towards the South Downs, hoping to eventually reach the sea. They didn't get anywhere near to the coast, where security seemed to be tightening. Several times they were stopped on the road while their identity documents were examined.

'We will go to the sea one day,' Sally promised, overlooking all her own former reservations about even thinking that Vaclav might have a part in her ultimate future.

The gentle hills of the countryside were beautiful, but they couldn't really enjoy the scenery. Every few miles they encountered some reminder of the war. If they weren't passing small landing strips, the nearby fields accommodated gun batteries or observation posts.

'I just hope we don't have an air raid spoiling everything,' said Sally. She had set her heart on giving Vaclav an enjoyable outing.

Her emotions that day were in the familiar vein that she first had recognized when she was longing to show Vaclav how the beauty of her beloved Yorkshire hills might provide relief from stress. And although their one trip to Halifax had been less than satis-factory, she couldn't regret the whole of that experience.

For the present, they were content to eat at a wayside pub where Vaclav was thankful to be able to tackle a meal with reasonable ease. He had been told his jaw had respond-ed well to the surgery, and so long as he felt no embarrassment dining with Sally, he was prepared to accept the operation was a success.

That day marked an upturn in Vaclav's luck. One week later he was discharged from the Queen Victoria Hospital, and after a brief convalescence rejoined his squadron. He kept in touch with Sally, and was pleased to pass on the news when, after only a short period on ground duties, he was back in the air.

Vaclav was based further away from her than ever, though. Meeting again seemed unlikely in the foreseeable future.

Seeing him injured had made a deep

impression on Sally. Even though her working life continued to be as busy as before, she could not push him to the back of her mind. Quite frequently her sleep was disturbed with dreams of how seriously his face had been damaged – dreams that never once reflected the great improvement to his features which had evolved during the weeks of her visits to him.

There were other reminders too, which would continue long after the true nature of the German site at Peenemunde was revealed. Vaclav might have been wary of explaining even to Sally the significance of that raid, but the facts about the experiments carried out by the Germans on that Baltic coast and elsewhere gradually emerged. The reality of what they were engaged in came as a very unpleasant shock.

The rest of 1943 and the first half of 1944 had seen the continuing destruction of towns and cities on both sides of the Channel. But then D-Day on 6th June brought, with the Normandy landings, fresh hope that the Allies might be heading towards victory. The whole of Britain appeared to be experiencing a renewal of spirit, where belief that the wretched war might be drawing to a close could be justified.

Just one week later, the first of Hitler's diabolical new weapons was sighted from an observer post at Dymchurch on the south Kent coast. An apparently pilotless plane which was spurting flames from its rear came roaring through the night sky. Its course was plotted from one observation post to the next. Each sighting confirmed the missile as heading straight for London, although it finally drove into the ground of open farming country in Kent at Swanscombe.

The facts were emerging. That raid on Peenemunde and others on similar sites might have delayed development of these new weapons, they had not prevented them entirely. While that initial V1 (or 'flying bomb' as they became known) was followed immediately by others, Sally grew afraid.

For years now she had evaded fire from enemy aircraft – with experience, becoming adept at avoiding a repeat of that one attack by a Messerschmitt. After witnessing her first flying bomb streaking through the sky, Sally recognized instantly that such a weapon would pursue its course relentlessly, regardless of anything in its path.

Any other aircraft it struck would be blown out of the air.

Ashamed of her fear, she discussed this dread with no one. Kept private, her obsession grew, and increased with each report of a V1 reaching its target.

When news of Allied fighters flying out to

161

destroy these V1s featured regularly in reports within the RAF, Sally could think of nothing else. And, to her, almost the worst aspect was the seeming waste of the attempts to disable sites like Peenemunde. Had Vaclav's efforts and those of others like him been entirely in vain? Would there be no hope now of defeating this current German attack?

The inevitable exhaustion of continuing with work that demanded the utmost concentration may have been partly responsible for Sally's depression. Whatever the cause, she couldn't help believing that Britain and the Allies never would succeed in winning. Wouldn't Hitler always come up with some other weapon, just as he had when everyone at home was celebrating D-Day? While compelling herself to carry on, she could find no relief from what felt like an enormous weight pressing down on her.

Even her friend Freda could not help, try though she did, to encourage Sally to enjoy their few hours of free time together.

'Why don't you come home with me for Christmas?' Freda suggested, as soon as they all began making plans for the season that was supposed to feel festive.

Sally thanked her sincerely, but shook her head. 'I've got to get home to see my dad, haven't I?'

Somehow, though, turning down Freda's

suggestion made Sally more reluctant to make the trip to Yorkshire. The novelty of having her own car had worn off, and the prospect of driving all the way on roads which could be hampered by fog or snow seemed anything but encouraging.

Sally was also becoming uneasy again about David's attitude towards her. Ever since she had rushed up to Halifax because he was ill, he appeared ready to assume that her feelings towards him were deeper than they actually were. Short of blurting out the bald truth that he really didn't excite her, she didn't know how to cope.

Throughout her two previous visits, David had tried to engineer more time alone together until Sally had even felt thankful for Henry Downing's possessiveness. With such a father, she could excuse herself from an excess of tête-à-tête meetings with David Saunders! She knew in her heart, though, that she could not rely on making excuses for ever.

Christmas Eve approached, and Sally waved Freda off regretfully, feeling still more miserable because she would not be spending time with her friend. Slowly, reluctantly, she was preparing to take to the road, when a telephone call came through for her.

The caller was Vaclav, a lovely surprise, for he had indeed rung her far less often since

163

returning to his squadron following that spell in hospital. They chatted for several minutes, catching up on news, exchanging details of how they were planning to spend Christmas. Vaclav would be on duty, he said, and wasn't entirely sorry. At the base he would participate in whatever celebrations could be arranged when they weren't actually flying.

'I still think of that one Christmas I spent with you, Sally. You have always been the only person over here who made me feel welcome.'

'If my father didn't!' she exclaimed ruefully.

They laughed together, at ease with Henry's attitude now, as they seemed to be at ease with their own circumstances.

For Sally, around that Christmas in 1944, her dismal suspicion that the Allies might not triumph, after all, was preventing any thoughts of a stable future. The factor of Vaclav's fiancée mattered less, now that she herself was feeling unable to look ahead very far.

With her own pessimism never far below the surface, and not having seen Vaclav for months on end, the old attraction had dulled. She could hardly credit that it once had flared within her, even at times while he was working a long way away.

I must be growing old, she thought wryly

after he had rung off; hearing his voice no longer aroused all that intense pining. So long as I do meet him again one day, she asserted inwardly, I can accept not seeing him, for the present.

The long drive up to Yorkshire soon began to feel wearisome, and so cold that Sally wondered how she might keep her gloved hands from going into cramp on the steering wheel. Her feet felt almost as bad, and she hoped that she would be able to continue to double-declutch when she needed to change gear.

Somewhere in the Midlands, Sally stopped to have a warming meal, but the distance still to be covered prevented her from lingering, she was soon pressing on again, willing the journey to end. She was thankful to see at last that, even after nightfall and in countryside blacked out for the war, she was among landmarks that she could recognize. Towns and villages through which she drove resurrected memories from her childhood and teenage years.

Her father would be anxious now, awaiting her arrival, and she could not condemn him for his tendency to worry. Her own spirits, these days, often felt so low that she could not criticize anyone for failing to feel optimistic.

Sally drove on through Rishworth and Ripponden, where the valley in summertime

165

normally presented an appealing picture of sylvan beauty. Suddenly, she heard the drone of an engine far louder than her tiny Austin. And she knew. Instantly alert, she felt her heart beating agitatedly, while that external engine noise increased. Almost above her head, she spotted the looming dark shape with its significant flaming tail.

Listening, she heard its engine die, and flinched. The flare of its tail revealed the V1's course while it sped towards earth among the hills over to her left. Sally instinctively buried her head in the hands clenching the steering wheel.

Feeling shattered, she opened her eyes, noticed she'd automatically halted the car at the side of the road, and was relieved. She had been so shaken by the sight of that thing at close quarters that she might easily have driven on to the footpath.

Ashamed of her apprehension, she wondered how ever she had managed to fly aircraft through the skies when she was daunted by driving along a familiar road.

But it's because this is my home territory, Sally thought. Away from here, in the south, she expected to encounter evidence of enemy action. From what her father said, throughout the war there had been very little in and around Halifax. They had experienced only the one severe bombing, plus some nights when incendiaries had been dropped.

Driving on again, she wondered where that dreadful V1 had landed. It seemed to have headed in the direction of Sowerby. Who did she know who lived in that area? Sally reflected anxiously.

She could at least feel certain that Henry Downing was a few miles away from the destination of that particular flying bomb. But was the whole country about to be attacked by these weapons?

Arriving at Downing House, Sally was glad her journey was over, and Henry's expression soon revealed that he was no less thankful for her arrival.

'You look fair worn out, Sally love, has it been a trying drive?' he asked after they had hugged.

'A bit. It always seems a long way in the dark. And then I saw one of those dreadful flying bombs coming down.'

'Further south, you mean? Just after you'd set out?'

Sally shook her head. 'Not so far from here, looked as if it would land out Sowerby way.'

'Go on! It must be the first as far north as this. Leastways, I've heard of none being reported.'

'Oh, well. We'll just have to hope no one's been injured. It might have come down in open country.'

'Aye. There's nothing we can do about it, is there? I'm afraid it won't help anybody if we let it spoil our Christmas. I've done everything in my power to ensure that we enjoy ourselves, and Mrs Holbrook has managed to get plenty of stuff together for some lovely meals.'

The few days of festivities did indeed pass very pleasantly. Sally was glad to have had much of the food prepared in readiness by their housekeeper, enabling her to relax between putting dishes on to cook. When David joined them for virtually every meal, he insisted on helping afterwards with clearing away and washing-up.

Sally appreciated that until, on her final day at home, he remarked that he loved to feel that they worked so well together they might be a much-married couple.

She tried to make a joke of it. 'You wouldn't really wish that on yourself, you know! I'm not at my best when I'm tackling the domestic scene, I much prefer work that gets me out of the house.'

'We could make a go of it, though. If we each did our share, I wouldn't grumble. What do you say, Sally?'

She choked back a sigh, gave herself a few moments before replying. There could be no doubting his meaning, this time. She had been so afraid this suggestion might come up one day. 'All I can say is there's still a war

168

to be won. From what I see of Hitler's new weapons, there's a long way to go yet.'

'You can't mean that. Look at the way we tackled them in Normandy – surely that gave everyone fresh heart?'

'Until the following week, when the flying bombs started. Sorry, David – you'll not find me looking to settle down for many a month.'

'Happen not. Happen not. But you would want to one day, surely? Settle down in a home of your own. We could begin now to talk over what we both want when the war's over. And we get on all right, don't we?'

Sally stifled a groan. Evidently, nothing she'd said had put him off. 'Please – don't persist with this. I'd hate us to fall out just before I set off back from leave.'

She could see he was deeply disappointed. David sighed, his pleasant features slowly formed a smile, he didn't want this to spark a major disagreement either.

'As you wish, love,' he said. 'We can leave this open until the war's over. Just promise me we'll talk then.'

Sally promised, but she suspected already that she was unlikely to say something that David would like to hear. He'd been even more ready for proposing than she had expected, and she would much prefer that he hadn't suggested anything of the kind.

Despite her misgivings regarding David's

attitude towards a possible future for them, Sally felt refreshed by spending Christmas at home. Driving away from Halifax, she also was grateful that they had all had that short period without any air-raid warnings.

Arriving back at her base, the first person she saw was Freda Turner. They spent their last free evening chatting over cups of tea and cake that her friend had brought with her.

Measured against Freda's account of several V1s falling near her home, the isolated one that had alarmed Sally began to seem less frightening. They had been fortunate. As she had been thinking on her way up to the West Riding, the area around Halifax had suffered so little damage throughout the war that she'd been relieved of a great deal of worry concerning Henry Downing's safety. She must not become obsessed now with the dread that he might become a victim of a flying bomb.

Being among people who had a more optimistic outlook on how the war was going once again influenced Sally's own thinking, and she began to feel less uneasy about the ultimate outcome of the fighting.

Another telephone call from Vaclav made her more cheerful still, especially when he told her he would soon be stationed somewhat nearer to her own base.

'We must get together again, if only for one

day,' he insisted. 'I want you to see that I am fully recovered. You haven't spent any time with me since that outing when I was still quite unfit.'

They met in Sussex somewhere between his base and her own. Vaclav had travelled by train and was standing outside the railway station when she drove up.

'Have you been waiting long?' she enquired after they kissed.

He smiled, shook his head, kissed her again. 'I would wait for ever to see you. Especially when you are looking so beautiful.'

'What have you been drinking?' she teased. 'Turning on the charm a bit, aren't you?'

Vaclav laughed. 'You surely do not wish that I should be miserable company? That came to an end the day that I was certain my jaw was repaired satisfactorily. Having that restored has convinced me that I must enjoy my life.'

He definitely seemed to have decided that he must ensure that they both enjoyed their day together. They drove out into the country quite near to Pulborough, and walked for miles along narrow lanes, pausing to see the first evidence of bulbs showing above the frosted ground. Birds were singing in trees whose buds witnessed to the promise of the spring which had seemed too far distant.

'Hope is restoring itself,' Vaclav declared. 'And we must be hopeful also. This year will see the end to fighting, and people everywhere will return to living for their normal work, and for their families.'

I wish I possessed such hope, such a positive belief, thought Sally, and wondered how much Vaclav's faith contributed to his outlook. Her own religion felt to be stagnant, lacking in resources. Was her own neglect responsible for that? She didn't attend chapel nearly often enough, and had no excuse beyond not liking the minister at the place nearest to her base.

'We *shall* live again for our normal work, and for families,' Vaclav reiterated.

But where will you *be?* wondered Sally, and would not ask him. Ever since he'd been injured and she realized how much he meant to her, she had needed Vaclav to reveal how *he* really felt about her.

'We must cling to our vision, even though no one can say what the end of this war will bring,' he continued. 'I cannot forget that my homeland is an occupied country.'

That told her nothing, as she might have expected. Vaclav evidently meant to keep silent about his own future intentions.

Sally could very easily have let that spoil their day, but she resolved not to do so. He could simply be reserving firm planning until the time when they were at peace. That was only what she herself was doing. She reminded herself that their friendship was too good to destroy on the grounds that it was not leading to something much deeper.

They talked a great deal, walking, and afterwards eating in a country inn. In the main, they were reflecting on the war and the changes it had introduced into their lives, until Vaclav announced that he would continue as a civilian pilot in peacetime.

Again, Sally might have enquired if that would be in his own country, but again she refrained. Deep in her subconscious she buried the suspicion that she was afraid of learning his answer.

On the way back to the station for Vaclav's train that evening, he suggested that she park the car in a farmyard. It was evident that the building itself was deserted, all but destroyed by bombing.

Drawing her to him, he kissed her fervently, holding her very close while his hands slipped into her coat to caress her through the silky texture of her blouse. Stirring immediately, Vaclav sighed between kisses, then his lips traced the line of her throat, his fingers found the buttons of her blouse.

His touch on her skin was electric, Sally felt all her nerve endings awakening, impelling her to reach for him, to caress. She had never wanted him more, had to steel herself to resist. But how would she live with such passion if it were never to be sated?

Vaclav groaned. 'Love me, Sally, love me. I have wanted you for years, I cannot wait to have us belong together. I need you so much, you are such a gorgeous woman.'

He was telling her *at last* that she was the one, the only one, for him. Sally kissed him feverishly, felt her body urging her on. Restraining her own impulse to caress him had grown impossible. His tongue was darting between her teeth, lingering with hers. His hand was on her leg, smoothing the skin above her stocking.

Vaclav smiled against her mouth, kissed her more insistently. 'This car is tiny, Sally, but I think we should find the back seat more accommodating...'

She had heard too many girls gossiping. She might not have been experienced sexually, but Sally understood what could often take place on the back seat of a car. And she had never intended that situation to be right for her – not for something that she considered so very special as loving the man with whom she would spend the rest of her life.

'Not here, Vaclav my love, not like this. When we make love it should be something that we would always remember.'

'And I would, I give you my word on that, Sally. Do you not believe that I could make you happy? I have changed, you know, become – become not so very selfish. I promise gentleness, concern for your needs...'

'I'm sorry, no.'

She would not, *could* not consent. Difficult though denying him was, Sally felt compelled to refuse to have their love-making continue.

'I do want you, Vaclav,' she assured him while they straightened themselves in their seats, and she fastened her blouse, composing her emotions in order to drive on. 'You must never think I don't. Please understand that, when the time is right for us, I shall be more than eager.'

Vaclav had said only today that this war should soon be over. And that had led to beginning to caress her, promising to make her happy. That could only mean that he was looking ahead to the future – a future that would be *theirs*.

It was ages and ages now since she had learned that he was engaged, near the start of this terrible war: romances didn't stand that sort of strain. And now everything appeared to have changed, Vaclav said he had changed. He must have had second thoughts about marrying that girl, whoever she was. This explained why he never did behave like a man who had a fiancée, no matter how far distant. Hadn't he spoken just now of wanting Sally herself for years?

'I can only accept your decision, naturally,'

said Vaclav coolly. 'And trust that you will understand my longing, as I must understand your – your inflexibility.'

'Of course I understand. And it shouldn't be long now before we can be everything for each other.'

The day ended quietly – almost dispiritedly on Sally's part – when Vaclav said very little during the journey to the railway station and their wait on its platform. He echoed her words to 'take care now, be safe,' but left her feeling uneasy.

For days Sally was preoccupied, even flying did not feel to be releasing her from the sense of anticlimax that followed their meeting. But eventually Vaclav phoned her again. Simply hearing his voice made her concern about their relationship begin to ease.

He sounded in good spirits, eager to tell her that he had been promoted, and had been commended for his part in the bombing of Dresden.

Sally had possessed lots of misgivings about the damage to that city, but she started to revise her opinion. After all, the airmen involved were only calling on the skills in which they were trained. Wasn't she herself to some degree responsible – if simply through delivering the aircraft for engaging in such destruction? She couldn't do the work that she had loved throughout this long war, and cling to ideals rooted in showing no aggression.

It could be that, much as she once would have relished flying on active service, her temperament would not have been suited to battle. It was true nevertheless, that the V1s, and later V2s, which continued the assault on Britain seemed to prove that any attack on German territory might be justified. Flying from her ferry pool to bases around the country, Sally witnessed far too much evidence of those dreadful weapons, and the destruction that they caused.

Sally was pleased for Vaclav that he visualized his peace-time occupation as piloting planes. For herself, she would be content for a while to settle for a quieter life, one less demanding on time and on nerves. She would prefer to devote some effort and attention to the other side of her nature, as a homemaker.

When she had spoken to David of her lack of enthusiasm for the domestic scene, she'd only been trying to deter him. He had made her consider the future, and recognize that she would like to create a real home. She was certain now that, with the *right* man, she would love to devote herself to doing just that.

Eight

Ideas for embarking on a very different life preoccupied Sally during all the weeks between the end of the war in Europe and the final conclusion of the fight against Japan. Overcoming the Germans had provided the hope which, for so long, had felt to be missing. And in other ways the stress was waning. With less pressure on her to keep up supplies of fresh aircraft, she arranged more home leave, relishing these visits to Yorkshire and sharing her father's satisfaction in starting the initial stages of restoring carpet production at Downing's. The family business could prove more interesting than Sally had once supposed.

She also enjoyed seeing more of friends like Emma Francis, although this could be quite disturbing. Emma was expecting another child, a fact which increased Sally's own awareness that time was passing. Her yearnings for a family quickly became too strong for her to ignore, and her dreams seemed fixed on Vaclav and the possibility of creating a home with him.

Since that night when she had been tempted to become his completely, she could no longer dismiss the familiar attraction which had returned and often was resurrected simply by thinking about him. When her longing for Vaclav combined with her need of children, Sally believed she had discovered where her fulfilment would lie.

She was thankful Vaclav did not seem to be upset by her decision to stop short of making love; he phoned her rather less frequently perhaps, but never without speaking affectionately of certain times they had spent together. Quite recently, he had said how delighted he had been when Sally visited him in hospital after his plane crash-landed.

'Your being with me then has confirmed how special you are to me, my Sally.'

She could understand why Vaclav did not contact her very often after VJ-Day. Everyone was busy looking towards the ending of service life and planning their future existence. For someone from the middle of Europe, making any plans must be more complicated. Sally focussed on his calling her special, and tried to be patient.

When Vaclav eventually suggested that they should meet in London, she began to believe everything was about to come right. He sounded so happy that she felt elated, sure that he had an important reason for choosing this brightly lit city which seemed to epitomize renewed hope. This had got to be because they now had the prospect of spending the rest of their lives together.

As soon as she arrived in London, Sally became too excited to think beyond the fact that, with peace, so many of the good things of life were gradually being restored.

Simply spending an evening in the capital was exhilarating, because she hardly knew the city. And Vaclav appeared equally happy that they were together. They hugged the moment he met her at the station, then he took her to one of the popular dance halls. The place seemed to Sally far grander than anywhere that she had danced ever in her life before.

Vaclav held her closer than close against him, kissing her frequently, and singing softly to the tunes the band was playing. She had always thought he was romantic but never more so than this, she had never felt such delight as all this attraction created by being so near to each other.

Sally couldn't help thinking ahead, and believing that, when they finally were married, the desire igniting between them would be utter elation. She smiled secretly to herself, supposing that much of the time in their future paradise would be spent in the loving which until now had been expressed in ardent promises.

They danced and danced until the band

stopped playing. Almost unsteady with the thrill of it all, she needed his arm around her as they went out to the car that Vaclav had bought after the war ended. He opened up the back immediately, and indicated the rear seat. The car was larger, more luxurious than her Austin, but Sally didn't notice any more than that. She was hungry for his kisses, desperate for greater passion than any permitted on the dance floor. All but delirious with longing, she sank on to the leather upholstery.

The instant he sat beside her, Vaclav kissed her again, deeply, his lips insistent with desire. His fingers sought her breast, caressing until yearning seemed to scream through all of Sally's senses. She returned his kisses feverishly, every pulse dancing to the music that had drawn them close for hours. How she would resist Vaclav this night, she could not imagine.

If *she still felt compelled to resist*, she thought: she would have to make sure he understood how much she yearned to make him happy. And that had got to be soon – just as soon as they could arrange their wedding.

'You have always been so good for me,' Vaclav told her huskily.

'And you for me, Vaclav. We've not been able to meet all that often, but it has always been enough to convince me how well we get on, *in every way*,' she added, determined he

181

must be certain how much she wanted him.

Demanding kisses again prevented Sally from speaking; she felt his hard body pressing at her. Vaclav felt so powerful, she was more sure than ever that he would be a dynamic lover. She reached out, laid a hand on his thigh.

'You have meant so much to me, Sally, throughout my years in England. I shall remember that always.'

'Remember?' she asked, puzzled by his sudden gravity.

'Naturally. And you will remember also, surely? You would not wish to forget what we have been to each other, I trust?'

'No, no. Of course I wouldn't.' *But I thought* … Sally continued silently, the words locked firmly inside her head. She could feel dismay clutching at her throat. Hastily, she withdrew her hand from him, leaned away. How could she have been so mistaken, so – wrong?

She swallowed hard, eased back into her own corner, away from him; away from the torment he was introducing between them.

'I shall take to my homeland the dearest of memories, Sally, of your enduring concern, and of your affection. When any person talks about England, I shall think always of you.'

'I trust your fiancée will appreciate that,' she said dryly, and marvelled that she retained enough composure to speak at all.

'Magdaleny was – *is* always understanding of me.'

'That's good. How – how soon shall you see her?'

'I cannot be certain as yet, there is much to arrange. This is why I wished to see you now, to speak of returning home. When word comes that I may leave, there could be no time for goodbyes.'

'I always hate them, anyway. Much better having had this brief opportunity to wish you well.' She prayed he did not notice how her fingers trembled as she turned back a sleeve to check her watch.

'Sally? Forget the time. You're not leaving London already? Tonight? I did not intend that we should cut short this visit. I have reserved accommodation in a fine hotel.'

'But *I* have not arranged to stay there. Please drive me to Waterloo Station, then you can take up your hotel room.'

'No, no. I cannot let you do this.'

'You won't stop me. I'm going back to the ferry pool. If you don't take me to the station, I'll make my own way there.'

'But it is the middle of the night.'

'And we've both been accustomed to travelling around at all hours, throughout the war. And now we're at peace.' *If no longer at peace with each other!* thought Sally grimly.

Sighing weightily, Vaclav got out of the back of the car and assisted her as they moved to sit in the front.

'I would spend the night more tenderly, if you permitted me,' he told her.

Sally said nothing. If he couldn't understand why she could not remain with him, Vaclav had far less comprehension than she credited him with.

Waterloo station looked very large, and more than a little forbidding. Vaclav offered to wait with her until the early trains began running. Sally refused to consider that.

'I've said I hate goodbyes, I do not mean to extend this one.'

He hugged her close, attempted to kiss her fervently. Sally clamped her teeth together. When he leaned away from her, his blue eyes were full of tears. She shook her head at him.

'This is it, Vaclav. Just go.'

Alone, any relief at no longer needing to contain emotion failed to compensate for the stark reality of her surroundings. And of her situation. Although barely able to see through the tears now rushing to the surface, Sally grew aware of the dismal concourse, with its rank of deserted platforms. Closer to hand, wooden benches provided seating which she might in time welcome, but they offered that facility to several men who, from their garments, appeared to have encountered misfortune of one kind or another.

I hate it here, thought Sally, more perhaps

than I would have hated a prolonged fare-
well to the man I love. But she could, at
least, console herself that she had main-
tained some degree of dignity when they
parted. She would keep that in mind, steel
herself not to go to pieces now.

If only everything did not feel so strange –
the whole atmosphere of this place now
devoid of the crowds of uniformed forces
regularly packing the railways to suffocation
throughout the war. Worse than that, though,
was the strangeness of her own future. Soon
she would no longer be rushing off to the
work that she had loved: and now with
nothing remaining of those hopes of
spending her years with Vaclav.

Most of the other women who had passed
the war delivering aircraft had left her base
already. Sally herself had discussed her
future. With her father, she had hedged all
questions, delaying a firm answer, antici-
pating that this meeting with Vaclav could
offer plans for her new life. At the base, she
had prevaricated in the hope that she might
be staying there only until moving on to
create her own home.

How had she become such a fool? *How* –
when she had known originally that Vaclav
had a girlfriend in Prague – had she allowed
herself to dream? She could not credit that
the same person who'd required such determination to fly had possessed too little sense

185

to comprehend what was happening. Vaclav had desired her, just as she had wanted him, and if more had existed between them that evidently had been no deeper than friendship.

Could the trouble today be because, recognizing her career as a pilot was ending, she'd been so desperate for a settled life that she had woven this fantasy future around Vaclav Capkova?

What remained *now*? Returning to Yorkshire, she supposed. Henry Downing would be delighted to have her around, if the carpet mill suddenly seemed less interesting. Sally recalled that he'd suggested she might take on some accounts work. She hadn't really been listening to what Henry said, her own sights had been fixed on a far different prospect. In a far distant country.

And so now Vaclav was gone, out of her life, and shortly to be out of England. She wasn't prepared to contemplate how it might feel to exist with the knowledge that he was all those thousands of miles away. She had loathed the war years whenever he'd been based a long distance from her. But then Vaclav had been in danger. This *ought* to be different, the war was long since over. It had got to be different, there was no alternative to living with the situation.

By the time the first train that would take her back to base arrived, Sally had ceased weeping, and was resolved to put everything that had happened in London firmly behind her.

Despite steeling herself to endure, Sally found the following weeks very hard, all the more so because of Vaclav's phone calls – calls in which she refused to say any more than that she was 'fine'. By the time that she arrived back in Yorkshire to begin a new life in her father's office, she had decided that initially she must devote all her attention to Downing's mill.

Czechoslovakia came into the news all too frequently for her peace of mind. The Russians, who had featured in the freeing of Prague in 1945, still exerted considerable influence. The only thing for which Sally could be thankful was her father's forgetting where Vaclav came from. That spared her any discussion on the matter.

She herself could not avoid thinking about him, wondering how greatly Prague had suffered during the war, and what he might find there when he eventually returned.

His city looked much as it had in the mind pictures he had carried with him over the years. His first impression was of the river Vltava flanked by the exquisite architecture that had thrilled him since he was a boy. Away on the hill, above the red-roofed houses, Prazsky Hrad, and his beloved

Katedrala sv. Vita still dominated Prague. The castle bore witness to its survival through numerous changes of power, while the cathedral epitomized strength to endure all vicissitudes that changes evoked.

One month ago elections had been held, a fact that had seemed encouraging, although Vaclav was waiting to see if the majority won by the Communist Party would help his Czech people.

The little-changed outward appearance of Prague was the only reassuring feature. Life in his homeland did seem to entail a mass of restrictions. It was purely due to the influence of an old friend, now working for the new regime, that he had at last succeeded in entering his own country. He had learned of too many of his fellow pilots who were denied entry because of their service with the RAF.

Vaclav had been obliged to conceal the occupation he had followed during the war: even charges of treason were being brought against a lot of the other airmen returning home from England.

He had been depressed by having to disguise his profession when all the while he yearned to fly civilian aircraft, but he was discovering he had ties greater than his ambition as a pilot.

News of his parents and brothers had remained sparse throughout the war, and even up to this summer of 1946 he rarely had managed to contact them. Vaclav had learned little more than that they had all survived and still were living in the old apartment a few streets beyond Staromestske Namesti, the Old Town Square.

He had come in by river, and paused now in his walk to glance across the Charles Bridge towards the far bank of the Vltava, to where tomorrow he would visit Magdaleny. Months ago she had sent word to him in England, relating how she had left her parents' home to lodge with a former university friend in one of the quaint houses of Golden Lane, near to the castle.

Vaclav turned his back on the river to stride on, willing his steps not to slow, despite the increasing reluctance he suddenly was feeling. What would he find in his old home – he himself had altered beyond belief, would his mother and father also have changed? And what of his brothers, men now, rather than the impressionable youngsters he had left behind? Tales of the reactions of the young men of Prague to the German occupation, and since then to Soviet influence, suggested great disharmony. From what he recalled of Jaroslav and Bedrich, they were able candidates for participating in any rebellion.

Again, Vaclav paused, this time to gaze, smiling, at the astronomical clock, and to

189

wonder if it could have remained as undamaged as it looked, quite capable of performing its mechanical ritual to draw the crowds.

He could delay no longer, and hurried onwards across the square and through a narrow street, until he stood at the once familiar door.

Vaclav knocked twice before it was opened and he was drawn into the huge embrace of his tiny mother. Johana appeared to have shrunk during his absence, or was memory painting less accurately the woman on whose stability he once had relied?

Crying with joy and shrieking her excitement, Johana was summoning Karel, her husband. He came at a run, a man tall as Vaclav himself, but thin, so very thin that he seemed emaciated.

Vaclav opened his arms wider, hugging them both to him, while the three sobbed out the seeming eternity of anxiety and separation.

'We all see now who is the favourite son,' Bedrich exclaimed in the language which, across the years of absence, today sounded quite unfamiliar to Vaclav.

Prepared to tease over the show of intense emotion, Bedrich glanced back as he was followed more slowly by his brother Jaroslav.

'No longer boys, are they, your brothers?' Johana remarked. 'Grown men, both – and sceptical about such displays of affection.'

They were still his brothers though, and hugged Vaclav warmly, slapping his shoulders and asking how fit he was.

Vaclav wished they could have seen him in uniform.

He reassured everyone immediately that he was fine, never better. His mother was gazing up at him, shaking her head. He felt her work-roughened fingers tenderly tracing the scarring of his face.

'A long time ago now,' he told Johana lovingly. 'A long time.' And it had not all been bad, Vaclav added to himself. But resolved hastily that he would not reflect again on Sally's concern for him.

Prague was his life now: all the people he loved in his homeland. And in this household those people were no less busy than in the past. Johana might look to have aged, but she was the same energetic mother, bustling out to make coffee and to find a cake that she had baked, tomorrow was Sunday.

'She will be sad that we did not know the precise day of your arrival,' said Karel. 'Since the war is over, my Johana plan to bake a special cake for you.'

Vaclav hesitated to say that a special cake did not matter. He knew that, to *his* mother, it would.

'We show you your room first, I think,' Karel suggested. 'When we drink coffee, we talk long time, I believe.'

Snatching up Vaclav's baggage and parcels, Bedrich and Jaroslav followed, insisting on accompanying their brother to his room.

The bed, though merely a single person's, looked large, but only because the rest of the place appeared tiny. So small that it might never have been his, the bedroom seemed unfamiliar because of the way he misremembered every feature. The wardrobe and chest of drawers were plainly enough *his*, yet both looked so little that they might be useless for storage. But at the same time they were crammed into this space in such a manner that moving between these objects and the bed would challenge ingenuity. How had he once lived contentedly here?

'Is good, yes?' said Karel, beaming. 'Your mother have polished for you this lovely furniture. She knows how you love your room, and she makes for you fresh counterpane.'

'It – it is beautiful. I will tell her at once when we go to drink our coffee.'

'Never – never, all the time that you were absent, was I allowed to sleep in here,' Jaroslav confided, ruefully. 'Every night I was compelled to sleep in the one room with Bedrich here.'

'You have all been very kind,' said Vaclav, embarrassed.

His brothers both laughed. 'No, no. Be truthful, Vaclav – you know, as we know, that

Johana Capkova arranges everything here most rigidly!' Jaroslav had seemed at first unable to decide what to say to him, but appeared to be relaxing now.

When their mother called that coffee was ready, Vaclav quashed his immediate reaction to his personal region of the house. He became able to enthuse about the manner in which she had prepared his room for him.

'I have never seen the furniture so well tended. And that bed now looks so splendid. How you have made everything so exquisite, I cannot think. Were there no shortages here in Prague?'

Johana smiled up at him. 'You should not need me to tell you, Vaclav, that difficulties exist only to be overcome.'

Her words were light, but Vaclav read in the shadow behind her eyes that life here had been anything but easy, even since the ending of the war.

His brothers began asking, eagerly, for tales of his life as a pilot: 'That must have been such a thrill!'

'How many German aircraft did you destroy?'

Frowning, their father stopped them instantly. 'What have I told to you? Have you no regard whatever for your brother's safety? No one is to discuss the work that he has done.'

'But here, Father, in our home...?' Bedrich

protested. 'Who is to hear?'

'Not here, not anywhere. I said to you how it must be. You cannot be so stupid. Can you not see that one mention, one tiny word that slips off the tongue, could mean that Vaclav will be tried, imprisoned.'

Johana was weeping. 'Please to remember this, my sons. We must not lose our Vaclav now that he is restored to us.'

The relief of at last being in his home was marred slightly by unease. He hated discovering that the threat to his remaining was precisely as real as he had been given to expect. Joyous though the subsequent meal and the rest of the day were meant to be, Vaclav went to his little room that night decidedly uncomfortable. Could he ever feel happy again about his presence in this family house?

The emphasis in their references to his situation had rested upon his own safety. What concerned Vaclav now was a grave realization. If he were ever to be challenged on account of his RAF service, his whole family could suffer recriminations.

Further problems arose on the next day. A Sunday, with his brothers still at home, Vaclav anticipated that they would all attend mass in his beloved Cathedral. Never in all his life more thankful for deliverance, he needed to express his profound gratitude.

He had never before seen Johana's eyes

194

fearful to such a degree, and his father appeared no less alarmed by the prospect of participating in a service.

'I think perhaps it would be unwise, as yet, to let everyone note your presence there,' said Karel carefully.

'We are not encouraged to worship...' Jaroslav began.

Vaclav sighed, but did not argue. He resolved to discover what was happening to his city. Later, he thought, later, I shall see Magdaleny, she will tell me how things really are. She is not a girl to be afraid: always, I have loved her for her spirit. *She* cannot permit any circumstance here to intimidate her. I shall see – together, we will construct the kind of life that we must live.

His parents were disappointed that he must go out, but accepted Vaclav's explanation that he had to see his fiancée as soon as possible.

'You must bring Magdaleny back with you this evening, to eat with us all,' Johana insisted. 'She is such a lovely girl.'

'Have you seen her at all recently?' Vaclav wanted some reassurance that Magdaleny had not altered in any way.

His mother shook her head. 'Not for some long time now – I think perhaps since she go to stay with her friend near the old castle.'

'OK.'

Vaclav saw how this western expression

195

caused a glance exchanged between Karel and his wife. Initially amused, he turned to wondering if his years in England might have rendered him rather more 'different' from his own people than he had supposed, or wanted.

Setting out to see Magdaleny quickly drove all other thoughts from his mind. Striding energetically in the direction of the river, he found her image superimposed so strongly before his eyes that he scarcely saw the streets and picturesque squares for which he had ached throughout those years of exile.

Reaching the tower that marked the Old Town end of the Charles Bridge, Vaclav paused to inhale, savouring the sheer delight of being home once more. Today, the sun was beating down, glinting off the Vltava with such intensity that he was all but blinded. He felt sweat drenching the collar of his shirt.

He should have worn something less formal, and shorts. His long absence had dulled memories of the heat of a Prague summer, he had not thought beyond grabbing trousers and shirt from among the now forgotten clothes once left behind there.

Even the urge to be with Magdaleny wasn't powerful enough to prevent his lingering near the middle of the bridge. He went to lean on a parapet, first to one side and then the other, to gaze and gaze up and downstream. God, but this was where he belonged!

On the way back home with Magdaleny, they must pause here *together* to savour it all. He would assure her of his love, reassert in the tenderest of words the longing which, within this hour, his body would be expressing.

Vaclav strode out more swiftly, driven by the desire reawakening and his thoughts of their future. He reduced his pace hardly at all when steep streets and steps took him upwards towards her. Nothing now must delay him.

Sparing no time for either castle or cathedral, Vaclav hastened around the walls towards the fifteenth-century street once know as Goldsmith's Lane. There, he finally hesitated, trying to regain breath lost in the climb, and to compose himself.

The woman with whom Magdaleny lodged was, from what he heard, an old university friend, no one he knew. He felt a little unsure now, and unprepared with an explanation of his arrival. The suddenness of his departure for Prague, and the secret nature of his journey, had not allowed recent opportunity for contacting his fiancée. Although certain that Magdaleny would only need to see him to thrust herself into his arms, if the first confrontation were instead with her friend, that could prove difficult.

His fiancée sounded to be very glad to be sharing this house; he himself could only resent the fact that some strange woman might prevent this reunion from developing into the scene he visualized so dynamically...

Sighing, Vaclav chided himself for his feeble spirit. Could he really be hesitating now? Surely nothing could really render him reluctant? Had he not yearned during five – *six* wearisome years, dreaming constantly of nothing but his meeting with Magdaleny? No matter who was present, being reunited with her would be the only thing that counted.

The house looked rather better than some of its neighbours, its paint on walls and woodwork more recent than others that seemed neglected. The door stood slightly ajar, moved fractionally when Vaclav rapped on its panels.

No one came. He waited, rapped again. Again, there was no answer. Through from the kitchen, the aroma of his favourite *gulas* stew with dumplings reached him. Vaclav smiled, and hoped the interior would be much cooler than these city streets. They might then enjoy the meal together. Afterwards...

Assured by the smell of cooking that someone was at home, Vaclav pushed the door wider, and called: 'Magdaleny...'

When no one answered, he dredged

memory for her friend's name, called again: 'Iva...'

Looking around him as he stepped over the threshold, Vaclav found the entire dwelling was poorly illuminated, its tiny windows masked with blinds. Again, nobody responded. In a room somewhere above his head, bare feet began walking across floorboards. A woman whispered a few words then giggled. A man's voice laughed, confidently.

The man appeared first at the head of the stairs; tall, broad-shouldered, completely naked. A young woman followed, trailing the bedcover hastily anchored over her breasts. In the dim light, her long tresses gleamed golden.

Her hair looked just as pale as Magdaleny's, his thought that they might have been sisters made Vaclav feel easier. At least this Iva did not seem embarrassed by her situation. Explaining who he was should excuse the way he had intruded on them.

'I do apologize,' he began.

He was interrupted.

'Vaclav!'

Magdaleny recognized him more readily than he recognized her. Very slowly, she came walking down the stairs towards him. As she caught up with the man, she grasped that firm, bare shoulder. He glanced back at her, asked some question in a language that Vaclav didn't know.

Her reply seemed to be in the same tongue: from her tone, a reassurance that she was all right. The pair continued down the last few steps, together.

Vaclav turned his back on them, plunged through the gloom towards the outer door. Fumbling for the door handle, he was impeded by finely woven cloth. Glancing upwards, he identified a Russian army uniform hanging there, beneath its smart cap.

He did not wait for any explanation.

Nine

He would not, *could not*, go home. His parents, and Jaroslav and Bedrich too, were expecting to see Magdaleny with him. He would never endure their questions, any more than he might stuff his mouth with the food Johana Capkova would have prepared so lovingly. For her future daughter-in-law.

In the old days (and how old they were now) Vaclav had always been delighted that his mother and Magdaleny got along so well. He could picture the two women now, chattering and laughing while they cooked together in the kitchen of which Johana was so proud. And if his fiancée had confided to him that she'd found the place too small and old-fashioned, she had uttered no hint of that to his mother.

He even recalled overhearing her remark to Johana that, when she possessed a home of her own, she would equip its kitchen in similar fashion.

Had Magdaleny been laughing privately then, at his family, at Vaclav himself? He could find no reason now to convince him

201

otherwise. He loved her for her brightness, her vivacity, had marvelled that she who *sparkled* so vividly was interested in him.

They had known each other at school, though it wasn't until some festivity preceding Easter that he had really noticed Magdaleny. Vaclav could see her now – seeming to dance along as she hastened towards him, bearing traditional green branches bright with ribbons and decorated eggs. No one more closely symbolized spring, *returning life*. In the old custom, all the girls were rushing away from the ritual destruction of a person dressed to represent Death. For Vaclav, from that day, Magdaleny *had become his new life*.

She had seemed so sweet originally, almost childlike in her delight at having fun, never conscious of her own keen intelligence. Even when both studying hard, they had spared time always to enjoy being together. Within a few months they had matured a great deal, but he had been good, or fairly good.

Aware of their Church's teaching, conscious of Magdaleny's virginity, he had restrained his fiercer desires. They had kissed, of course, frequently, had explored with eager fingers, tongues; exciting, inciting, eliciting delight.

Vaclav had loved her with his entire heart, with his eager, young man's ardour. Only when evil war foreshadowed their parting had he made love with her completely. It was Magdaleny who had insisted, tears filling her beautiful eyes, on the night when she'd received his ring to betroth them.

Where was that ring now? How had it come to mean so little? How could she have contemplated making love with another man?

The desire surging an hour ago at the mere thought of her, pulsed on, paining him, straining at his clothing as it strained within him. There could be no relief, or none that he could imagine seeking.

With Magdaleny no longer his, he was condemned to perpetual torture. How could she have done this to him? Who would consider that he deserved this betrayal? He had travelled that long, dangerous route to England, had remained there for years to fight his war in the skies.

The thought of all that he'd endured sickened him. Or was it revulsion generated by that scene he had recently witnessed? Whatever its cause, the nausea persisted, driving him to stagger into a neglected courtyard and vomit.

Leaning against a wall, Vaclav reviewed the dreadful reality. He had come home to her, had saved himself for *her*, he did not deserve such treatment.

Wiping his lips, he shuddered. He'd rarely been sick, could count the occasions.

During his student years perhaps, or afterwards with the RAF, drinking into oblivion a bad night's flying.

He had never really needed that amount of alcohol, life was good without it, the life which he'd believed had a future. *He* had been true to their commitment, true to Magdaleny.

Truth asserted itself abruptly, the truth he'd been ignoring. Honesty made Vaclav acknowledge that he had not been blameless. So many times, his intentions had been superseded. Throughout that war. His will had been obliged to surrender to Sally Downing, or he'd have made her his with all the force of a full-blooded suitor!

Today, and for all time, he was settling the account.

Sally had opted for remaining in the office of Downing's, could blame no one but herself for the decision to keep the firm's books, even when the work generated little more than the satisfaction of balancing figures. She no longer felt miserable, but she wasn't happy either. Days and weeks turned into months. Through Emma Francis and her husband, Sally increased her circle of friends, but none of them mattered deeply.

David still featured in much of her life. Since returning to the mill, he was shouldering more of the responsibility delegated by her father, and as Henry continued to relish his company of an evening, David often was around her home.

They talked a lot, enjoyed walking together through the Yorkshire hills, and occasionally visited a theatre or cinema, but a certain unease existed between them. Her relationship with him continued to count for more on David's part than ever it did on her own. For some time now Sally had been in no doubt of that.

David had asked her to marry him. She could still picture the night as though it were happening today, still felt the flood of embarrassment she'd experienced when compelled to turn him down.

They had been to a cinema in Leeds, where the film had been very enjoyable, and quite erotic. In the car, after he'd driven her home, David kissed her fervently, and Sally instinctively responded. They both knew that Henry would have retired to bed, David insisted on seeing her into the house.

Kissing Sally again in the hall, he held her close, smiled into her eyes. 'I do wish you would marry me,' he said earnestly. 'We are so good together.'

Although hardly surprised by his proposal, Sally was shaken. She could not trap herself in a marriage based on no more than fondness. And she must not let him believe she felt anything deeper. Feeling gauche and

205

inept, she blurted out the truth.

'No, David, that would spoil everything. We're all right as we are. We're good pals, aren't we? And always will be, but I don't want to get wed. Besides, it'd complicate things here, with Dad.'

'Don't make Henry your excuse, it won't wash. You know as well as I do he'd be highly delighted if we made a go of it.'

'You don't know him like I do, David.'

'You're not the one he confides in, not the way he does with me. He wants to see you settled, Sally. Settled with me.'

'If he *has* said that, it's not with my agreement. He'd no business to go talking that way with you.'

'Sally love, that's just something fathers do, hope to see their daughters find a good partner.'

She shrugged, sighed. 'Whatever. Just – leave it, will you? I don't want to fall out with you over this, but that doesn't mean I'll come round to thinking as you do.'

Having always known how greatly her father would love her to marry David made everything worse. Sally couldn't avoid suspecting the two men had been conspiring. If she consented now, she could lose the freedom to make her own decisions.

She must remain adamant: David wasn't her ideal, she could see from his rather outmoded home that they were not sufficiently alike. Fortunately, after one further attempt to persuade her, he agreed to drop the subject.

Ironically, the fact that he ceased referring to the possibility of marrying did not solve the problem for Sally. Another dimension was introduced between them. She could almost believe he had willed it to happen that, whenever she and David were together, she experienced a strong attraction towards him. It was not something that she'd ever felt for him in the past, and it was the last thing she wanted now. Even when he came into her office, she would feel blatant longing surge through her, often so fiercely that concentrating on columns of figures grew impossible.

During an evening out together, desire would threaten her composure until the simple touch of his hand on hers would make her yearn for love-making. Sally became so perturbed that she wished she'd never declared what good friends they were. If her need continued for this man she'd no wish to marry, she would feel compelled to stop their outings.

Several times when they sat for a while in David's car, or afterwards in his home or her own, Sally wondered how David would react if she encouraged him to make love with her. They both were mature adults, after all, and neither of them had any other commitment.

Such love-making might be one solution.

So far, her natural restraint had made her hold back, and Sally was half-convinced that it always would. Only with one man had she ever believed she might yield to desire, and she loved Vaclav, didn't she? Without love, she wouldn't really give herself. Would she?

The weekend that everything changed wasn't all that long afterwards, in the February of 1947. The whole of the West Riding, plus other parts of the country, suffered massively heavy snow. No one could recall such deep drifts and, despite power cuts, lots of people were thrilled, marvelling at their altered landscape.

David and Sally spent much of the Saturday morning taking buses and then, when routes were blocked, walking out into the countryside. Places like Wainstalls on the edge of the moors were scarcely recognizable. Snow had drifted almost to the rooftops of many houses, obliterating doors and windows, while, beside the roads, most of the gas lamps were barely visible.

Exhilarated by the spectacular scenes they'd discovered, they returned to Downing House expecting to spend the rest of the day near the fireside. They could not believe that any previously arranged functions would still be taking place. But Henry told of a telephone call for Sally, announcing that a dance to be held in the chapel Sunday School had not, after all, been cancelled.

'We've got to go,' Sally insisted to David. 'Lots of folk will be put off by the weather, it's up to us that don't live so far away to make the evening worthwhile.'

It was fun trudging through snow to the hall, and the fun continued while everyone was changing Wellingtons for dancing shoes. Because there was no electricity, the music was provided by an old wind-up gramophone, but that only added to the enjoyment.

The room was cold and the occasion attended only sparsely. She and David danced constantly in order to keep warm. They laughed a lot with other couples, and relished a set of The Lancers and one or two Scottish dances among the ballroom numbers. By the time they were leaving, both were feeling exuberant.

'I don't think I'll sleep for ages, I'll never quieten down after this lot!' Sally exclaimed ruefully.

'I've got just the thing for that,' said David swiftly. 'We'll call in at my place before I walk you home.'

As soon as they reached the warmth of his house, David took her coat, and told her to change out of her boots.

'Now, what'll you have?' he asked, leading the way into his rather old-fashioned living room. 'A brandy would be good, make sure you don't cool down too suddenly. And it would help you to sleep.'

They stood near the hearth, sipping their drinks, and Sally felt the spirit warming her from within while the embers in the grate gave off enough heat to prevent the room feeling chilly.

After a few moments, David took her glass and set it aside with his own. He pulled her close against him, so near that Sally was shaken by his need of her. He kissed her deeply, fiercely, his tongue parting her teeth while his hands pressed into her back, anchoring her against him. Instinctively, Sally stirred in response, her hips swaying, expressing the intensity of the familiar yearning. Her fingers traced the line of his spine while her mouth welcomed his.

'Let's find somewhere more comfortable,' she said huskily, taking her hands from his back, stretching them out sideways while she still retained some control over her fingers. She hadn't seriously visualized herself as provocative.

'I don't think you know what you're saying,' David protested. But he remained closer than close, leaving her in no doubt of what he was feeling.

'Don't be so sure. David love, if we're grown-up about this, we'll soon both feel a heck of a lot better.' This had to be the solution, the sensible way to make the best of the situation.

'I can't believe what you're suggesting.'

She scarcely noticed her arm going around him again. Her other hand struggled with his belt.

'Stop that, Sally. You seem to forget we're not married.'

'We could still—'

His bitter voice interrupted her. 'If this is what you thought when you turned me down, you can think again! Casual sex isn't on my agenda. *I'm* not like that.'

'Are you implying I am?' Sally was feeling dreadful now. Did David think she was common, *cheap*? 'Actually, you'd be the first.'

'Really?' Aware of her fondness for Vaclav Capkova, David had always wondered how far Sally might have gone with the Czech pilot. That question had become quite an obsession.

'Yes, really,' she retorted. 'But that's irrelevant. I know where I stand here.' She reached for her drink again, gulped it down. 'Where did you put my coat?'

'You're not leaving yet, not while this is unresolved?' Her evident passion was a surprise, and convinced David she could be keen enough now. Ready to agree to marrying. 'When we need each other so much, it surely is time we considered our options again. You know what I want, Sally.'

She could never agree to marrying now without seeming obsessed with sex. 'That's not something I'll discuss. If you'll fetch my coat, I am going home.'

David insisted on walking her to the door of Downing House, which didn't surprise her, but did create a difficult few minutes. Sally had never been more thankful to arrive home. They hadn't spoken again before she slid her key into the lock.

She was on the point of saying goodnight when David kissed her cheek.

'Still friends?' he asked.

'That's up to you,' said Sally, and went into the house.

Dismally, she closed the door behind her and leaned against its panels. Because of the snow there was no sound of David walking away. Eerily, she felt that he could still be standing out there. Waiting for her.

By the following morning, Sally felt intensely uncomfortable. It hadn't been like her at all to try and convince any man that they should make love, least of all a rather old-fashioned man like David Saunders. She dreaded seeing him again, her only relief being that their next meeting would be at Downing's. No matter what he thought of her now, he was unlikely to voice his opinion in front of anyone in the office or elsewhere about the mill. And they did have more than enough work to keep their attention on the business.

Although raw materials were difficult to obtain, some supplies were coming through, and there seemed to be more demand for carpets than ever in the past. The long gap in production enforced by the war certainly had resulted in masses of orders from people who were beginning to look to refurbishing their homes.

All the new houses now being constructed also would require floor coverings, it seemed that the prospects of having full order books would continue for years to come. Henry, naturally, was greatly pleased by the future work this presaged. If only the rest of his world appeared equally satisfactory, he would be a happy man.

Henry was too concerned for his only daughter to fail to notice how uneasy she'd suddenly become, and just one day at the mill confirmed that David was no less preoccupied. When his old friend declined the suggestion that he dine with them that evening, Henry delayed tackling Sally only until they reached their home.

'Has David been asking you again if you'll marry him?' he enquired as they were hanging their coats in the hall. 'You could look a lot further and fare a hell of a lot worse, you know.'

'I dare say, Dad. I just don't happen to love

David. You surely wouldn't want me to set up with him in a loveless marriage?'

'Love can grow, have you considered that?' When Sally said nothing, Henry pressed on, relentlessly. 'There's something else you might consider, an' all – you're not being exactly fair to him.'

Her father hesitated and Sally sensed he was searching his mind for acceptable words. 'I've no idea, really, how much you understand about men. If your mother was still alive, she'd be better at this. I'll try to handle this delicately, love...'

Henry sighed, moistened his lips, cleared his throat, twice. 'Men aren't made like you young ladies, you know. They have needs, needs that force them to find the right partner. Once they get married, that kind of thing – well, sorts itself out. When they're not wed, though, it ... makes it ... *difficult* for them. Happen you ought to bear this in mind, not spend quite so much time on your own with David, not if you've no intention of marrying. It's actually unkind to be leading him on, while you're compelling him to restrain what he's feeling for you.'

Sally felt her lips twitching, pressed them together. If only her father knew how the very opposite of his assumption applied!

Almost as soon as her amusement had arisen, it died. If Henry Downing *could* know the truth of the situation, he would be totally horrified. And even though the matter really should be none of his business, she couldn't rid herself of the feeling that by encouraging David like that, she had let her father down.

Despite her father's interference, Sally rationalized her own reaction to David's rejection of her, recognizing that nothing in his life so far had prepared him for more than the norm of falling for a girl and marrying. He wasn't the one who had been away throughout the war, mixing with people from other parts of the country and from other cultures. He hadn't lived among men and women who faced death every single day, and were driven by that to find comfort – *happiness* – wherever they could.

Whatever he felt for her – and Sally believed it was genuine – the emotion had grown steadily over the years, a development from their friendship. But that slow emergence of feeling must surely be responsible for the way he was prepared to wait, and wait, for his ideal circumstances in which to consummate their relationship.

'If only he'd shown a bit of real passion...' Sally murmured aloud in the privacy of her room one night.

She might have settled for that, could eventually have agreed that marriage might be a solution to this physical attraction which was so unlike her old response to

David Saunders. Perhaps she only needed to be assured how greatly he wanted her?

Sally had always been determined to avoid comparing David's attitude with Vaclav's. She thought of each of them quite differently, did not believe them to be in the least alike. But once the word passion surged into her mind, there could be no excluding Vaclav from it. There was no chance of dissociating the Czech pilot from all her most secret yearnings, any more than there was any prospect of ceasing to be concerned for him. Caring about him was not something that she could just switch off – as she had found throughout the long months since seeing him.

Daily on awakening, and each time among her nightly prayers, Sally remembered. She ached for word that Vaclav was safe, while she longed with a physical pain to have him near. The pain she could endure, the caring seemed to eat into her.

There had been no word from Vaclav and, although none had been promised or expected, Sally felt wounded. Admittedly, they hadn't parted on good terms, but she felt nevertheless that the understanding they once shared might have proved stronger than any disagreement.

As time had passed, she had willed herself to accept that this chapter of her life was closed, and she must get on with the rest.

Unfortunately, Sally was discovering that her once effective will power had developed certain flaws. Her only comfort became the knowledge that her inability to surrender memories of Vaclav Capkova was quite private from everyone else.

Being fully occupied at Downing's mill, and continuing to indulge in the social life that Emma and her friends encouraged, continued to help the months to pass quite swiftly. Following his years at sea, Emma's husband Paul seemed to relish his home life, and was happy to spend an evening looking after their daughters and the new baby boy. Emma, meanwhile, loved every opportunity to go out for a meal or to see a film with her women friends.

Sally managed for a while to avoid tête-àt-tête outings with David, but eventually she was obliged to listen when he insisted that they still could go out together without her fearing that he might propose. He was being straight with her, and Sally admired straightforwardness.

If they were not entirely comfortable together any longer, at least he hadn't mentioned her suggestion about love-making! She soon discovered they hadn't completely lost their former rapport, and was relieved everything between them hadn't been ruined.

David was still an interesting companion

for visits to the theatre or for exploring the Yorkshire countryside – rather more serious than some of her acquaintances. And Sally had always loved to introduce debates on matters she considered important. There were times when she suspected he was the only person who really listened to her thoughts on politics or the potential conflict between religion and the sciences.

He also remained her staunchest ally in looking after her father. Now that Henry was ageing and seemed troubled by a number of little ailments, having someone else to hand was a support she appreciated. Someone to rely upon.

Without fully realizing it, somewhere at the back of her subconscious, Sally was perhaps beginning to acknowledge that the idea of *some day* ending up with David Saunders was no longer entirely impossible. He was such an agreeable man with anyone who behaved reasonably. Their working together had increased their mutual understanding, and could prove more important still in the future, if her father relinquished more of his own contribution within Downing's.

Any prospect of commitment to David was driven from Sally's mind instantly on the day that a letter arrived from Prague. The unexpected nature of the letter increased its importance to her, even when nothing in its pages conveyed any hint that she might even see Vaclav again.

Dear Sally,

It is so long that we have been apart, and I can only hope that you have not forgotten who I am.

As you see from this address, I did arrive quite safely in my own country, and I was happy to learn that both parents and my brothers were in good health. Our dear city has survived the war years in better condition than I had feared. From what I saw during my long journey here, the same applies for much of my homeland.

There have been changes, as one would expect, and not all of them good ones, but I make a living now, if not in the work that I would have chosen. Jaroslav and Bedrich (my brothers) are doing well, but no longer in Prague. They work now for an uncle who farms near to the Polish border.

I hope that you and your father are well, and that carpet production at his factory has recovered from the reorganization enforced by the war. What kind of work are you engaged in? I hope that you are not prevented from continuing to fly.

From the day that I arrived home in

Prague to find it still so beautiful, I have
wished that I might show to you all of my
favourite places here. I do so want to have
you love my city as deeply as I myself
love it.

Your affectionate friend,

Vaclav

*And what exactly would his wife think of my
visiting them?* Sally wondered immediately.
How could Vaclav suppose that the woman
might readily accept as a guest some girl
remembered from his years in England? In a
similar situation, she herself would soon
become curious about the significance of a
'friendship' which seemed so important that
memories of that person still persisted.

Although greatly relieved to learn that
Vaclav was alive and appeared to be fit, Sally
did not intend replying swiftly to his letter.
She had used those many months which had
elapsed to school herself to live with never
seeing him again. Managing without Vaclav
Capkova in any part of her life was instinctive now, she read nothing in his words to
suggest that situation was likely to change.

Her decision to ignore his letter was
reinforced within days, while Sally was still
feeling quite unsettled after hearing from
him. She needed to concentrate on people
nearer to home. Suddenly, and with little to

indicate that any further problem was developing, David collapsed with another heart attack.

Sally was with him at the time, and soon began blaming herself for his collapse. It was a Saturday in spring, hot for so early in the year, and they had taken a walk over Norland Moor during the afternoon. Following a meal at Downing House, they had gone together to a dance being held at the local army barracks.

Sally always relished dances held by the army regulars, which naturally reminded her of the comradeship she'd enjoyed throughout the war. If David was less keen, he never said, and he always seemed to join in enthusiastically, just as he did when they attended occasions organized by his church or her own. They danced a lot, partly because neither of them drank a great deal, therefore the bar didn't appeal very much.

The evening was drawing to a close when David fell. At first, Sally thought his foot must have slipped, but then she saw his face was twisting in pain, and one hand clutched at his chest. Moments after she had dropped to her knees beside him, the army medical officer was there, edging her out of the way so that he could tend David.

Sally had never seen an ambulance arrive so swiftly. Praying that he would survive, she dashed to David's car in order to follow the ambulance.

On the previous occasion when he'd collapsed, she hadn't seen David until he was in bed, beginning to recover. This time, Sally witnessed every alarming second following his admission to hospital.

She couldn't recall ever feeling more perturbed. By the time she had parked his car, David was on a stretcher in the casualty department; the army MO was speaking urgently to one of the nurses, and a doctor came running towards them. Listening to the uniformed MO, the doctor felt the pulse in David's neck then tore open his shirt to apply a stethoscope to his chest.

Sighing, he raised his head to seek the nurse. 'Barely in time! We've caught this one, I think, but it's a near thing. Admit him at once, to the special heart unit. I'll be there before we have him into bed. We'll need all possible monitoring to hand.'

'You mean – we could lose him?' Sally was horrified.

'Let's hope not. Is he your husband?'

Sally shook her head. 'A friend, but I was there when he collapsed.'

'You'd better follow us to the ward. First, though, it'd help if you'd leave the patient's details with the desk.'

Sally finally reached the ward as David was being connected to some monitoring machine.

'Is it the first time this has happened?' the ward sister asked her.

'No, he was rushed here before. Quite early in the war, could have been 1940, or '41.'

'Right, I'll send someone for his records.'

'And this time – had he indulged in a lot of exertion?' the doctor enquired over his shoulder from David's bedside.

'We had been dancing. All evening, I'm afraid. And we'd had a long walk during the day. This is all my fault, isn't it?'

The doctor smiled. 'Not necessarily. None of that would have harmed a fit person. And, you must remember, Mr Saunders is quite old enough to say for himself if he'd done enough.'

'Even so...' Sally felt sickened that she hadn't given the least consideration to David's history of heart trouble.

'Does he have any close family?' the sister enquired.

'None that I know of, not really close. His parents are dead, he's lived alone for years. But my father's a great friend of his, I'd like to let him know as soon as—'

'You could do that now, there's a phone outside in the corridor. And there's nothing you can do here for the present.'

Although Sally tried to begin telling him carefully, Henry was terribly shocked to hear that David had suffered a further attack.

Asking which hospital he was in, he told her that he would be there without delay.

'There doesn't seem to be much we can do though, Dad,' she warned him.

'Happen not, but when he comes round he'll be glad to have somebody there that he knows.'

In fact, when Sally returned to the ward, David was fully conscious. She was cautioned, however, to be careful not to disturb him, and not to expect him to talk.

'This could be a long, slow haul, I'm afraid,' the consultant added before turning aside to instruct one of his junior doctors in the care required for David.

Sitting beside the bed, Sally took her friend's hand, and was reassured when his fingers tightened briefly on her own as she told him to rest.

Henry arrived half an hour later, accompanied by a nurse who was explaining the patient should have complete rest, and should not be expected to converse.

'I understand,' Henry told her. 'Me and my daughter were here before. You pulled him through that time, let's hope this won't be any worse.'

Sally had expected to feel relieved that her father was there, sharing the concern. Instead of that, she began to wonder if she had been wrong to contact him before there was more hopeful news of their friend's condition. She had never been blind to the fact that Henry Downing was ageing, but tonight she became aware suddenly of the dark shadows beneath his eyes and the mass of lines etched into his face.

'I should have spared you this, shouldn't I, Dad? For a bit, at least...'

He shook his head, but indicated she should leave the bedside for a moment so they might talk in private.

Outside the ward doors, he grasped her by the shoulder. 'David's the one you ought to have thought of sparing, you know.'

'I do know that. And I feel ever so guilty, I just didn't think how much exercise we'd had today.'

'That's not what I mean.' Henry's voice was sharp. 'You should have been looking after him for years by now. As only a good wife could.'

David was in hospital for weeks, but began improving within the first few days, which meant Sally and her father felt their anxiety reducing. They visited him together occasionally, but mainly individually to cover more of the allotted visiting hours. One or two senior staff from the mill also went in to see him. Before the war, and since, David Saunders had won their respect for being entirely conscientious.

Henry didn't refer again to his own remark

that Sally should have been caring for David, as his wife. That didn't prevent her from thinking repeatedly about the idea, and growing increasingly alarmed by such a thought. The fact that it only confirmed what she'd always understood of her father's wishes made her feel no better. And if David gave no hint of his own feelings, that was little consolation. He was the last person who would have reproached her on such grounds. Hadn't she been thankful for some long while that he seemed unlikely to remind her of his proposal?

Sally did resolve, nevertheless, to do her utmost to help when David finally was released from hospital and went home after a short convalescent break. The rest and medication appeared to have been highly successful, and he looked and sounded fitter than he had been for some months before the attack.

He had been given a list of things he ought to avoid. Strenuous exercise was one, but walking was encouraged. That was where Sally decided she could best assist. Together, they began walking to and from the mill instead of driving. They also went rambling through woods and meadows and over the local moors whenever time permitted. She could ensure, initially, that only short distances were covered, and they were never far from transport in case that should become necessary.

David had returned to Downing's shortly after his stay in the convalescent home, but with a fresh attitude to work. Still conscientious (he'd never really be other than that), but prepared to accept that delegating certain tasks might now be acceptable.

Sally took over some of his responsibilities, and particularly relished being introduced to the intricacies of calculating costings for the carpets they produced. She found this work interesting, and especially satisfying whenever her control of the company balance sheets revealed she'd accurately estimated the cost and potential profit margin for producing a particular line.

Feeling more truly involved with Downing's than ever before, she often told David how pleased she was to have taken on additional responsibility within the firm. Late one afternoon, he laughed, as he was tending to do more frequently.

'So, neither your father nor I need to worry that you'll ever quit then?'

'You hadn't worried on that score, had you? I'm only a glorified bookkeeper.'

'Don't think "only" – you're special, Sally. Always will be, to me as much as to Henry.'

Sally steeled herself not to sigh. She might enjoy her work more than ever, she did not wish to begin to feel trapped there. Any more than she had wished to feel trapped into marriage with David. Actually, the latter might never happen. Sally was beginning to feel easier because, these days, she was seeing him less frequently. Although most weekends they took one short walk together, he rarely joined them at Downing House of an evening. Sally wondered if her father had embarrassed him with the opinion that she should be looking after David, as his wife. From what she knew of their old friend, he could be reluctant to discuss the subject.

Whatever the cause, Sally felt able to shelve that particular anxiety. She was afraid, nevertheless, that David's words about the job were making her consider her own future more carefully. Was it high time that she asked herself whether she wanted anyone to take for granted that she'd always work at Downing's?

The months since the ending of the war hadn't obliterated memories of how much she had loved that job, and not only for the exhilaration of flying aircraft around the country. She had relished meeting people from other backgrounds and different countries, an experience that provided a wider appreciation of the world as a whole.

She was earning good money, especially since taking on additional responsibility, and was beginning to cherish hopes of travelling beyond Britain. During that late summer of 1947, however, Sally could see little evidence that the near future would provide many such opportunities for herself.

In addition to the limitations enforced by the probable expense, she anticipated that Henry would be far from happy to see her go off alone to explore. So much of the world appeared to be in turmoil. Not only was India on the point of accepting partition as inevitable, the Middle East was severely troubled by action against the Jews, while eastern Europe seemed to be changing beyond recognition. Sally might long to experience something of the excitement enjoyed during her years with the Air Transport Auxiliary, but she felt compelled to accept that she could not justify seeking out excitement.

All at once she was struck by the thought that she might have been an utter fool. If only she could agree to marry David Saunders, she would be provided with the companion who would reassure her father regarding her well-being. With David, she would be able to travel wherever and whenever she wished.

Ten

Sally had heard very little about Czecho-slovakia since the ending of the war. The one letter from Prague had told her no details at all of the life its people were leading. She had assumed that they were enjoying a peacetime much like the situation in Britain. No one over here could claim that life was good, rationing continued, along with other econ-omy measures, to remind everyone that more should be achieved, but the country was free.

She was jolted suddenly when news filter-ed through in September that 142 people had been arrested in Czechoslovakia for plotting to murder their President, Edvard Benes. The number of people taken into custody seemed to indicate that there must be a great deal of unrest over there. She could imagine that the strongest of these reactions would be in the capital city, Prague.

Sally was seized by a massive dread that Vaclav could be involved, that something might happen to him. Why on earth hadn't she answered his letter? He could then have written back to her, and they would have continued to keep in touch. She would always have *known* that, at least until his most recent correspondence, he was safe. Instead of that, suddenly she was just as fearful for his safety now as ever she had been throughout the time when he was flying with the RAF.

Sally could speak to no one of her fears. With David and her father she continued to feign indifference to whatever Vaclav might be doing. This was not difficult, no one mentioned him. With Emma and their friends, meanwhile, Sally adopted the air of enjoying the present – an attitude that had become acceptable in that crowd. They went out as often as they could afford, and the women among them vied with each other to treat themselves to the New Look fashions that were being introduced.

Laughing and chattering their time away might be no more than an antidote for the war years they had endured, and subsequent shortages and disappointments. Sally could not expect any of them to become more serious and share this concern for her Czech friend who now lived thousands of miles away.

If people around her seemed preoccupied with their own circumstances, no one Sally knew could miss the news in February 1948

231

when the Communist Party seized control in Czechoslovakia. Sitting in the cinema, they watched newsreels that showed the squares and streets of Prague packed with its citizens, while the Communist leader Klement Gottwald addressed the rally from a balcony of the Kinsky Palace.

Reports revealed that Gottwald was announcing the new government, stating that President Benes had accepted the resignation of twelve centre and right-wing ministers.

Shortly afterwards, Benes twice cancelled radio broadcasts that he had intended making to the nation. Everyone agreed with Sally when she suggested it seemed that his ideas were being suppressed.

Sally found herself scouring the upturned faces in every film shot and staring hard at any newspaper photos. She felt sure that Vaclav would be there, and she couldn't believe he would do other than oppose this new regime. Concern for his safety increased to alarm. Most nights she could hardly sleep for worrying about him.

The next news sounded hopeful initially, when a counter-demonstration by students in Prague struggled and got through to the President's Palace. Those who opposed oppression could triumph after all. And then word came that they were turned back by police and works militia members.

Unable to endure the suspense regarding Vaclav, Sally wrote to him, mentioning that, earlier, she had been pleased to receive word that he was all right. Suspecting that mail over there could be censored, she refrained from asking how things were for him as the new regime strengthened its control.

Sally's letter arrived with the envelope opened and resealed, but it appeared to be intact. Vaclav could have described to no one his delight on hearing from her. During all those months since writing to England, he had convinced himself that Sally was married to David Saunders, too happy in her new life to even think about the Czech pilot who had shared so much of her war.

Learning her address was Downing House was a bonus, important in the implication that she was still single, living at home. As he himself was, in that small dwelling in Prague, and perhaps duty-bound now to remain there. Johana and Karel Capkova had aged dreadfully since the previous September. Knowing Bedrich and Jaroslav were relatively safer, living as farm workers well away from Prague, had only partially eased their general anxiety. The city felt to be constantly alert with unrest. Friends and family had seen sons and daughters arrested last year, and now others more recently were seized by the militia.

Perhaps worst of all, though, had been witnessing Gottwald, the Communist Prime Minister, speaking to the crowds assembled in their own Old Town Square. With a home so close to the heart of such upheaval, Johana had wept that the enforcement of this new regime meant nothing would ever again be the same.

Vaclav's father too had wept, but only with his son: the elderly man remained proud to protect his wife as best he could, and that entailed being dry-eyed in front of her.

It was Karel a few weeks afterwards who told Vaclav that he would understand if a new life elsewhere should beckon.

'For your mother and myself, life will go on, as we do all we can to ignore the government forced upon us. But you, Vaclav, have earned more freedom – if only by all you did to assist when war confronted the British and their allies.'

Vaclav had protested that he would always be there for his parents. But with a menial job the best that he'd been able to obtain, and his disgust for Communist principles increasing, he recognized that staying in Prague would be far from easy.

As if to confirm that, the situation worsened quite rapidly. Since the day that he had returned to Prague, Vaclav had tried not to be deterred by the way that those who followed his faith were being victimized. Today, with the 'Concealed Church' of priests, who practised their religion covertly, becoming proof that Christian worship was being obliged to go underground, he could not entirely ignore what was happening. Along with his parents, he still attended Mass, but stories were emerging of more and more churches being closed, or permitted only to open within certain hours.

In no time at all it was becoming evident that anyone loyal to their Church was being discriminated against. Names and details of church attendances were being noted by officials, and those parishioners were then denied privileges granted to their neighbours.

Vaclav's distaste for all that was happening within his homeland increased when he met Magdaleny one day, by chance, and was shocked to see her in the company of a Communist government minister. He wondered, briefly, what had become of the Russian soldier, but Magdaleny was determined to speak to him and, face to face as they were, there was no avoiding her.

She was looking well, her hair elegantly styled, every item of clothing immaculate, and expensive. *So much for adhering to Communist principles*, he thought.

Magdaleny was resolutely introducing the two men, but Vaclav could not force himself to shake the other's hand. He turned instead to enquire if his former fiancée was well, then excused himself abruptly, mentioning a previous engagement.

Vaclav remained disturbed, no longer feeling any of the old love for Magdaleny, that had died many months ago, but nevertheless shaken by her current allegiance.

He should not have been surprised, her liaison with the Russian had indicated that she was not too particular about her friends' loyalties, but Vaclav would have preferred to be ignorant of her recent commitment.

His yearning to get right away from all that Magdaleny represented had surfaced previously. They had met on only one other occasion throughout the months since that initial disastrous encounter. Roughly a week after he had seen her with her Russian lover, Vaclav had been shattered to arrive from work to find Johana and Magdaleny chattering in the kitchen.

It might have been the old days: *to his mother*, it seemed that the former situation still existed. The two women in Vaclav's life were resurrecting their original friendship. To Vaclav himself it seemed the grossest intrusion.

Magdaleny had been smiling, and extending a hand towards him, he recalled. He could see and hear her still. 'I am come here to talk with you, to tell you how things are.'

'I have nothing to say to you, except that

you must leave. I do not want you to enter my home ever again.'

Vaclav had remained motionless, glowering, while Magdaleny set aside the vegetables and the knife she was using and stalked ahead of him towards the outer door.

His mother had rebuked him severely for such discourtesy the moment his former sweetheart slammed the door behind her. Vaclav had felt more deeply the pain of being obliged to reveal that Magdaleny had been unfaithful. He was not certain even yet that Johana had begun to believe him.

Reminders of Magdaleny, however, were minor troubles compared with the terrible situation developing in Prague. Daily it seemed that restrictions were increased, while their government appeared intent on welcoming increased Soviet influence. At the same time, contact with non-Communist countries was fiercely discouraged.

Vaclav began to feel that his home city was turning into a prison. The day that they first heard the loudspeaker systems indoctrinating them through the streets, he found his mother weeping dejectedly.

'I shall take you to the country, to the farm, to be with Bedrich and Jaroslav,' Vaclav promised. 'You will find life pleasanter there, with none of this stress.'

Johana would not hear of it. 'I could never contemplate leaving your father here alone, and he has his work. Do not forget that Karel and I have put our lives into our home, we cannot desert it.'

During the following evening, both of his parents spoke gravely of Vaclav's future.

'You need not remain here, as I have told you before,' Karel began. 'You are still young, deserving of a better future.'

'We have done whatever we wished with our lives,' Johana added. 'Until the war years and – and all that has occurred here since then. This is the time when you should make *your* choices.'

'And without being restrained by anxiety on our behalf. We have learned care and caution, know how to survive here.'

Vaclav would not have contemplated leaving home if he had not met Alois, a former colleague from his pre-war days in the Czech air force. Chancing upon each other in one of the city bars, they sat over glasses of the good local beer, reminiscing about the escape routes each had taken in the effort to reach England.

'Would that there were such possibilities of getting out now,' said Alois ruefully.

Vaclav nodded. 'So often today I think of all that we did. I did not fight throughout that war in order to live beneath these degrading restrictions.'

'You would head for the West then, if you

could find some means?' Alois enquired pensively.

'I should feel compelled to do so. I need to live in a land where discussion and debate are employed to settle differences, I cannot accept this continual resorting to force, violence and killing.'

'Would you really be willing to get away from Prague?'

'Leaving family behind would be hard, but the time might come when – when, if I were to remain here, I could bring reprisals on them. Quietly accepting this regime does not come readily to me,' Vaclav added in a whisper.

'To me neither. Likewise, with several others.' Alois hesitated. 'I can trust you, can I?'

'But naturally. What are you planning?'

Alois glanced over first one shoulder then the other. 'Not here. You come with me to my lodgings?'

The room was near to the Charles University, had the appearance of a student's quarters, but was tidier than it might be with a younger occupant.

Alois gestured towards the one simple chair, seated himself on the bed. Glancing about him, he sighed.

'You see that I have hit bad times, I was not permitted to continue flying. I found work of a sort, labouring in the brewery.'

Vaclav grinned. 'For me also, all ambitions were forbidden. I earn a little money in a factory, making valves for radio sets. But enough of that, you must tell me what you have in mind.'

'Not myself only. There are three, four of us already. Old friends who approached me because of knowing how I am a pilot. One of them is a member of the works militia, but do not ask where his loyalties truly lie. Sufficient to know that he gains certain information. For weeks now they have been urging me to agree. I would not consent while I was the only pilot. This is their plan...'

Vaclav had overcome his own immediate reservations and become part of the team. Emerging from the strictures of life in his homeland could justify what he initially saw as proving a traitor. As Alois assured him, once away in the West, they might work for the good of their own people. Here in Prague, they could do nothing. They had seen enough of fellow citizens being jailed, or worse, for presuming to oppose the regime.

Unable to tell either parent his intended destination, Vaclav said little more than goodbye. 'Forgive my going, but I must seek better work elsewhere.'

Looking tinier than ever to Vaclav, Johana wept while she kissed him, but less copiously than if she could have known how far away he was going.

His father hugged him close. 'Remember, Vaclav, that our love is constant,' he said, and somehow conveyed that he could guess where his eldest son was heading.

Closing the door of his home behind him, Vaclav allowed himself a few private tears, but quickly dashed those away as he strode off through the night to meet Alois and the others.

He laughed to see the car, a battered, pre-war object covered in grime wherever rust had failed to eat through the bodywork.

'Do you not fear that its decrepitude might draw the attention we intend avoiding?' he asked.

The car's owner, Pavel, eyed him sharply before indicating that he get into the car. 'I trust that you do not believe the vehicle unworthy of you?'

Vaclav laughed again. 'Not at all, my friend. I only hope that you will not regret surrendering it before we leave.'

'Surrendering? But no. Its future is secured already. Is arranged for my cousin to go where we shall abandon it. Long before daylight this little motor will be many miles from here.'

Hints of humour evaporated into the misty air early in that May morning. The vehicle rattled and bucked its way along the track

241

they had selected to take them away from the centre of Prague.

Vaclav willed himself to avoid looking back, steeled his spirit to consider only the plans which must be accomplished. The success of this venture would depend upon himself as much as Alois, his fellow pilot. The aircraft would be strange to them, and rendered stranger by the long months of not flying. Their concentration must be absolute, their awareness acute while every sense scanned their vicinity for hazards. And the hazards might not be confined to those encountered in the air.

The airport perimeter eventually loomed through the darkness, appearing reminiscent of some of the RAF airfields that Vaclav had known. One of their party descended and crossed to a section of the wire fencing already darkened by the accomplice who had removed a crucial light bulb. When the man tackled the wire mesh with cutters, Vaclav flinched, instinctively resented interfering with security.

'Come now, come,' Alois insisted. 'No time for reservations.'

Pavel had killed the car's engine, was silently assisting the others to unload their small amount of baggage. No one carried much, and all in packages little enough for passing through the gap in the wire, and later for stowing in tiny spaces.

Once everything was through on to the airport, Alois gave his friend a signal. Pavel drove off into the night, to dispose of the car to his cousin.

'Surely he is flying with us?' Vaclav was puzzled.

One of the others grinned, teeth gleaming in the darkness. 'He did not tell you the whole story. His cousin waits already, will bring him back to within a few metres of us.'

Their own waiting time seemed interminable, but was actually no more than four minutes. The moment they all were reunited, Alois led the way stealthily across the grass in the direction of the nearest hangar.

'We shall find cover now, until we reach our plane,' he hissed. 'Our reconnoitering was thorough, you will see that each building here lies adjacent to some other.'

This proved to be so, and Vaclav vowed that his own eventual part in this escape should be equally efficient. Alois needed a co-pilot, and every one of them would rely on Vaclav's knowledge of that Kentish airbase. If he should fail them today he would not deserve the freedom for which he yearned.

The aircraft stood on the runway as planned. A lone figure emerged from the shadow of its bulk, murmured a word or two to Alois, and waited while one of their team kept watch and the rest scrambled aboard. It

243

was completely black in the cockpit, and Vaclav wondered how anyone would find the controls, but Alois was taking charge already. Engines fired, their friend on the ground slung aside the chocks.

Lights blazed to illuminate countless dials, and the runway ahead. Too late now to be impeded, their flight was on its way.

One of the men on board had maps at the ready; another, binoculars to scan the terrain below them, while Vaclav and Alois strained to adapt to unfamiliar controls.

We're taking a terrible risk, thought Vaclav, but remaining behind would have been more terrible.

His eyes had become accustomed to night flying again by the time Alois handed over control to him. Exhilaration surged, and he steeled himself to calm it. He must remain absolutely composed. The lives of these friends were his responsibility. And, suddenly, after months of indifference, *he* wanted to live. He had got to make it to England.

They had had no say in the type of plane that they borrowed. Vaclav soon realized he had never previously handled anything at all similar. He steeled himself to remain undaunted, prayed that the general principles of flying would prove sufficient.

He caught Alois giving him a sideways glance, and grinned back at him. 'Have you flown one of these before?'

The other pilot laughed. 'You should not ask that question!'

'Let's hope that, between us, we shall learn enough as we carry on.'

'What was that saying in the RAF – "A wing and a prayer ..."?'

'But in those days, Alois, we had back-up from experts who knew their machines.' *And, he added silently, I had more faith in praying.*

Whether through prayer or remembered skills, by the time that dawn was brightening the sky behind them, they had brought their aircraft as far as the stretch of sea that Vaclav recognized as the Dover Straits. Distantly, a gleam of early sunlight revealed the narrowest of strips of land, cliffs whiter than the wave caps tossing beneath them.

'That coastline ahead is Kent,' said Vaclav. 'Do you wish to take the controls?' He himself would soon be scouring the ground below for landmarks, hoping desperately that little had been redeveloped during these years of peacetime.

He saw an airfield at once, just slightly inland from Dover. But that was too near to the town.

'I think we need to head due north,' he told Alois.

'*Think?* You ought to be certain.' The tension was getting to his fellow pilot.

'Please try to the north, I shall know it when I see. The coast on that north-east corner of Kent has several towns.'

'Ramsgate, Margate, yes?' called their colleague with the map.

'Due north will be on course,' their navigator confirmed.

Along with the expected scattering of towns and villages, large tracts of open countryside remained, some wooded, other areas grassland or fields sectioned by hedgerows. Vaclav spotted evidence of bomb damage, recalled how savagely this corner of England had suffered. But there Manston was, at last, clearly recognizable still.

'We're there!' he yelled triumphantly, laughing and crying with relief.

They had half hoped that the airfield might be deserted, to afford a landing as covert as they could desire. Several figures were visible, even from this height, some leaving vehicles parked near offices or hangars, a few of them striding out towards planes standing in readiness.

'Question time ahead,' Alois announced, circling as he prepared to land. 'I hope that we are ready.'

Vaclav smiled. He hadn't anticipated that any of this would be easy. The flight had been carried out to plan, they were *here*. Everything that ensued would, at the very worst, be tolerable.

David's news shook everyone at Downing's factory and made Sally smile to herself despite her surprise. He would be marrying one Saturday before the summer was out. Henry was badly shaken, and furious with his daughter, who he believed was missing out on what he termed 'a chance in a lifetime'.

'That could have been you,' he snapped at Sally on the day when David's plans came to light. 'You know it's what I always wanted for you. You'd have been comfortably off, set up in a good house from the start, without any need to scrimp and save.'

Henry was, in fact, doubly annoyed because the truth had emerged without any attempt on David's part to be what he saw as straightforward. One of the foremen had relished coming to Henry's office with word that details of David's engagement were all around the church that they both attended.

'Ruth's one of the nurses who was on his ward during that last spell in hospital. Apparently, they'd been meeting up occasionally ever since, and things sort of came to a head just recently, like.'

Initially, Henry was inclined to disbelieve the news. 'Can you be certain? This doesn't sound at all like David.'

'You haven't seen 'em together. He's a different chap when he's with Ruth.'

After imparting the news to Sally and

reproving her for failing to snap up David herself, Henry remained beside her desk.

'Was there something else, Dad?' she asked him. She wanted a bit of peace in which to relish the relief she was feeling.

Her father didn't do peace – and he did need her company while he tried to accept that nothing would ever be the same again.

'Even if David remains just as efficient as ever here in the mill, he won't be popping round to Downing House nearly so often of an evening.'

'But he hasn't been doing that, has he, Dad? Not for some time.'

Worst of all, though, for Henry, was the decimation of his dream of David Saunders becoming his son-in-law. He had been ready with an offer of shares in the mill, would gladly have left this place in safe hands.

They were still together in Sally's office when David came in. 'Hope I'm not interrupting anything important?' Without waiting for their confirmation, David continued: 'I dare say you've been told my good news.'

'If you call it good.'

'Congratulations, David. I'm very pleased for you, and I hope you'll both be very happy,' said Sally, before her father could say something downright upsetting to their old friend.

'Thank you, Sally, I hoped you'd be glad for me.'

Henry sniffed. 'When's it to be, then? Or are you to keep that a secret an' all, until you're bound to tell us?'

'No secret, Henry – neither me nor Ruth have any reason to be other than delighted to broadcast the news. The date's fixed for the end of June, a Saturday, naturally. You'll have your invitations by the end of this week. The only reason I've delayed putting you in the picture is that I wasn't sure until this morning just when I'll be leaving.'

'Leaving?' Henry exclaimed, sounding feeble, quite unlike himself.

David smiled. 'Ah – that part of my plans hadn't filtered through then?'

Sally began to hope he wasn't enjoying this. Her father most surely was not.

'You might have given me fair warning about replacing you, David.'

'I believe this is fair, actually. Ruth and I don't begin our new jobs in Edinburgh until a month after we're wed.'

Two months after would not have eased the prospect for Henry, not even three, four...

'Why Edinburgh?' he demanded.

'It's Ruth's home city. She's always intended going back there. And, with all the experience I had of different production during the war, I haven't found it difficult to secure myself a decent position.'

Henry was saying nothing about expecting

David would remain with Downing's until his actual departure from Halifax. And David did need to know.

'If you wish, Henry, I shall be here to see that the new chap you bring in is beginning to get a grasp of how we work here,' he volunteered.

'Happen so, I'll have to see how we're placed. I'm not shelling out two wages for one job for so long, you know.'

David let it go at that, although he later made sure of having a chat with Sally.

Certainly that evening she recognized the trepidation with which her father faced a future without his very able right-hand man. Henry scarcely tasted the meal that Mrs Holbrook had left ready for them, and, speaking hardly at all, appeared the epitome of dejection.

'David can't be the only good manager in the whole of the West Riding,' she assured him. 'You'll find somebody else that's glad to come to Downing's. We've done that well, production's picking up really grand since we've got raw materials coming through more readily again.'

'You reckon? I wish I shared your optimism. It looks to me more like we're heading for a downturn soon as David quits.'

Yet again, before they went up to their beds that night, he was blaming Sally for David's decision to leave.

'This is all down to you, you know. If you hadn't been so high-minded that you wouldn't even consider his proposal, none of this would have happened. You'd have been in that lovely house, doing everything *your* way. Don't look at me like that, either – I know you like to do things in your own fashion.'

'And that includes choosing who I'm going to settle down with,' said Sally, with a degree of asperity. 'I've never understood how you could believe that I'd plump for a husband, just because he suited you.'

'There's no need to put it like that, lass. I've always respected your ideas, ever since you were little. Always.'

Sally was not prepared to argue the point. If Henry wished to cherish illusions about his own attitude, he'd be no happier for having them destroyed. And she had taken one decision without consulting him.

Before leaving the factory that day, she had located David beside one of the looms and learned that he'd intended having a chat with her. She wasn't surprised by his rueful admission that he had put off telling Henry the news because of dreading his reaction.

'That's understandable,' she said with a grin, then reiterated her delight regarding his plans. 'I'm suggesting that you bring Ruth along for lunch sometime soon, next Sunday, if you've nothing else arranged.'

She wanted to get to know her, and was

251

determined that Henry Downing should not treat David with such bad grace.

Ruth appeared slightly older than Sally herself, smartly dressed in a blue silky dress that had the full skirt so fashionable since the longer New Look was introduced. Her eyes echoed the blue she was wearing, and seemed to smile constantly, while her short blond hair gleamed in the sunlight as Sally welcomed her and David at the door.

Henry was in the dining room already, sharpening the carving knife on its steel, and with an expression on his face suggesting that their guests might sample the efficacy of its blade. Had Sally not known he always gave that knife its weekly sharpening, she might have been fearful of its significance.

She had lectured her father that morning, as she had on several earlier occasions, rebuking him for his evident refusal to accept that David was free to marry whoever he chose, and to live wherever he thought fit.

'Even if I *had* been the one wanting to be his wife, you'd have had no say in where the pair of us might have moved on to.' She had curbed her tongue rather than saying more, but she was tempted to add that his current attitude would have driven anyone to get right away from Halifax!

When Ruth was brought through to the dining room and introduced to him, Henry thawed slightly. Watching, Sally noticed him appraising their new guest's nicely rounded figure, and saw his gaze returning to relish the smile in Ruth's beautiful eyes.

David did appear to be altered in his fiancée's company; he was decidedly more relaxed, and had rediscovered a sense of fun from somewhere, an asset that had been waning during the past year or two.

Sally had decided that serving the meal as soon as they arrived would give Ruth and David some focus if conversation flagged. Henry, however, seemed to have taken to the young woman, and immediately began talking about the roast lamb he was carving.

'We've always liked a nice shoulder of lamb, Ruth. Our housekeeper, Mrs Holbrook, cooks it just right, even better than my late wife used to. Though, naturally, I wouldn't have wanted my Gwen to know I say that! I come from a family where the man's always done the carving of the Sunday joint. I was taught by my father, as I suppose he was by his.'

'That's really nice, Mr Downing. I'm afraid I don't remember my dad very clearly, I was only three when he was killed in 1918.'

'Does that mean he served in the Great War?'

'That's right. He had a bad time of it, I believe, in the trenches.'

'Aye – well. There weren't so many came

253

out of that lot without some sort of adjustment to be made, if they came back at all. Some of my old pals have never been the same to this day.'

'We can only hope that the last war really has convinced people that it mustn't happen again. I began nursing in a military hospital, and we saw some terrible injuries there.'

'My Sally, here, spent the war delivering aircraft to the RAF. Has David told you? I'm right proud of the way she tackled flying.'

Her father smiled towards Sally and she felt a blush rising from her neck. His words had pleased her, if only because they proved he no longer resented her long absences from his life.

Ruth glanced towards David and then across to Henry once more. 'I understand your normal factory production had to cease during the war. You must have hated that.'

'I did indeed. Least said about those years, soonest mended. I wouldn't have minded if we'd been given any challenging stuff to make, but a lot of it was creating camouflaged articles for the army, and miles and miles of webbing.'

'But David came back to Downing's afterwards. Did most of your workforce?'

'Those that I wanted, yes, designers and our best dyer. I was fortunate.'

Sally had been placing dishes of vegetables on the table and urged them to help themselves as soon as Henry passed around plates of meat. She was pleased to see that they all continued to talk quite readily, and by the end of the meal, it seemed as though Ruth was feeling just as at home there as David always had.

When the other woman offered to help wash the dishes afterwards, Sally felt that she had made a new friend, and was quite sorry that Ruth and David would be moving to Scotland. She was astonished, nevertheless, when Ruth asked her to be her only bridesmaid.

'Oh, that would be nice. But are you sure?' Sally couldn't believe that Ruth didn't have a closer woman friend who might resent not being asked.

Ruth grinned. 'My best friend's married, and she's expecting a baby the month after we're getting wed. We had a laugh about it, but agreed she wouldn't quite look right!'

The rest of the visit proved equally pleasant, and by the time that David and Ruth were leaving, Sally was happy to be arranging with her to shop together for a bridesmaid's dress.

'It's only the second time I've been asked to do this,' she confided. The first occasion had been when Emma married Paul.

The next few weeks became quite hectic, almost as much so for Sally as for the bride to be. They had failed to find a dress that

255

seemed suitable for Sally, but discovered some beautiful artificial silk in a deep shade of dusky pink that was pretty without looking too young-girlish.

'I'm making my own frock, anyway,' Ruth told her. 'Do you sew at all?'

'I was taught how to at school, but I can't say I've practised what I learned.'

'If you did want to have a go, I'd be glad to give you a hand with cutting it out and fitting, and so on.'

'Would you have the time? You say you're making your own dress.'

'That's almost ready now. With me working shifts, I have a lot of time on my own when David's at the mill. He wouldn't mind if you and I got together to sew on the occasional evening.'

'That sounds OK, could be fun. But only if you think I could manage to make something presentable.'

'It's worth a try. There's only one problem, though – I don't have a machine. I borrowed one from our ward sister, but I had to let her have it back. That didn't matter to me, I've only got hand-sewing to do now.'

'Mrs Holbrook has a sewing machine, she's let me use it in the past when I made fresh curtains for my bedroom.'

'You can sew straight then!' Ruth exclaimed, and grinned. 'Let's do it, Sally.'

The material was exquisite, it might not be

real silk, but it felt quite heavy, and would drape beautifully. The shade was its best feature, such a warm pink, yet nowhere near bold enough to shock, and as it caught the light, every fold seemed to possess a lustre.

Inhibited about tackling the task, Sally was greatly relieved that Ruth was helping with laying the paper pattern on the cloth and beginning to cut out. This new friend knew a lot about materials, and was able to show her how to place each piece of pattern so that the weave ran in the same direction.

'It's easier to understand when you've got a design in a material, like printed flowers, say – you get them the same way up. With something as plain as we've got here, you have to concentrate more, but it's well worth it. You see the way the skirt flares out towards the ankles – all you've got to do is make sure the widest bit of each paper pattern is—'

'Placed towards the same end of your cloth. In this case, the part that's last to be unfolded,' Sally put in, pleased to have grasped one factor of dressmaking.

'Got it in one. When we've cut this out, remind me to show you the different appearances of the texture that you might have if you weren't taking care.'

Sally became enthralled, and when Mrs Holbrook was involved in demonstrating her old treadle machine, she, too, developed an interest in what the young women were doing.

'I'm glad I left that machine here instead of having it back in my little place. It seems right for what you're making. I sewed my own wedding dress on this,' the elderly lady confided one evening when she had stayed late at the house. 'I thought I was the bee's knees, I can tell you.'

Ruth was helping Sally with her first fitting. 'You must show us a photograph,' she suggested, while Sally wondered why she had never seen a picture of the housekeeper's wedding. She had been to Mrs Holbrook's little home several times, if never in recent years.

'I don't think I can find one now. It's all a long time since,' said Mrs Holbrook hastily.

There was something odd about the way the idea was dismissed that made Sally so curious that she asked her father if the Holbrooks' marriage had been unhappy.

'On the contrary,' Henry told her. 'You won't remember, but she was an old friend of your mother's before she came to look after us. Her husband died very suddenly, and Mrs Holbrook reacted quite strangely. She tore up every photo she had of the poor man and threw them on the fire. I didn't understand, not for a long time, but she evidently didn't forgive him for dying and leaving her alone.'

'And she must have found any photos of him aroused too many emotions.'

That seemed so sad that Sally was glad when the housekeeper continued to be interested in her dressmaking. She was more pleased still when Ruth came up with the idea of inviting her to the wedding.

'We haven't got so many guests that we're unable to squeeze in one more, and the meal is a buffet. Do you think Mrs Holbrook would enjoy it, Sally?'

'She'd be thrilled. I think she would have gone to the church, anyway, to see David married. He's been such a regular here for so many years.'

Henry and his daughter shared one or two private smiles over Mrs Holbrook's elation at receiving an invitation. Scarcely a day went by when she failed to mention the occasion and the outfit she was buying especially.

'I wish I was more wholeheartedly in favour of the entire business,' Henry admitted as the wedding day approached.

'You'll miss him a lot, I know. But you've a successor lined up at the mill, Dad. Things might be worse.'

'Not much. Although I suppose I'm thankful to see you're not perturbed that David's going out of our lives.'

'Dad, of course I'm not. I turned him down ages ago, remember.'

'More fool you.'

'You know my opinion. And I hope you're not going to drop hints to Ruth that I received the first offer long before he proposed to her.'

'Don't be certain that he hasn't told her that.'

Sally wondered if David had confided the fact to his fiancée. She shrugged. 'If he has, that's their business, nothing to do with us.'

All Sally knew was that she still relished the prospect of David Saunders being safely married to someone else. And having that someone be as likeable as Ruth was an added bonus. She herself was going to enjoy their day. She was elated already; somehow, she sensed that, with their wedding, she would be freed to enter a new phase in her own life.

Eleven

Vaclav was holding his breath, trying to contain the emotion surging right through him. He had found the house without difficulty, and realized then how much the place meant to him. This was *it* – his opportunity to, *at last*, see and speak to his dearly loved Sally again. He heard footsteps approaching on the other side of the door, saw its handle turning...

Nervously now, he inhaled, raised his gaze, ready for meeting hers. He tried to smile, but was feeling far too serious, this was so important.

The elderly woman looked vaguely familiar, he remembered a housekeeper, someone who prepared the meals here. But this person, despite her evident age, was dressed in a bright, lilac suit, white hair was embellished by a matching hat – a hat so small that it defied his attempt to guess how it might be anchored.

'You will not remember me, I am a friend of Sally, from the years when we were at war. Vaclav, Vaclav Capkova.'

The lady cupped a gloved hand around one ear, she coped better with voices familiar to her. 'I beg your pardon? Can't hear so well nowadays.'

'I need to see Sally.'

'You'll be on your way to the church, for the wedding. She left here a few minutes since, with her father, of course. If you run, you'll happen get there just as the ceremony's beginning. It's not far – that High Church, the Anglo-Catholic one.'

High Church? Anglo-Catholic. If his Sally was marrying in such a ceremony, that surely must mean only one thing. She was marrying David Saunders. Today.

Vaclav turned away, tears were blinding him. He felt embarrassed, far worse than that – *broken*.

'There's a car waiting for me, you can have a lift, if you like,' Mrs Holbrook suggested. The poor chap looked in a bad way.

Dismally, he shook his head, struggled to force his brain to accept the terrible irony. After years of separation, an eternity of yearning for her, he had arrived at her home only minutes before Sally was to commit herself to David Saunders.

The fact that he liked the man made Vaclav feel even worse. Able to hate the person who was taking Sally from him, he might have believed – even hoped – her lack of taste was condemning her to uncertainty. As things stood, finding him likeable rendered David quite – *suitable* as Sally's partner.

If only this did not hurt so dreadfully...

Vaclav weighed the idea of going to the church, entering, against all his deep reluctance, witnessing ... But no, he would not, *could not* steel himself to watch while she promised herself to another man. He would be compelled by all the months of pent-up longing to halt that ceremony, to force her to reject Saunders.

And then what...?

There was not even one glimmer of a hope that Sally would, at this very last moment, turn instead to himself.

He would control his emotions somehow, then walk down that long, long hill towards the town, would wait again at that rail station, would take the train destined to carry him away, right away, back to London, with dignity intact. No one need ever know that he had been here.

In all the excitement of Sally's wedding day, their housekeeper would forget that someone had knocked at the door. She was old, wasn't she, likely to be forgetful? She had not recalled Vaclav Capkova's previous visit. Amidst all the celebrating, the guests, the drinks, her weary memory would neglect to dredge up anything about his arrival at Downing House. He must leave.

Vaclav turned sharply, began striding away,

past the garden wall of Downing House, past further substantial houses. Houses so different from his own home. He should have recognized that he had no place here.

Even this far away from the church, the sound of the organ wafted towards Vaclav. With it floated memories of that Christmas. The first, the only one spent with Sally. He must see her. From a distance only, unobserved. This one, final, time.

Trees lined the pathway to the church door, large trees, well able to conceal him. Vaclav would do nothing to disturb her, to mar her day. He would instead furnish his future memories with this one, last, image of her. An image to instil greater sense: to remind, whenever foolishness arose, that he had reached this day when he must resign himself to defeat.

A photographer approached from somewhere to the side of the building, set up his tripod in line with the door. The church was an impressive structure; despite its soot-blackened walls, it would enhance her wedding pictures.

Behind Vaclav, just outside the gateway, a group of women gathered, making him recall how in his own country a wedding attracted onlookers. To see the bride. This other man's bride. The bride *he* needed.

Some of the trees were conifers, the heat of the sun was drawing out their scent, a heady aroma that sickened him. Or was the sickness from that gnawing ache of loss?

He could bear no more. Turning his back on the church, he started off down the path. The gateway was blocked by the group of elated women. They stared at him.

Embarrassed by further tears, Vaclav could not push a way past them. Obliged to remain, he faced the church again, stood in the middle of the path, and felt dreadfully vulnerable.

The door was open now, triumphal organ music mocked his misery. He steeled himself to focus on the newly-wed couple, forced a smile on to lips that felt frozen. Sally must not see him so deeply affected. This was not the day for distressing her.

Vaclav's smile faded, he frowned, puzzled. Saunders was recognizable, but older, temples greying, although his grin was wide. The bride on his arm shocked Vaclav by her appearance, she seemed less tall than he recalled, but heavier, her hair was very different. Her veil, thrown back, revealed a fair head, as light or lighter than his own. He could not believe his Sally would peroxide her hair. Artifice was no part of her.

How altered she was! Or had he totally misremembered her appearance? How could that be when he *cherished* everything about her? None of her gestures were the same, and nor were her hands, the hands that had caressed ... Vaclav recognized nothing in the tilt of her head when she turned towards her bridegroom.

He rubbed his eyes, must clear them of tears. And then he saw Sally, emerging from behind the couple, moving to one side when the photographer focused on bride and groom alone. And how she *glowed*! That lovely gown captured every gleam of sunlight on its folds, swirling about slender ankles, while the matching deep pink roses in her mid-brown hair seemed to echo the flush of her cheeks.

She was here, she *was happy* – happy to see Saunders married to another woman.

'Sally!' The name flew ungoverned from his lips, startling Vaclav himself as it startled the woman he called.

'Vaclav...'

His name was spoken wonderingly, her tone uncertain, unwilling perhaps to expose her emotions to disappointment? Were they both still so alike?

'Yes, oh yes.'

They ran: she, extracting herself from other guests, to speed down the steps, he, to greet her at their foot, his arms extended wide to embrace her.

'Thank God! Thank God, my Sally!'

She did not speak, could not. Tears cascaded from her brown eyes, but she was smiling, her lips parting, inviting.

They had kissed before, many times and fervently, but never in their lives so whole-heartedly. He held her close, felt her breasts pressing at his shirt, the silkiness of her gown enticing him. Opening his arms had flung his jacket wide, unnoticed perhaps, but so symbolic. There would be no concealment, no holding back, nothing to mar their union.

'I shall love you for ever,' Vaclav promised.

'And I you. And I you, my darling.'

Pausing, hugging and kissing, they ambled towards the church entrance.

Henry was waiting on the steps. If he recognized Vaclav, he gave no sign.

'Don't you see who's here, Dad?' Sally prompted him. 'You must remember Vac-lav...'

Henry wore dark-rimmed spectacles now, he peered through them. 'I suppose – well, yes. But you have a role here, Sally. One you're neglecting unforgivably. Ruth chose you, don't forget, you've no right to desert her.'

'I'm not deserting, I wouldn't. Any more than I would be discourteous to someone who's come thousands of miles to visit me.'

Ruth was listening, and walked with David towards them.

Sally smiled at them. 'Ruth, this is a very dear friend of mine, Vaclav Capkova. Vaclav, I'm so pleased you're here to meet Ruth on the day she's married David.'

They were all shaking hands, Vaclav was congratulating David, asking how he was, telling Ruth that he hoped that they would be very happy. Behind her, Sally sensed her father turning away. She resisted the impulse to ignore him. Instead, she followed, took his arm, slid her hand down to grasp his fingers.

'I need your understanding, Dad. I love Vaclav, I won't let him leave my life again.'

'You'd arranged that he was coming here?'

'Not at all. It's a complete surprise, the best surprise in my life.'

'I don't wish to know that.'

She swallowed down a sigh. 'I do need you to make him welcome, you know.'

'You've asked him to stay?'

'Not yet, there's been no chance. You wouldn't wish us to spend our time together elsewhere?'

'Is that what you plan? First you let David go right away from us, now you're threatening to leave me entirely bereft. Have you no consideration?'

Vaclav had turned from the others to join her, was standing behind her. She felt his hands grasp her shoulders, conveying strength, his support. Sally let herself relax to lean against him, faced her father squarely.

'It *is* all right for Vaclav to stay with us, isn't it?'

'There's no room prepared. Mrs Holbrook

will be going to her own home after the reception.'

'I can manage to make up a bed! You're not going to object, are you?'

'It's your home as much as mine.'

Even Henry Downing had no power to dampen Sally's elation. David and Ruth approached again to insist that Vaclav was welcome at their reception, then introduced him to Ruth's mother, whom Sally had already decided was adorable. A lady in her middle years whose elegant composure belied her sudden admission that she'd made herself a fool by weeping throughout the ceremony.

'But emotions are good, surely,' said Vaclav to her. 'In my country, for men also – concealing how we feel can lead to needless heartache,' he ended, looking at Sally.

Still wiping her eyes, the bride's mother glanced from Vaclav to Sally and back again.

'It's really grand that a friend of Sally's is here today. I'll be able to think of you together. I've met so many lovely people in Halifax that I've almost felt sorry that Ruth and David won't always have a home here.'

Vaclav turned to David. 'Where do you intend living?'

'Scotland, near Ruth's old home.'

Vaclav nodded, smiled. He could like David Saunders, without feeling sorry that he would be moving right away.

After more photographs were taken, Sally took hold of Vaclav's arm. 'I shall have to do my bit, at the reception, but I'll keep an eye on you as well, see you won't feel out of place.'

He laughed. 'And my eyes will be focused all the time on you! You must not worry, my love. To be in the same room as you is fulfilment of all my dreams.' He paused, smiled again. 'Until later.'

Sally was too elated to eat, which freed her to help David, Ruth and their best man to ensure that everyone was happy. Ruth's mother had insisted that she had no desire to take an active role in the reception, and was leaving any speechmaking to the nephew who had given Ruth away. He, the best man and David himself kept their speeches brief, which seemed appropriate for a rather informal occasion.

Vaclav was quite thankful for that, and relieved that they hadn't all been seated around tables clothed in white linen. He couldn't be unaware of the general curiosity about his sudden appearance, and was happy to explain that he was a wartime friend of Sally.

One or two people remarked that they were pleased that she had someone at her side, and Vaclav was quick to reveal how delighted he was to be that person. More than once, he had caught Henry Downing giving him a long look from across the room, and wished that the man would come across to speak to him. Vaclav knew that he could not win everyone round, certainly not instantly, but he would have appreciated some small indication that he might one day be accepted.

In the end, he strode across to speak to Henry, willing a smile on to his lips and making sure that his own blue eyes made contact with the sombre grey ones.

'I can understand that my unannounced arrival would take you by surprise, but I truly had no idea what an important day this was. All I had in mind was to meet with Sally again, and for that I have travelled thousands of miles.'

'I suppose you would,' said Henry slowly. 'Since that distance away is where you're from. As ever, my concern is for my daughter's happiness. I can only ask myself for what good purpose you have made this trip. I trust that she's not about to be distressed when you disappear off again.'

'Indeed not, Mr Downing. I am in England to stay, I shall live over here.'

Henry opened his mouth to speak, but seemed perplexed by Vaclav's assurance. Sally was at his side, however, very sure of her feelings.

'Thank heaven for that! It would break my heart if I lost you again. We need to talk, of

271

course, but David and Ruth will be going off on honeymoon shortly, the reception's all but over. In fact, we shall have the place to ourselves this evening. Dad and a few others are going on somewhere with Ruth's cousin and her mother.'

Henry went back to Downing House initially to change into something less formal, and Sally sensed that he was reluctant to leave her alone there with Vaclav. Deciding immediately that they must have a fresh understanding there, she announced that she would make up a spare bed for Vaclav, and insisted he go upstairs with her.

'Just a minute,' Henry began, frowning. 'Aren't you overlooking something? The two of you were not the ones getting wed today, you can't intend going up to the bedroom together.'

Vaclav concealed a smile, but immediately began to look perturbed. Mr Downing was very serious.

'Actually, Dad, that's what we do intend,' said Sally firmly. 'I'm thirty years old, mature enough to make decisions for myself.'

'But – he's only today turned up here.'

'And we've loved each other for years. Whether or not we've consummated that is our business, as is whatever we do today.'

Henry sank on to the nearest chair. He had never heard explicit language in his home, and certainly did not expect such words from his daughter. Whatever her age.

'Enjoy your evening, Dad,' Sally called over her shoulder. Reaching for Vaclav's hand, she headed swiftly towards the staircase.

'This is the room you can have,' she told Vaclav, opening a door when they arrived on the landing. 'Unless you'd rather share mine...'

'Sally? Your father...'

She smiled, tilted her head to indicate the staircase. 'I meant him to hear. Your coming here is the most wonderful thing that's happened. I don't mean to let him spoil one moment.'

Vaclav gazed and gazed at her, his blue eyes widening. 'You seem so different.'

'Oh, I am. You are here, for me. Even before learning all the ins and outs of that, I know nothing else matters.'

As the bedroom door closed after them, Vaclav drew her towards him, kissing her insistently, his lean body hard when he held her near.

'Marry me, Sally. That is why I am here.'

'I will, I will. That is the reason I exist.'

They kissed again, hugging, their mouths and hands feverish with longing. She could not ignore his desire – nor her own, startling her as it ranged through each nerve ending.

'Do we wait?' he asked her gravely. 'We do

mean to marry...'

'*Can* we delay?' Sally could promise nothing that would curb this passion.

'We could try waiting. If you'd forgive, should I need you too greatly.'

'Would we marry soon?' She couldn't endure a prolonged period of waiting.

'How swiftly are weddings arranged in England?'

More urgent than any formalities, distance-nurtured longing took them to the bed. Unmade as it was, the sole *un*readiness in that room, the mattress felt warmed by the sun streaming through a nearby window, but could not match the heat they might generate.

'Feel how much I need you,' Vaclav gasped between kisses. 'Hold me, hold me.'

They should have undressed, but passion sought no such refinements. Her fingers travelled swiftly, desire-driven.

'Slip off your dress, though,' Vaclav insisted. 'We'll keep it for ever, you wear that colour so beautifully.'

'It fastens down the back,' Sally explained and sighed. She had used a long, long row of tiny buttons designed to enhance her rear view while standing in the church.

Tenderly, slowly, Vaclav released each button, pausing to kiss her spine while his mouth travelled downwards. The dress was lined, needed no more than a waist petticoat.

He reached its waist, she felt his tongue testing her skin beneath it.

'That dress has to go,' Sally moaned. 'Quickly.'

Vaclav smiled, kissed the nape of her neck, the tender flesh that covered her collar-bone, then turned aside to lay her dress on a chair. Her breasts were encased in white lace, alluring to his gaze, fragile to his fingers. Silky beneath the lace, her skin made desire surge.

'Hold me, hold me,' he said again, and welcomed her touch. He kissed the hollow of her throat, each breast in turn, his mouth travelled downwards. 'Show me what you need, Sally.'

They lay there till darkness fell, exploring, enhancing, relishing their closeness as much as each sensation. Downstairs in the hall, the outer door opened to Henry's key, Vaclav sighed but Sally smiled.

'I'll dress,' she said, and did so, neglecting the long line of buttons. 'You'd better get your clothes on.'

She was at the door, her back to it, preventing her father's entry.

'He wouldn't, would he?' asked Vaclav.

'He *won't*, that is certain!'

Sally was thankful, though, to hear Henry's steps heading towards his own room. She had no wish to believe he would interfere to that degree.

'Tomorrow we'll tell him our plans,' she said. 'He's not going to accuse me of keeping anything from him. More importantly, he needs to understand that we belong now, nothing will be allowed to change that.'

Vaclav glanced at his watch. 'It is almost Sunday. Would he be happy, do you think, if we accompanied him to chapel?'

'Dad ought to be. It can do no harm, and we do need to know where we would hold our wedding. If your being a Catholic will be a problem, I want to change my religion. Would I have to study, or something?'

'For your country, I do not know. But there is no need for you to make changes. I love you, that is enough. We make our promises to our God, he will hear us in your chapel, as he would in my cathedral.'

'A chapel wedding would please my father.'

'A small concession that might win us a few grains of his favour. I shall do my utmost, you know, my Sally. One day, your father shall see that we are so good together.'

They talked some more, as they made up the bed for Vaclav. He had found work in England, he told her, would explain more in the morning. It would be great if they could marry within, say, four weeks.

Sally grinned. 'Can't it be sooner?'

'We have much to discuss. Do you work with your father? Will that continue?'

'Perhaps for a time. I can't withdraw from everything immediately. Staying on in the office will help. I've certainly no wish for us to live in this house.'

'You have no such wish...?'

'You're surprised? Vaclav, you haven't seen what it's been like over the years. And you can't pretend he'll accept you readily, no matter how truly you intend to win him over.'

'I shall be happy wherever you are.'

'Being together will be all that counts.'

'We should be starting now, I long to have you sleep in my arms.'

Sally chuckled. 'There's an old question about how much sleeping there'd be! For the present, we need to fortify ourselves with a bit of rest, for all the decisions we must make.'

Vaclav kissed her goodnight, his mouth lingering on her own while she felt his heart hammering at her through the silky texture of her gown. Reluctantly, she left to walk slowly, pensively, towards her own room.

Further along the landing, a door opened. Henry came striding towards her, his eyes keen. He might have been searching her face, or beyond it, for signs of the activity engaging her.

Sally kept her back turned well away from him, conscious of the buttons no longer fastened, determined to reveal none of the clues her father was seeking.

'You're not in bed yet.'

'No, nor is Vaclav. We've a lot to discuss.'

'If discussing is what you're up to!'

'I'm not your little girl any longer. You've no need to curtail my wishes, whatever they—' Sally stopped speaking, sighed. 'And we are planning to marry, *soon.*'

'So – you *are* about to desert me.'

All at once Sally felt sorry for him, could read in his troubled grey eyes the dread of having her live in Czechoslovakia.

'Stop worrying, Daddy. Vaclav told you – we intend living here in England.'

'I see.' Henry looked no happier. After a moment he spoke again. 'You need to give thought to all this, Sally, a great deal of thought. Hasn't it occurred to you at all that Vaclav will be marrying you simply to ensure his settling here? With British nationality.'

Her father's assumption about Vaclav's motives for their wedding was dreadful. But Sally resolved before going to bed that she would not permit it to perturb her. The fact that Vaclav wished to marry her was suffi- cient. By coming all this way to Halifax to propose, he had brightened every aspect of her future life.

Before setting out for chapel the following morning, Henry drew her aside again as she washed the breakfast dishes while Vaclav went off to finish dressing.

'You're not really about to make arrangements for a wedding already, are you, Sally love? Give it time, eh – get to know him a bit better.'

'And do what – demand to know if your disgusting insinuation is true? I wouldn't insult any man with that, least of all the one I have yearned for since the last day I saw him.'

'Yearned? Isn't that an exaggeration?'

'Actually, it isn't. If you hadn't lacked the perception to discover what I was feeling, you'd have seen, but it doesn't matter any longer. Vaclav understands, nothing else is of any consequence.'

'How do you expect me to just – well, hand you over to him?'

'*How* really isn't my problem, Dad. I can only expect that you will do so. Willingly might be nice. With some sort of good grace would be even better. You have had the first thirty years of my life, it isn't logical to anticipate your having the remainder.'

'I have cared for you.'

'I know, Dad. I do know that. And we will care for you, even if that should be from some little distance. But that caring would continue only if you didn't shut out the pair of us.'

'You're a couple already,' Henry murmured dismally.

'I'm glad that you can see that.'

The three of them spoke with the local minister after the chapel service. The Rev Frank Bell was a pleasant man, slightly older than Vaclav himself and very interested to learn of his second escape from Prague.

Sally listened while Vaclav explained about the plane that he and another pilot had 'borrowed' to fly out with a few friends who, like themselves, had loathed the Communist regime.

'For me, Sally epitomizes everything that is good about your country,' he continued. 'I could not think of leaving my homeland except that it should be to spend my life with her.'

'And your own faith?' Frank Bell asked him.

'I am Roman Catholic, have been proud to witness to that. At times, when our government chose to discriminate against such witness. I believe in justice, you see. Oppression of any kind is evil, but we do not always have the power to fight it. There is so much that is wrong about my country. And it was not to see all freedoms restricted that I once came here to fight.'

'Vaclav served with the RAF throughout the war,' said Henry.

Sally smiled. It was the first good thing her father had said about him.

'Excellent,' said the minister. 'But I do

need for you to comprehend more fully. We Methodists are of the Nonconformist faith.'

Vaclav nodded. 'I do know that. Since meeting Sally I have been concerned to discover as much as I can regarding the things that matter to her.'

Frank Bell was relieved. 'Good. Very good. But about your wedding – would you really be willing to marry before this simple altar table, in our chapel here?'

'Before our *same God*, yes.'

The minister nodded, he was looking pensive. 'I may have to confer with someone – every Church has its own orders of seniority, and I must confess to having no experience of a Roman Catholic from abroad wishing to marry here.'

Vaclav was smiling. 'I do understand. And if it should be that you need to speak with someone from my own Church, I could suggest whom to contact.' He paused, sighed. 'All that I would ask is that you could exercise some discretion. No one in my homeland can guarantee that conversations are not overheard, even recorded. My escape to your country could impact quite seriously upon my parents or brothers.'

Frank Bell nodded. 'I shall bear that in mind, although I believe it may not be necessary to speak with anyone in Prague. My chief concern will be to ensure that you yourselves will be happy that your marriage signifies all that you wish it to.'

He turned slightly to include Sally more closely. 'As you may know, because neither my own chapel nor the Roman Catholic is the established Church in England, the ceremony must also have a civil registrar in attendance. This will certainly mean your union complies with legal requirements.'

Vaclav smiled yet again. 'And, with promises made in a sanctified building such as this, we should be well satisfied.'

The minister brought out the chapel diary, and they began discussing likely dates for the wedding. When a Saturday six weeks ahead was suggested, Henry Downing sighed heavily, and looked towards his daughter.

'Before making firm arrangements, shouldn't you perhaps wait a little while? If only to be sure that – well, to be sure that you and Vaclav still get along?'

Sally sighed over his persistence, and shook her head. 'Vaclav has proclaimed his belief that we still do – by risking his life to join me. I'm not going to prove I can't match that.'

Henry's dissatisfaction continued through the preliminary arrangements for Sally and Vaclav to marry, and afterwards throughout the rest of the day at Downing House.

By evening, although Vaclav appeared unperturbed by the atmosphere, Sally had had enough.

'Let's go and see Emma and Paul,' she suggested to Vaclav. 'I'm dying to tell them our news.'

He smiled. 'You do not wish, then, to wait until you have my engagement ring on your finger? I thought that we should go into the town tomorrow so that we may choose one.'

'Having a ring will be lovely, but it's more important to me to let all our friends see how happy we are together.'

Emma and Paul welcomed Vaclav with all the enthusiasm that had been lacking from Henry Downing. Their two daughters were equally excited when told who their visitor was and how far he had travelled.

'Did we really meet you when we were little, was I very tiny like our baby?' the younger girl asked him. 'I should have remembered, if you'd come all that way then.'

Vaclav smiled. 'But I did not travel far in those days. My job was in England, flying aeroplanes. Like Sally.'

'But how on earth did you make it, this time?' Paul asked solemnly. 'Your country endures a strict regime, doesn't it?'

'It does indeed, one that causes many people to wish to evade the restrictions obligatory there. Which is part of my reason for getting out. That – and to meet with Sally again.'

'How did you manage to get hold of a plane, love?' Sally asked him. 'We've had so much to say to each other, you haven't told me the details yet.'

'I met in Prague another pilot who had served with the RAF. It seemed like chance, at the time. *Now*, I know it was God's will. Alois knew several others who were anxious to get away to the West. As soon as he learned my own intentions, he explained that he needed a second pilot to ensure the success of their plan.'

'And the plane itself...? Did Alois work for an airline?' asked Sally.

A slight smile curved Vaclav's mouth. He shook his head. 'Like myself, Alois had not been permitted anywhere near aircraft following what our government saw as the treason of working alongside British fliers. He did, however, have some knowledge of the airport near to Prague, and one trustworthy friend who showed how we might gain access within the perimeter.'

'You didn't steal an aeroplane?' said one of the girls.

'We "borrowed" one, certainly. Alois is negotiating with someone over here to have it returned. But that is a further story.'

'Were you the folk who landed at Manston?' Paul enquired.

'That is so. My wartime experience was useful coming in to land. But it took more than that to extricate us from a difficult situation. The authorities here needed some convincing that we intended nothing more sinister than seeking sanctuary, and offering to work in England as soon as permission might be granted.'

'Do you mean you were interrogated?' Sally enquired, shaken to learn that Vaclav might have endured serious hardship to reach her.

'Repeatedly, but in a civilized fashion. There was nothing to compare with the brutality engaged when questions are pursued on the other side of the iron curtain. However, the experience did feel neverending. None of us felt easy until we were released.'

'Were you and the other pilot treated differently from the rest of your group?' Emma wanted to know.

'A little more severely, but that was inevitable. We were the ones capable of taking the aircraft, and of putting down on an airbase over here. Not an everyday occurrence, you must agree. They were right to investigate.'

'But you truly are free now, Vaclav?' Sally checked. 'Nobody could take you away again?'

'Entirely free. No one over here would do a thing now. I still have my service documents from the war, you see. Confirming my identity became possible because of them.'

'I suppose they will now be treating you something like the way we've accepted Latvians and Poles,' Emma suggested.

'I believe that to be the case, yes.'

'And work – what do you contemplate doing?' Paul enquired.

'Anything that will provide a living. I have a job of a kind, which will serve until after our marriage. I do hope to fly, one day, but pursuing that end will be difficult. Perhaps too difficult. I also am interested in studying aircraft design. Again, though, I fear that I may be barred from accessing work with such potential for acquiring confidential information.'

'There's a long way to go, then, before you're settled in a job,' said Emma.

Vaclav smiled. 'A *good* job, yes. But in Prague I was making valves for radio sets. The work was undemanding, did not fulfil, but I would not refuse to do the same here in England.' For Sally, he added silently.

Sally herself was gazing around her friends' home, thinking how serious life had become, however happy the future promised to be. The atmosphere was very different from the occasions when she had gathered there with other friends, to laugh and fool an evening away. She had felt very different then from the Sally Downing who had risked her life delivering aircraft to RAF bases: today, she was different again, quite awed by all that

Vaclav had experienced in the effort to reach her.

Looking back to the inconsequential light-heartedness enjoyed among Emma's acquaintances, Sally realized that she had simply been marking time. She rather regretted that now, but could understand her own reaction to the belief that she never would see Vaclav again. Perhaps in those days they all had needed that period of relaxation in which to recover from the tensions of wartime.

'I'll never take you for granted, you know,' she told Vaclav as they walked hand-in-hand back to Downing House. 'I need to prove I deserve all that you've done to make certain of returning to me.'

Twelve

Once all the formal arrangements were in place, and Frank Bell was content that no problems would arise in having a Roman Catholic from Czechoslovakia marry in his chapel, both Sally and Vaclav began to look forward unreservedly to their wedding day.

She had taken very little holiday from the factory office that year. In addition to the fortnight's honeymoon that they were to spend in the Lake District, Sally insisted on having the occasional day off work in order to show Vaclav favourite parts of her beloved Yorkshire. She still had her little car and they drove as far as York, where they wandered contentedly around the Minster, then, after a late lunch, walked along the old walls to admire the views of the city.

On another day they set out in the same direction but continued on to Whitby. There, the light was brilliant, the sun silhouetting the ruined abbey and gleaming off the boats anchored in the picturesque harbour. Despite Vaclav's laughing protest, they climbed the 199 steps to explore the church and abbey before pausing to admire the view over the town and out towards the North Sea.

'You are making me to love your Yorkshire almost as much as I love you,' he exclaimed as they drove back to Halifax.

'I've always wanted to help you feel that,' Sally confided. 'Ever since those first few days after I met you.'

'Can you learn to forgive that I did not remain with you after the war ended?' Vaclav asked, suddenly grave.

'That's forgiven already.' She paused, tried to quell a sigh. 'I suppose you went home to your fiancée, was that it?'

'Fool that I was.'

'Fool? But if you were engaged, you'd have been wrong not to return to her, surely?'

'To me, it did seem the – honourable thing. Unfortunately, I had been entirely misled by her. She – I found her with an officer of the Russian army. Their troops had taken part in the liberation of my city in 1945, you know.'

'You must have been devastated. I hope having your family around helped?'

He shook his head. 'I told no one. Until this day, have told no one the whole of it. To my parents, I was obliged to make plain that I would not have Magdaleny in our home, I indicated only that she was unfaithful. And she did not trouble us a second time.' Vaclav could not force himself to speak of that other

289

alliance the woman had forged, with someone from that unspeakable government!

When she drew up outside Downing House, Sally leaned towards him and kissed him fervently.

'I just wish I could make up to you for all the terrible things that have happened in your life.'

'You do that already, by promising me a good future with you.'

Henry was not particularly pleased that Sally had requested several days off work, but she had waited until David returned from honeymoon before being absent. By this time, of course, her father was becoming depressed about David's ultimate departure from the firm. Sally was thankful that the new man who was taking over from David appeared to be efficient and fitting in well there, but her father seemed to be devoid of any feelings of thankfulness. Whilst she found his mood understandable, she did not mean to have it curtail her own activities.

She and Vaclav needed to spend hours discussing where their future home might be, they hadn't as yet reached a firm conclusion. The temporary job that he had found locally would still be there after they had been away. Beyond that, he was looking to find an occupation that utilized his interest in aircraft design, but obtaining such work could entail all kinds of problems, plus a great deal of patience.

In the interim, therefore, Sally was expecting to continue working at Downing's after the honeymoon, and was determined no one would take advantage of her being in the office.

'I *know* Dad,' she confided to Vaclav. 'He'll do his utmost to have me compensate for David's absence. I won't have that. He's engaged a perfectly capable successor as his second in command, I don't intend nursemaiding them!'

Vaclav laughed, but was relieved to see that his bride-to-be was no longer dominated to the same degree by her father. Vaclav himself had achieved a kind of neutrality with Henry; neither of them provoked the other, but nor did the older man attempt to befriend his future son-in-law.

Sally wished that her father could relent and make Vaclav feel welcome in Halifax, but he seemed disinclined to do so.

Perhaps Vaclav had a point when he said that only Henry Downing himself could reach the conclusion that a better attitude towards him would result in seeing more of the couple who already were spending less time in Downing House.

Sally was shopping for her wedding dress and trousseau. She hadn't bought a lot of clothes since the end of the war, and meant to make up for that for such a special occasion. She hadn't the courage to attempt making anything as important as her gown, but she did sew a couple of frocks to take on honeymoon.

She had asked Emma to be her matron of honour, and her two daughters bridesmaids. The four of them had spent an afternoon having fun while they selected outfits.

As soon as David and Ruth returned from their two weeks away, Vaclav had asked David if he was willing to act as his best man. Sally was pleased that her old friend was delighted to be asked, and that he and Ruth would naturally be happy to come back from Scotland for a weekend in Halifax.

Vaclav was privately beginning to feel distressed. Since their wedding plans had begun, he frequently pictured his mother's dear face, and his father's. No one from his own family would be able to be present. Sally didn't immediately recognize the significance of his inviting David to be best man until he explained how he had written to his brothers to let them know he was in England, and about his forthcoming marriage.

'They work so many miles distant from Prague that restrictions there should be less severe, and no one is around to link them with myself. I asked them to tell the news to our parents, and prayed they would have the sense to do so in the utmost secrecy.'

'Are things really that bad over there?' Sally was appalled by the evident situation.

'I have learned that the escape to Manston attracted great attention in my homeland, we must take no risks that my parents could suffer as a consequence. I do not know for certain if the authorities know the identities of those of us who got away.'

He did not doubt that Johana and Karel would be interrogated if the secret police were to discover that Vaclav Capkova was among the few who had escaped by air.

Sally sighed. 'This is all so sad. I do long to meet your mother and father, and I want them to share our happiness. We must be sure to visit them just as soon as we can arrange that.'

Vaclav hadn't the heart to explain that it was unlikely to be possible to venture into or out of his country. For someone born on the free side of the iron curtain, that would be virtually impossible. And if he himself were ever to go home...? He could not believe he would ever again be permitted to leave.

Despite such limitations, Vaclav was looking forward to their wedding day with increasing excitement, and was elated that he and Sally had found a tiny house they might rent as a temporary home. He had half suspected that she might surrender to her father's insistence that Downing House could well accommodate the three of them, but Sally was adamant.

'If I don't get away from there at this opportunity, there'll always be some reason conjured from the air to keep me there. In this way, we'll have made a sort of break, while the rented place in Hanson Lane isn't that far from Dad's home at Highroad Well. We don't know where we'll end up when we buy a house near work that you really want to do, but this will be an easy stage in that direction.'

'Easy' was not quite the word for the way Henry viewed what he could only term Sally's desertion of him. Even though they had included him in their plans by taking him along to view the rented property as soon as they agreed to move into it, Henry behaved as he might have if they had been emigrating to Czechoslovakia.

'There are times when I wish that we could do just that!' Sally admitted to Vaclav, but he was determined not to voice one word of what his ideal future could have been.

Instead, he insisted that he could sympathize with the older man's anxieties. Without discussing the matter with Sally, Vaclav later decided to make a determined effort to establish a better relationship with her father.

The wedding was almost upon them and Sally and Emma had chosen to have an evening out together one week before the big day rather than closer to it. In quite a frivolous mood, for she privately was glad of a change from the exhaustion of looking after the baby and the girls, Emma had suggested that they should go dancing.

Sally was quite shaken, she hadn't thought that married women would choose that kind of a night out. She herself couldn't even visualize dancing with anyone but Vaclav.

'Are you sure that's what you really want, Emma? Isn't it just a bit...?'

'Unwise?' Emma laughed. 'I wondered if you might think that. You being so devoted to your other half and all that. Just wait until you're tied down by two little girls plus an infant! OK then, tell me what you want to do.'

'We could go into Leeds or Bradford.'

'If not to a dance! OK, OK. We could see a show, or have a meal out or something.'

'A meal, I think. Somewhere very special, with a nice glass or two of wine.'

'Do two women on their own go for that?' asked Emma. She and Paul liked an occasional drink, but that was in a pub as a rule.

'Who's to say that we shouldn't? Especially if we didn't choose anywhere too far away. Then I needn't take the car.'

'Not take it?' Emma had been looking forward to feeling independent for once. She herself didn't drive.

Sally laughed. 'None of this sounds very exciting, does it?'

In the end they decided to visit a new restaurant that had opened in Halifax town centre. That way they could use the bus quite easily, and if they chose to have wine they need not worry about the journey home.

'Didn't you drink any alcohol in wartime then?' Emma enquired when they were facing each other across the table laden with the food they had ordered. 'You were driving the car in those days, weren't you?'

Sally grinned. 'I was doing a lot of other things that might be considered dangerous, as well. I'm not aware of the odd drink affecting the way I drove, but you've got to remember that I had less of an incentive then to stay alive. I didn't have the prospect of marrying Vaclav, did I?'

'Didn't you have even an inkling that you could end up together?' Emma hadn't fully understood how it had taken them so long to become serious about each other.

Sally shook her head. 'He was engaged, wasn't he? Whatever I might have wished didn't come into it.'

'I didn't know that. Fancy you still seeing him, and all that, when he had someone back home.'

'Seeing him was all that I did. We never...'

'I wasn't asking, Sally. Just surprised, that's all. So, what happened, then – to that woman?'

'She let him down. That's all I'm saying. Vaclav's never told anybody but me. Think it hurt too much, at the time. Still, I'm going to make it up to him.'

'Which you'll do splendidly. You are so right for each other. Now – tell me where you're going to live, I don't mean just that place you're about to rent. Which, by the way, you haven't shown me yet.'

'It depends where he finds a job he really wishes to do. That light-engineering work is only a stop-gap, till we're settled.'

'And that will be over here? Paul was saying that Vaclav would find it difficult to go back to his own country – now he's escaped like that. And he didn't believe you'd get the papers to live there anyway.'

'That's probably true. Just as well, you know how my father would react if that was on the cards. I only hope that we shall be able to visit Prague some day, Vaclav is very cut-up about his parents and family missing the wedding. I'd give anything if we could somehow share it with them.'

Henry was surprised that Vaclav was at the house that evening while Sally was not. The unfamiliar situation made him uncomfortable, on edge. In all the years that he had

297

been in business, he had never previously felt short of conversation. Yet here he was in his own home, tongue-tied for want of an approach with this young man who (all too soon) was to become a part of his family.

'How wonderful it would be if only my own father could be sitting here with us.'

Startled, Henry faced his daughter's fiancé, drew in a deep breath. 'You're missing him then? Missing all your folk...?' Hadn't this chap been only too thankful to get away to the better life offered with British people?

'So very greatly – almost as hurtfully as I once was missing Sally. Only for her would I ever have come back to England.' Recently, he had been distressed further by being unable to locate any of the friends who had dispersed after escaping together to England. There would be no one of his own at this marriage.

'But I thought it was the regime drove you to leave? Them Communists?'

'Oh, yes. I hated what they were doing to my country. But, if it were not in order to find Sally again, I should not have moved so far away. To some other mid-European country perhaps, certainly one close enough to visit my mother and father afterwards. He is not at all like yourself, you understand. A mild man, kind, protective of my mother and of his sons, but never equipped for standing

298

firm against injustice. I fear for them both, but most of all for him, because I feel that his inability to resist oppression is hurting. Hurting greatly.'

Her father was surprised, perhaps most of all by Vaclav's implied assessment of Henry himself. He liked to believe he could be strong. 'You reckon then that I would stand up for me and mine, against – what – a government, them in power?'

'Naturally. You made your way in the world, did you not, and continue to run a successful company. That speaks of the man you are.'

Henry contained a private smile, sat upright in his chair. 'I suppose – I suppose then, in the absence of your own father, I might be asking if there is any way in which you require my assistance. With regard to this wedding, and so on.'

Vaclav smiled. 'I certainly could use advice, on what is customary in your country, about the ceremony itself and – and perhaps the reception that follows. I feel sure that, in England, you may be more sophisticated in many ways, than in my homeland.'

Coming from the capital city, as he did, Vaclav could not really think that this Yorkshire industrial town would be more socially advanced, but he was eager to comply with Henry's apparent urge to be needed!

He was rewarded with a widening of grey eyes, and a smile. 'Well, ask away – since David won't be arriving until the eleventh hour, as they say, I'm only happy to fill you in.'

Vaclav considered for a few moments. He and Sally had discussed most of the arrangements in detail, but there must be *something* not yet covered ... He had got to find it.

'Perhaps the nature of a chapel ceremony is something on which you could inform me more closely. You will have witnessed other weddings there, of course.'

'And my own – my dear Gwen and I were wed in precisely the spot where you and Sally will be standing. I have photographs, let me find them...'

'So, our marriage will be a family tradition. I am delighted to know that.'

Studying the old photographs provided a source of further discussion, one which led Vaclav to ask more about Downing family history, and enabled Henry to explain at length their long-standing involvement with the Methodist chapel. The dedication to their religion was something Vaclav well understood and approved, however different its nonconformity might feel to a Roman Catholic.

The abyss between the two men appeared to be being bridged, Vaclav allowed himself a brief inward feeling of relief. It could be that he was discovering one route to the heart of his future father-in-law. For his own sake, and mostly for Sally's, he hoped sincerely that was so.

Sally herself certainly was surprised to find the two still sitting together and talking, apparently amiably, when she returned from her outing with Emma. The relaxing evening with its excellent meal and a glass or two of wine had helped her to unwind amid all the preparations for the wedding. Finding her father and Vaclav like this was a delightful bonus.

'How did you win my father round?' she asked Vaclav as soon as they were alone.

'You think that I have done so then?' he said with a smile.

'There's certainly a remarkable improvement, and I'm not convinced he would trigger that.'

'We talked, and that was good. I am hoping that the better feelings may continue now.'

The mood certainly seemed to prevail up to and including the Saturday of their wedding, and on the morning of that day Vaclav was elated to receive a small parcel with a note from his mother. He could not know what difficulties his family might have faced to get it to him, but it was some compensation for their enforced absence.

He wanted to rush to show Sally, but she

had been adamant that he must not see her on that day until they met in the chapel, otherwise they might risk bad luck. Vaclav was afraid already that the timing of this gift that he'd unwrapped was unfortunate. No bride would have neglected to arrange every detail of what she would be wearing. He was nevertheless deeply touched, and warmed by the thoughts flowing across the continent towards him from his own people.

Vaclav was standing in the entrance hall of Downing House, rereading the note from Johana, when Ruth came dashing down the stairs.

'Have the flowers arrived yet?' she demanded agitatedly. 'I've had to ring them and ask for another spray of stephanotis. Don't think Sally'll mind me telling you she's in a right state, and it's all my fault! I promised to lend her my veil, and in the rush to get away from Edinburgh I clean forgot to bring it.'

Ruth was astonished when Vaclav laughed. And then she hurried across to see what he was holding.

'My mother has sent this for us – I was afraid that it had arrived too late. I felt sure that Sally would have purchased a veil.'

'But this is exquisite!' Ruth exclaimed.

His fingers handling the white lace tenderly, Vaclav held out Johana's veil towards her. 'Would you tell Sally, please, how this has been sent to us.'

'Of course, of course. She will be so thrilled. Gosh, isn't this romantic!'

Vaclav read his mother's note yet again, folded and tucked it inside his wallet before placing them in the pocket of his suit. The suit was new, very English, he felt, and strange, but Sally had approved his choice. He was longing to see her, kept glancing at the time, this morning felt interminable.

He had scarcely slept, he and David had talked at length last night. Vaclav had been enthralled to hear about David's experience of setting up house and adjusting to married life, and the account had left Vaclav excited and a little apprehensive.

Where David spoke of settling into a strange city, Vaclav knew very well that he would need to adapt to living in this fresh country which often felt very different from his own. More than that, he only need look around him in this house to be aware that, whatever home he might provide for his bride, there was little chance of its possessing one half of the luxuries present here.

He wasn't sorry when a ring at the doorbell announced the arrival of Emma and Paul with their family. His uneasy thinking required some disciplining today.

'My, you look smart!' Emma exclaimed, and kissed him. 'And you're ready nice and early.'

Vaclav smiled. 'I thought to use one of the bathrooms before anyone else was awake. And then David was not hurrying to change, therefore I did so in order to leave more space for others.'

'The best idea. Sounds like it was a good thing for us to get ready at home. And the girls couldn't wait to get into their dresses.'

'I can see why – they both look very pretty. As you yourself do, Emma.'

'The length of time that took, she ought to!' Paul remarked.

'Sally is in her room. Ruth is helping her to dress, I believe. She and David are staying here. Sally will be pleased that you are arrived.'

Emma left the baby with Paul and followed more slowly as her daughters rushed towards the staircase.

Henry and David were descending the stairs, talking animatedly as though to catch up after the few weeks apart. Smiling, Henry greeted Paul, and with Vaclav led the way through to the dining room.

'I don't know about our bridegroom here, but I'm going to have a drop of something to steady the nerves. What do you all say...?' Whatever else, Henry Downing was known for being a good host.

They had barely swallowed down their drinks when the first of the wedding cars drew up in the drive.

'Now for it, old chap!' said David, grinning at Vaclav. 'And it is too late already to back out – don't forget that Sally is a friend of mine, I've got to look after her interests.'

'You need not worry, David, I have waited all these many years to make Sally my wife.'

'And travelled thousands of miles,' Paul put in. 'We've got to admire your commitment.'

The second car drew up as Vaclav and David were setting off for the chapel.

Paul called up the stairs to Emma and the girls. 'And make sure Ruth comes with you too, we're all travelling together.'

Left alone, except for his daughter, who remained upstairs, Henry suddenly felt all energy draining from him. The presence of the others, especially David, had prevented him from dwelling too gravely on the step that was about to be taken.

All at once, the enormity of handing her into Vaclav's keeping hit home. Despite the better relations between himself and his son-in-law (and they were greatly improved) he was dreading the rest of this day, but, most of all, the days that would follow. The fact that, for a time, the young couple would be living quite near to Downing House did not mask the reality that they could at some stage in the future choose to live a great distance away.

Henry turned to pour himself another

whisky, then decided against it. He liked a drink, not something he'd been brought up to, rather a habit acquired through business associates, but he did not mean to rely upon alcohol. If that young chap Sally was to marry really did think him strong, he wasn't about to prove himself otherwise.

Distantly, he heard the closing of a door. Sally was coming. He owed her a day of undiluted bliss, the one thing he could give to her. His own emotions would be contained, he was well practised in that during all the years since losing Gwen.

The resolve not to shed a tear was almost broken when Henry reached the foot of the staircase. She was descending slowly, pensively, radiant yet with a familiar seriousness behind her brown eyes, which even that veil didn't conceal.

'Sally love, you look wonderful! So lovely, it scares me a bit. I want to hug you, but...'

Sally would not contemplate any misgivings. She ran from the foot of the stairs to hug her father. 'Bless you, Dad. I'm glad you're going to feel proud of me today.'

'Proud? I'm always that, lass – even if I haven't always wanted you to tackle the things that have made me think how grand you've turned out.'

'You'll always be special to me, and to Vaclav, you do know that, don't you?' she said eventually, easing away to look into his

306

eyes. She needed that reassurance.

'Aye, love, I do. We all know there's going to be changes. It'll be up to us all to make things work in the future.'

The car was there already, the short distance to the chapel would allow little time for more than composing themselves. Henry might have said more, but there should be opportunity afterwards. If he wasn't too choked for speaking.

Vaclav's first glimpse of her made him catch his breath. His mother's veil and the gown Sally had chosen glowed white against the dark wooden panelling of the chapel. On her father's arm, she walked so smoothly, elegantly, that she appeared quite ethereal as she moved towards him.

Along with his sudden feeling of awe, Vaclav reflected that this impression of her was very strange, totally different from the Sally he knew to be so vital, dynamic, the pilot whose skill delivered aircraft.

The strangeness evaporated when she stood at his side, Johana's veil reminding him of old sepia photographs, her smiling lips and eyes shining through the lace to assure him that this was real, this was the beginning of their new life.

All the way through the ceremony, Vaclav was conscious of Henry's gaze upon them and, surprising himself, was thankful that one parent was present – to witness to these changes, to family worth. He would be good to the old man, not only for Sally's sake, but as a commitment to his own belief in the values instilled in him.

Sally seemed light-hearted when they reached the legal registration of their marriage, as if her commitment, like his own, was dedicated in the sacred promises. She smiled and smiled again, into his eyes, and around at their friends. Vaclav had eyes for no one else, until Henry grasped his arm.

'You'll do, son, you'll do,' he told Vaclav.

'I did not understand, Sally,' her new husband whispered later under cover of the final hymn. 'What must I "do"?'

She chuckled softly. 'Nothing more than you have already, love. It's a thing we say round here. "You'll do" means you're approved of – you've made the grade.'

'Are you certain of that?' he asked as they turned to walk towards the open chapel door.

'Positive. And you know Dad, you're unlikely to get a longer speech than that, you'd better make the most of it!'

Vaclav laughed silently, hugged her to his side as they stepped out into the sunlight.

Feeling his arm about her, Sally noticed her smile was widening, and wondered if their photographs would show that she was grinning! Somehow, she could not compose her face to form a more sedate smile, something perhaps more suitably bride-like. Whether she wished it or not, she couldn't do anything but grin. Vaclav bent towards her ear and whispered, 'You, Sally Capkova, look not only beautiful but very, very sexy!'

She laughed out loud at that, exhilarated by love and desire, and in the knowledge that both would now be expressed without reservations. They had wanted each other for so long, had feared so many times that they should not attach any hopes to their personal yearnings.

They would laugh a great deal during the following few days, the utter relief of at last being together and committed to their future was so very heady. On the day of their marriage, though, Sally experienced several solemn moments.

She could see how intensely Vaclav was moved by not having his family witness his wedding. Whatever might happen in the future, she resolved, she would try somehow to compensate him for all that he had sacrificed by needing her.

Epilogue – 1992

Their plane circled, descending through wispy cloud. Vaclav grasped her hand, they smiled at each other. The glimpses they'd had already of Prague's many red rooftops were just as Sally expected from photographs, from Vaclav's constant descriptions.

'St Vitus's cathedral,' he said excitedly, leaning across her to indicate a large building roofed in grey. 'And the castle beside it. We'll go there tomorrow.'

'And there's the river – quite wide, isn't it?'

Tantalizingly, the plane executed another turn to head towards the airport.

'I was enjoying that,' Sally told him.

Her husband grinned, squeezed her hand. 'At last. You were not keen on the rest of the flight, were you?'

She sighed. 'Was it that obvious?' Sally had surprised herself, felt rather ashamed. This was the first time she had flown since those distant war years, and she hated *not* being in charge of the aircraft.

'You should have obtained a civil pilot's licence, I did tell you.' Vaclav teased. He himself had qualified for one shortly after they were married. But he had been extremely fortunate: utilizing his understanding of aerodynamics and with further study, he had found work in aircraft design. Progressing through the company, he'd even won the right to test-fly several prototypes in development. Having had such satisfying work, he now felt content to enjoy these retirement years.

'I seem to remember I was heavily pregnant with young Karel when you first suggested I might take up flying again!'

'I know, I do know, my love, and with another baby arriving only eighteen months afterwards, you were fully occupied.' Vaclav thought better of mentioning that, throughout their lives together, Henry Downing also had continued to demand a great deal of Sally's time.

They had been fortunate in Karel and his sister Johana, both had studied hard at school, afterwards at university. Karel had surprised his parents by choosing to go into his Grandfather Downing's carpet factory, where he had worked his way up through all the processes. His chief interest was design and his comprehension of technology equipped him for introducing developments there.

Since her father's death in 1988, Sally was content to see that the shares she still held in Downing's were reflecting her son's expertise. It was Johana, however, who really brought Sally her greatest satisfaction. Perhaps through listening to Vaclav's accounts of his studies, their daughter had grown up with an understanding of aircraft and an appreciation of what kept them in the air. Following her mother's example, she had qualified as a pilot while at university. Her career with a civilian airline had flourished until she had left to start a family with the Australian pilot she had married.

Ted's work had meant that he and Johana settled quite close to Heathrow Airport, his unsocial hours meant that they rarely arranged a visit to her family in Yorkshire. Johana and Ted's sons were twins, twenty, very fit like their father and currently spending a gap year in Australia. Some of Ted's family were farmers. Sally dreaded the possibility of her grandsons deciding to settle out there.

She hadn't been reassured by Vaclav's reminders that the two of them could easily fly out there to visit their grandchildren, should the opportunity arise. This flight had been a far more modest distance, and tackled, on her part, with a deal of nervous anticipation. Only today, coming in to land, could Sally feel that this trip was about to prove rewarding, a joyful success after all the years of promises which for one reason or another were aborted.

The last occasion when they should have come had been cancelled hurriedly when her father had succumbed to a nasty bout of flu which left him weakened and susceptible to pneumonia. Henry had lingered for weeks in hospital, responding not at all to antibiotics, worrying the pair of them while he himself became totally miserable.

The end should have felt like a massive relief, but instead had left Sally feeling that she ought to have done more to save the old man. The depressing effect had seemed all the keener, for she and Vaclav should have been celebrating their fortieth anniversary here in Prague.

'It will be far more enjoyable *now*, the way things are in my country,' Vaclav was saying, his reading of her own thoughts acute, as so frequently over the years.

As a result of the 'velvet revolution' the whole population was experiencing greater freedoms. In Vaclav Havel as President, they had a worthy head who had suffered with their people along the route to national stability. In the not too distant future the Czech Federal Republic would become well established.

'I feel that I am bringing you to a home that has become worth adopting – if only during what I hope will be the first of many visits here,' Vaclav continued.

'I certainly hope so too.' Sally had been

distressed in the past when family troubles had brought her husband back to Prague alone. The worst had been that first instance when his father Karel had died of a heart attack after Vaclav's brothers were both involved in unrest following the crushing of the 'Prague Spring' in 1968.

In that period, under Alexander Dubcek, efforts to provide 'Socialism with a human face' had been welcomed by the intelligentsia and most of the population, but such liberal developments were abruptly suppressed in an invasion by many thousands of Warsaw Pact troops equipped with tanks.

After Vaclav set out for Prague amid reactions to that Soviet repression, Sally had been unable to sleep because of fear for his safety, but even worse was being tormented by the belief that she ought to have travelled at his side. At the time Vaclav had emphasized that young Karel and his sister, who both were sitting important exams, needed one parent at home in Yorkshire. Only afterwards had Sally begun to understand that her travelling in and out of Czechoslovakia would have proved difficult, if not impossible. She still had required some convincing that she had not failed the husband she loved so deeply.

Today, a confident traveller, far more assured than many a man in his seventies, Vaclav smoothed their way through all the formalities of arriving in his homeland. Their hands touching as they steered the baggage trolley, they hurried out to be greeted by his brother Bedrich.

Shaking hands and offering her cheeks for his kisses, Sally was astonished to find Vaclav's brother looking almost as old as her husband. She had heard so many stories of the involvement in demonstrations of both younger Capkova sons. How could she equate this white-haired person with the regular agitator who had risked imprisonment for his belief in greater freedom?

Bedrich was taking charge of their baggage, leading the way towards a dark-blue Skoda parked at the kerb. His daughter Lucie was at the wheel, eager to greet them, and to whisk them away to her home, where all the family were to gather.

She told them in impeccable English that, as well as her parents, and her own son, they were being joined by Vaclav's brother Jaroslav and his wife.

'I will help you to get to know each of them,' Vaclav assured Sally, taking her hand as they settled into the car.

She certainly hoped that he would, she was already having difficulty in recalling everything he had told her about them, and as for remembering their names ... In her own familiar Halifax, there were times when she could not always put the right name to the face of some friend encountered in the street! It was old age, she told herself on bad days, and tried to feel reassured that perhaps seventy-odd years of memories could understandably become a little tangled.

Their welcome into the home of Lucie and her husband was so enthusiastic and wholehearted that Sally soon dismissed all her anxieties. Just seeing Vaclav so elated to be with his own people was a delight from the moment that she followed his lead and slipped off her shoes, as customary on entering.

Embraces and kisses seemed to go on for ever, while excited Czech voices surged all about her. Sally relished the opportunity to rely on the few phrases of his own language which Vaclav had taught her, while she observed his family welcoming him home.

Quieting slightly, and out of respect for her lack of their tongue, the few among the younger ones who knew English started asking Sally how she had enjoyed the flight.

Vaclav began answering for her, explaining how she had not been entirely happy to have the aircraft handled by some other pilot.

Sally gave him a look. Was he making her appear too difficult, or (as she herself feared might be true) a fragile old lady who'd become nervous of flying?

She smiled. 'It is so many years since I was in any kind of aeroplane. I feel sure that by the time we are compelled to leave your lovely country, I shall be happier about being in the air. My one dread then will be saying goodbye to my new family.'

Her response pleased them, and Vaclav squeezed her shoulders as they stood together before being invited to sit at the large table where a meal was prepared.

The room was quite big, but seemed less so because of the number of people it accommodated. They all were chattering again, most in their own language, two or three younger ones, who knew English, remembering to use it.

One of Vaclav's early questions was regarding his mother. Johana was well over ninety years old now, living in a residential home that was opened by nuns shortly after the success of the 'velvet revolution'.

'She is well, in some respects,' said Jaroslav carefully. 'Her memory is poor, though, and this distresses her.'

'We shall see her tomorrow,' Vaclav promised, and enquired where exactly the home was situated.

Throughout the family meal and the evening that followed, Sally was included in all conversation, with someone translating whenever excitement led every word to lapse into Czech.

Greatly though she loved participating, and much as she relished seeing Vaclav with his relatives, Sally was tiring. With her own children approaching middle-age, and grandsons so far away from England, she was no longer accustomed to the noisy exuberance enjoyed by many families.

Vaclav seemed not to notice how quiet she was growing. Sally interlocked her fingers in her lap, gripping them fiercely while she willed herself to remain awake. They had drunk wine with the meal, and more than the one glass which had become her custom. She must not let Vaclav down by drowsing.

Despite his elation, he did notice her condition and, smiling, suggested to Jaroslav, with whom they were staying, that perhaps their long day might be concluding.

Not unexpectedly, Jaroslav's car was another Skoda, but the surprise for Sally was the length of the journey, which seemed to take them way beyond the elegant buildings of central Prague. She hadn't anticipated that the city suburbs would stretch so far. En route, they passed a great many drab blocks of apartments which, Jaroslav told her, had been constructed for workers during the Communist regime.

The home of Jaroslav and his wife, however, was in a pleasant square, just one floor up above a small grocery shop. While Sally admired the good, if old-fashioned, furnishings, Vaclav was exclaiming over several items which had come from his old home.

He remarked to Jaroslav that he would tell their mother how well her furniture was looking there.

His brother shrugged. 'You may do so, naturally, but I have already told her. I fear that she does not really comprehend.'

They had learned from the rest of the family that afternoon was the best time for visiting Johana Capkova. Because of this, Vaclav and Sally spent the next morning near the centre of Prague. As she anticipated, he insisted that they climb the hill to make St Vitus's Cathedral their first destination.

Before going through the doorway, they stood motionless to admire the surround of carvings depicting historical and biblical scenes. Although impressed by the size of the building, Sally was a little disappointed by how dark the interior seemed compared to the bright sunlight outdoors, until her eyes adjusted. She then felt her attention drawn to splendid stained-glass windows, some of which, Vaclav explained, were as recent as 1968.

They spent some time wandering around while he showed her various treasures, and where his family used to sit when they attended Sunday services.

'It certainly is very different from our chapel at home!' Sally exclaimed. And felt thankful that Vaclav had so readily accepted her place of worship for their wedding. She was gaining a more complete understanding of his religion today, an understanding that was willing her to learn yet more.

Leaving the cathedral, Sally realized how vast the surrounding area was when they walked in and out of various courtyards, while Vaclav pointed out different palaces and towers, and he promised that they would return on another day and spend several hours exploring. For the present, they contented themselves with pausing to admire the view from various sides of the surrounding walls.

Vaclav needed a few moments to steady his composure. Looking with Sally across the Stag Moat towards the royal gardens, he was heeding a massive compulsion to avoid recalling the proximity of the picturesque Golden Lane. All these years later, it seemed incredible to him that he could still feel hurt by finding Magdaleny with that Russian officer.

Seeking a distraction, he pointed out the Strahov Monastery and wondered aloud if it could still be in use for its original purpose. 'Religion suffered so greatly over here that I cannot be sure what has remained the same.'

Sally was awed by the sight of the many impressive buildings in varied styles which surrounded Hradcanska Namesti, the near-by square. The square itself was so spacious that she longed to linger. Only Vaclav's reminder that they would revisit made her content to descend the Castle Steps as they headed back into the town that looked so picturesque spread out below them.

He was smiling again when they reached the Charles Bridge and he encouraged her to turn around when the view up to the cathedral and castle was particularly splendid, and conveyed an impression of how extensive the castle was.

'Where now do you wish to walk?' he asked Sally as they made their way through the crowds of visitors.

'You have told me many times about the square that has your name – Wenceslas, is it far from here?'

'Not if we take the Metro, and there is something which I am anxious to see in Wenceslas Square.'

The Metro system quickly took them to one end of the square, from where they strolled along admiring the floral displays. Vaclav was glancing towards the many imposing facades and stopped eventually before the Melantrich building.

'I have been longing for many months to see this, Sally. It was from this balcony in 1989 that Vaclav Havel and Alexander Dubcek spoke to all the people, an occasion which marked the end of Communist domination here.'

321

Looking sideways at him, Sally saw tears in Vaclav's eyes. He had missed so much, so many landmarks in the history of his homeland – and all because of her. She felt overwhelmed by the strength of his love, squeezed his hand and longed for some means of showing how deeply she appreciated his commitment to her.

It was time for them to eat, if they were to visit his mother during the afternoon. Sally had no idea of how far out of the centre of Prague they must travel to do so. She was pleased to sit with him at a shady table outside a restaurant, and rest the feet troubled by walking along so many stone surfaces.

The home where Johana Capkova was being cared for appeared to Sally to have been either a small convent or a Roman Catholic presbytery. Certainly the building was quite old, its interior darkened by wooden panelling, but, despite its age, bestowing a sense of what, in a more secular building, would be elegance.

They were met in the wide entrance hall by a lay woman whose grey dress nevertheless conveyed the impression that she would always be at home among nuns. She invited Vaclav to sign a visitors' book as soon as he explained whom they wished to see. Along a short corridor and through a door on the right, they were taken to a small sitting room which seemed to be reserved for private visits.

'My mother has someone with her already,' he told Sally as the woman who had admitted them spoke a few words then showed them through, and departed.

'Oh, my God,' he muttered, and halted in the doorway, staring.

Sally grasped his arm. This husband of hers evidently was deeply shocked to see how gravely his mother had deteriorated.

The woman who was seated beside the old lady faced them when she heard Vaclav speak, and she sprang to her feet. Extremely glamorous, it was only as she walked towards them that Sally realized Johana's other visitor was older than she looked, perhaps sixty or more, although her gleaming blonde hair belied that.

'Magdaleny,' said Vaclav huskily, and tried to recover his composure.

The woman greeted him effusively in their own tongue, hugged him, kissed both his cheeks.

The moment that Vaclav introduced Magdaleny to her, Sally sensed that this was his former fiancée. And now Magdaleny was speaking English, and informing them that she frequently called to see her old friend Johana.

Johana herself, meanwhile, was straining to hear what was being said, staring hard at the newcomers while she struggled to identify them.

Rushing to kneel before the old lady, Vaclav hugged her at last. 'Mother,' he exclaimed, while the tears streaming from his eyes conveyed to Sally the meaning of his Czech words. 'Mother. It's me – Vaclav.'

'They said that you would come, Bedrich, Jaroslav both, I did not dare to believe them. But I see now that they were right, I *feel* that you are my son.' Smiling, she leaned back slightly to gaze at Vaclav, smoothed away his tears and kissed him.

'And my wife is here also.' He paused, glanced over his shoulder and beckoned. 'I have waited so many years to have you meet my Sally.'

Johana's hands were cold on hers, but her grasp was firm despite the evident fragility of great age.

Smiling, Sally struggled through the few Czech words of greeting that Vaclav had taught her, then bent to kiss her wrinkled cheeks, while Vaclav sat back on his heels, still unable to move from Johana's feet.

Her mother-in-law held on to Sally's hands, said something to Vaclav, then turned back to Sally.

Vaclav translated. 'My mother is happy that she has lived to welcome you into our family, she hopes that you will enjoy your visit in our beautiful Prague.'

'Please thank her for me – and say how happy I am already to be here, but especially to be meeting her. Can you explain that I have a small gift for her.'

The present was a framed photograph, an enlargement of one taken on their wedding day. Giving it to Johana, Sally pointed to the wedding veil, then touched her own head and the silver hair of the woman now leaning forward to study the picture.

Johana became excited: a quiver in her voice, she exclaimed to see the veil that she had sent all those years ago to England.

'Can you tell her, Vaclav, how it was worn later by our Johana as a bride, and our Karel's wife also?' said Sally.

This elated the old lady further, causing her to kiss the photograph before grasping Sally's hand again.

Magdaleny had remained near the door. If she hadn't guessed from her husband's re-action who the woman might be, Sally would have been embarrassed to know anyone should stand there, neglected, while Vaclav and his mother chatted animatedly as though they would never have enough of each other.

But Sally had not only assumed who the woman was, she knew what Magdaleny once had done to Vaclav. For that cruelty, Sally would be unforgiving. The fact that, but for that unfaithfulness, Vaclav might have stayed in Prague, was irrelevant. He had been sorely hurt, Sally could find no cause for exonerating that woman for her behaviour.

Perhaps conscious of such thoughts, Magdaleny reached a decision, and strode towards them. Vaclav stood up as she neared the group, glanced towards her.

Determinedly, in English, his former fiancée began repeating that she visited his mother frequently, reminded him that the two women had been friends, always.

Whatever he said in reply, Sally could not translate, but she recognized in the coldness of Vaclav's blue eyes that such visits to his mother failed to impress him.

After assuring Johana swiftly that she would return before too long, Magdaleny turned and, hips swinging, she strode on stylish high heels towards the door.

Sally sensed that Johana was saying that Magdaleny had been very good to her.

Vaclav snapped out a retort, then translated for Sally. 'But not to me.'

She remained disturbed: if Magdaleny had known of their visit and contrived to be present, she could not have created more agitation. The woman was so beautiful, so very attractive. Sally was only able to conclude that if Magdaleny had not proved disloyal, she herself wouldn't even have been remembered by Vaclav Capkova.

The day was tarnished: but for their

assurances that this was to be the first of several visits to Vaclav's mother, this occasion would have seemed to Sally a failure.

Vaclav himself was quiet, withdrawn following the unwelcome encounter. Seeing Magdaleny with his mother had been the heaviest shock. Elsewhere, a chance meeting might have been regrettable, but this seemed to suggest that the woman might have some hidden purpose.

He explained this to Sally, and was surprised by her sudden smile.

'It felt like that to me, but I was being paranoid. We ought to be glad, I suppose, that someone other than family does brighten your mother's life with visits.'

It was time to return to Jaroslav's home, where his wife would be preparing a meal for them. Sally wasn't sorry. She felt exhausted by the afternoon, and perplexed as to how she might help Vaclav recover from that confrontation.

An evening with family and a night's sleep seemed to make them both feel better. In the morning Vaclav began telling Jaroslav about the wedding photograph and how it had pleased old Johana to see how well her veil had looked. He needed to concentrate on one good thing about that visit. He was recovering from the shock of finding Magdaleny with his mother, but that was far from being his only shock. Expecting Johana to have aged tremendously had in no way prepared him for how she looked. The silvering of her once bright golden hair had seemed for Vaclav to illustrate how she was fading from them. She was thinner too, hardly identifiable as the mother who had bustled about their home. He was so thankful that his wife had found a means of delighting the old lady.

He and Sally were reminiscing about their wedding as they set out again towards the centre of Prague. The sun was hot, as he explained it could be in June.

'We must make sure that we stop walking quite frequently to take a drink. We are no longer quite so young, after all.'

Sally instantly wondered if, by comparison, she appeared far older than his former fiancée. But then her spirit reasserted itself, and she resolved to forget about the woman. She must not permit Magdaleny to overshadow their entire stay in Vaclav's homeland.

She had believed he was taking her straight to Staromestske Namesti, the Old Town Square, but he led her beyond, into a narrow street, took a sharp turning between buildings, and then stood motionless.

'There,' Vaclav said, and pointed. 'There is the home where I was born, and to which I returned when the war was ended.'

Sally was thinking how tiny the exterior looked, when he confirmed that she wasn't mistaken.

'Is very small, I know. And seemed smaller still, that time when I came back here. I had to conceal my true feelings when I saw my own room. My mother had polished, and made everything nice for me, but I dreaded being confined within its walls!'

When they turned away and walked towards the Old Town Square, Vaclav grasped her hand. His voice was sombre when he spoke.

'You see this corner here – this is where we stood. It was 1939, March, I cannot forget. Hitler's troops marched into our city. I can see him now, an arrogant bastard sweeping through in his powerful car. We were ordered to give the Nazi salute, everyone all about us was weeping. Some jeered at the invading army. I was too scared.'

'Your opposition was more useful a short time later, when you got away to help attack the Germans.'

'Or made my escape. I think sometimes that fear might have driven me...' Vaclav paused, sighed. 'I lost many friends during that year, students who had remained in Prague, to be shot for demonstrating.'

'As I say, you *used* your life. Courageously too.'

'That day in thirty-nine we thought our

329

Prague was lost for ever – by nightfall, Hitler's standard flew from Prazsky Hrad, our beloved castle. But the Czech people are born to fight...' He turned to her and smiled. 'We become good, I think, at resisting oppression.'

Around them as they entered the square, crowds were gathering, heading in one direction. Vaclav glanced at his watch and laughed.

'You come with me, and see this spectacle. We are famous, you know, because we have a special clock. You will see in a moment if we hurry. On the old Town Hall, is very elaborate, astronomical. And that is not all, there are many figures – automata. But we will watch it.'

Hastening across the large square, they gained the edge of the throng just as the clock was beginning to strike. Vaclav encouraged Sally to stand in front of him, she felt his hands, protective, on her shoulders.

The mechanical figures did indeed parade, as promised, while the clock went about its business of marking the hour. Somehow, though, Sally was not quite so impressed as she'd expected.

Vaclav laughed as he took her arm to lead her away. 'Not very exciting really, is it? A brief amusement perhaps.'

'And one that we could have needed?'

'I tell to you too many sad things?' he

suggested anxiously, his accent sounding so strong that he might have been the young stranger pilot in England fifty years ago.

Sally shook her head. 'It's all a part of Prague, a part of you. There will never be an end to the things I need to learn about you.'

He reminded her that they had rested not at all since coming out, and indicated seating outside a bar at one side of the square. With a glass of lager before him, and the coffee Sally requested, they lingered to gaze all around while Vaclav pointed out several structures to be noticed.

Sally admired the varied architecture, some evidently very old, also the lovely, mainly pastel, colouring of many of the buildings. She eventually enquired about one ornate facade which he hadn't yet mentioned.

Vaclav frowned. 'Ah – the Kinsky Palace – baroque and beautiful, of course. But spoiled for me in 1948 – from its balcony Klement Gottwald addressed our people as the Communists seized power. The beginning of what could have been the end.'

'Oh, dear. Shouldn't I have asked?'

'You said – you wish to know. And is over now, after all. But history must come with its lessons, or we do not grow. We should tell our son and daughter at home, have them understand.'

A shiver traced Sally's spine, a special kind

331

of thrill. Vaclav had called England 'home'. In all these years she had never quite been sure.

And this place, Prague, the whole Czech Republic – where did they lie in his affection, in her own...?

She was falling in love with these large squares, which appeared so very different from anything in the West Riding, where parks, many of them nineteenth-century, relieved the urbanization of regions given to industry. Sally supposed spaciousness, for lots of Yorkshire folk, was found only by leaving their soot-darkened towns for wooded hills and moorland. Here, space was an intrinsic part of their city.

Overhead an airliner soared, making her think of the day when they must leave Vaclav's homeland. Not yet, she prayed, there was so much that she hadn't seen, so much to comprehend more fully.

Across the table, she reached to grasp his hand, the hand now thin-skinned with age, its veins pronounced.

'I'm so glad you've brought me here, Vaclav. This is becoming my second home. I could feel that I belong here.'

He smiled tenderly, blue eyes seeking her gaze while he raised her fingers to his lips.

'That is so good, very good. Only remember, my Sally, that my home always is where you are.'